IN LIKE FLYNN

DONNA ALAM

1

CHASTITY

I'M IN BED.

With my rabbit.

And I don't mean the fluffy, toothy kind.

Quite honestly, I could be in bed with Liam Hemsworth, and it wouldn't make a blind bit of difference because, queen of erotica or not, my orgasm is ruined, and it has been for months.

The whole thing just makes a mockery out of what I do for a living.

Because my name is Chastity, and I run an ethical porn company.

It totally is a thing.

I prefer the title cinematographer. I just happen to film people having sex. I also pay them to do so—pay them very well because my market isn't the *Porn Bub* demographic. Fast Girl Media produces porn and erotica for women and couples, and my images and recordings are tasteful and sensual and very high end. According to Camilla, my elderly aunt, my work very much *gets the job done*. Though why I'm recalling my ancient relative's enthusiasm for my subscription-based website, I don't quite know. *Because that's not going to help me right now, is it?* It really is no wonder I haven't orgasmed in six months. Who thinks of their seventy-three-year-old aunt and her hairy chin when trying to get a moment?

A moment. For a pornographer, that expression is probably a little coy.

Because my name is Chastity, and I haven't orgasmed in six months.

As much as I'd like to blame Camilla for my problem, I'd only be kidding myself. I am solely to blame for losing my orgasm following a recent weak moment when I slept with the cockiest, most infuriating man on the planet.

Flynn bloody Phillips.

We'd spent a glorious night screwing each other's brains out following the wedding of my best friend. He'd bent me in shapes I'd thought were impossible, while whispering things that still make the tips of my ears burn. And though I'm not sure how it happened, that night, he also seems to have stolen my ability to orgasm from me.

Bloody man. I'd both lusted and loathed him at first sight. Loathed because he's a loud-mouthed Australian who's far too full of himself—he knows *exactly* how good looking he is and seems to think a compliment and a cheeky grin will get him out of anything. *And into anyone.* But it's hard not to lust after him when he looks like a younger Henry Cavill. At least until he opens his mouth. Because when he does actually speak, a cocky jerk seems to fall out. He's so full of himself. So damned arrogant. And hell if that doesn't do something for me! Especially with his accent. What is it about an Aussie drawl that makes the elastic of a girl's underwear loose? I once heard him describe his accent as "true blue". I don't know about that, but he certainly turns the air blue in the bedroom. Yes, my poor burning ears. It's strange how I can still hear him whispering ...

Come on, Chastity. Come for me. Come all over my face.

It's unfortunate that I both have a thing for Henry Cavill—*The Tudors* anyone? That man rocked a codpiece back in the day—and a love of confident men. But there's confidence and then there's arrogance, and they just aren't the same thing, so I'm at a loss to understand why Flynn's inflated self-worth both turns me on while annoying the shit out of me! It's baffling.

He looks like he could be in the movies, and I mean that in the mainstream way. Though with his face and anatomy, he'd make a killing in my kind of movies, too. Broad shoulders and powerful arms, and the kind of abs that almost make you want to reach into the laundry basket to get a dirty shirt or two out.

Just to rub, because that's my kind of washboard.

Plus, the man is hung so he could definitely do porn. And then there's his magical tongue ...

But it doesn't matter how gorgeous he is, or how talented his tongue happens to be because what it boils down to is that I want my orgasm back!

How is it that I've been able to let my fingers do the walking quite satisfactorily since I'd discovered what fun a clitoris could be at boarding school, and now I can't even get myself to come? *Ménage à moi* used to be one of my favourite pastimes—a party for one where fun was always had! But now? Now I'm *broken*.

God knows I've tried—I've tried every trick in the book! Over the past few months, I've even acquired a drawer full of toys—a dildo, a rabbit, a wand, vibrators that bend in various ways, and something that looks like a vibrating pink rock that, though is very pleasant, has yet to seal the deal. I've tried lotions and potions and lube that promised tingles but delivered little more than an itch, and even bought a strange looking two-ended thing described as "the Swiss army knife of sex toys" that did nothing but rattle my teeth.

In short, I've been cursed since I spent the night with Flynn Philips and have been subject to more sexual frustration than any twenty-nine-year-old woman, never mind purveyor of tasteful porn, ought to know.

I push out a frustrated sigh, another attempt at reaching climax over for another night. Pulling back the covers, I swing my legs out of my bed and throw tonight's battery operated boyfriend into the open drawer. I'm so disgusted with it I'm not even going to bother giving it a quick wipe. I might just throw it away. Or maybe give it another go after a cup of calming chamomile tea.

Pulling the robe from the end of my bed, I slide it on, conscious that I probably shouldn't walk around naked these days. Not unless I want to give Max a heart attack. Max, my little brother, is currently staying with me after finishing his degree. *Last year*. At twenty-three, he appears to be experiencing a quarter life crisis and has no idea what to do with his life. Except badger his sister for a job with my company. *Dipping his dick*, as he so eloquently put it. Like that's ever going to happen. Our family may be dysfunctional, but we're not sick.

God, I hope he's not serious, I think as I walk into the kitchen to be greeted by the sight of him eating cereal while wearing nothing more than a pair of designer jeans.

'What are you doing up?' I flip on the light wondering why he's sitting in the dark.

'I was out with friends,' he replies, to which I roll my

lips inwards. Best to keep quiet. I don't like to nag. Okay, I *try* not to nag. Too much. But honestly, it's like having an overgrown teenager in the house. He's not likely to find a job if he doesn't wake up before noon!

Max glances out at the darkened garden, maybe watching the rain slicking the roof of the house opposite, maybe the dance of it as it hits the surface of the garden pond.

'God, I hate this place,' he grumbles. The spoon clanks against the side of the bowl as he pushes it away, propping his chin on his fist.

Again, I don't answer; it's not required. He wouldn't listen. I wish he'd just pull himself together and find something—*something!*—to do. He doesn't have to leave, just get out from under my feet. Our parents split when we were young, and as we were already at boarding school, I suppose we've never really felt like we had a family home. We never lived with our parents. Just spent alternate holidays with them.

'Do you ever feel like running away?'

His question jerks me from my musing. It might not be the first time he's asked, but I try to keep the notion of how ridiculous I find the question to myself.

'I like my life. I like my job, and I like my house. Why would I want to leave?'

'Because *like* isn't enough. Because love and passion—'

'Are constructs of society. What's wrong with just being okay? Why do we all have to strive for magnificence? Why can't we just settle for good enough?'

Max snorts derisively. 'That's a crock, and you know it. You only settle for mediocre outside of your art.'

His words sting, even if he's right. My job might be extraordinary, but my life is pretty dull. And that's how I like it. My work is my art. There's a beauty in erotica because that's what I sell—seduction, sensuality, and romance. Not sex. Not really. I studied fine art at university and became enamoured with the human form. I drew, painted, and critiqued the body. Became a little obsessed, I suppose. I sort of fell into pornography, but not like the guilty husband who insists he was looking for a new nanny yet somehow *stumbled* onto a spanking site.

I saw a gap in the market and began selling stylised erotic stills. All very innocent; the art in the dip of a spine, the beauty in the contouring of a firm bicep. And then a client asked for a tasteful penis pic—yes, there are such things. As far as I'm concerned, there's beauty in every-thing. I'll admit, I was a little shocked, and more so when I discovered how much she was willing to pay. She even supplied the posing penis by way of her husband's hard on.

I suppose my business concept just spiralled from there. Now I spend my days filming beautiful people enjoying their own bodies and the bodies of others. But it's not all art house fucking. I do spend a lot of time edit-ing, and nannying the website, promotion, and all kinds of horrid admin. Thankfully, I still have my best friend, Paisley, to help some days. Since marrying, she's taken on a few new freelance makeup artist gigs, though she still makes time to come and help on set. I thought being newly married might complicate matters—men can be such territorial creatures—but I'm happy to report that is *not* the case with her husband, Keir.

I fill the kettle, flick the switch, then turn back to Max, leaning back against the kitchen countertop.

He really is turning into a carbon copy of our father, at least physically. He has the same chestnut hair and brooding expression. *Byron-esque*, my mother once said. Though I don't think either my father or Max lean towards Byron's partiality for bum sex, not that I would care if they did. I sigh quietly. I've made no secret of my business, and in turn, my family have made no secret of their abhorrence and disgust. My aunt Camilla might be a fan, but I think she's the only one. The only one who admits it, at least.

I'm sure my mother would prefer Max to sleep on Genghis Khan's sofa rather than stay with me. She probably thinks I'll corrupt him—have him starring in one of my skin flicks. If only they knew how it's the opposite— how he harasses me, trying to persuade me to let him "have a go".

He doesn't understand. He's just an oversexed, overgrown boy. I don't think he believes that being an adult actor is hard work. Hard to remain focused over long days. Hard to fake enthusiasm some days. Hard to stay hard!

But I don't often talk of my work. And our family is dealing with my career choice as they do with all things: by pretending it's not an actual thing. Brush it all under the antique carpet and make-believe that everything is fine. Stiff upper lips, not penises. Lie back and think of England. Tradition and heritage over smut.

'Something will turn up,' I tell Max, tearing myself away from my thoughts again.

'Well, in the meantime, I'm going away.'

'Again?' He must have more frequent flier points than the Kardashians combined. 'I mean, so soon?' I amend, softening my reply in response to his glare.

'Yeah, Josh's parents have a place in Goa. We're going to hang out and meditate.'

Self-medicate, more like.

'Look, Max, you'll find the thing that sparks your interest—something you can see yourself doing. A thing you'll love.'

'Not like you did,' he answers morosely, still looking out at the dark, wet night. 'You've found a passion.'

Lost it more like. Who can't bloody orgasm? If I can't find it soon, I'll probably end up having a stress-related heart attack. And who will be to blame then? Flynn bloody Phillips, that's who.

I reach for the canister of tea to avoid Max reading my expression. I'm told I wear my emotions on my face, and no one wants to question my thoughts right now. Because Flynn Phillips has stolen my orgasm, and I need to come up with a plan to make him give it back.

2

FLYNN

'Barbecue. Tomorrow.'

'Fuck off. I'm not working Saturday.' My retort is immediate though Keir, my boss, doesn't bite. 'Working for you is like indentured servitude. And actually,' I add, another angle occurring to me. 'I think that invitation might be a little racist.'

'What was racist?' Keir asks, not really paying me any attention as he sifts through a pile of papers cluttering his desk, searching for the plans I have in my hand. It's late Friday evening after a hellish day, but I love my job. Almost as much as I love winding up my boss. 'The bit where I invited you to spend an evening with pleasant company, providing you food and drink, or when I asked you where the paperwork for Simmons had gone?'

'The barbecue,' I respond. 'Just because I'm Australian, don't think you can pigeonhole me. It's culturally insensitive.'

'I dunno about pigeonholed, but I wish you'd shut your hole,' Keir murmurs. 'Where the fuck have those fucking plans gone?'

Keir McClain might be a killer businessman, but he'd be lost without me. 'These plans?' I say, chucking them down in front of him. 'You left them on my desk this morning.'

'I've been looking for them for an hour,' he growls. 'You'd better not have been fucking with me.'

'I was prioritising your workday.'

'Manipulating it, more like.'

'It's called managing, you arsehole.' My words come out on a chuckle. 'Come on, admit it. You couldn't arrange a screw in a brothel without my help.' Not because he's forgetful or unfocussed. Quite the opposite. He just has too many plates spinning to tend to them all. Not without me behind him, spinning those plates just as hard. I say again: I love my job.

'Fuck, I'm done,' he says, standing suddenly straight at the same moment his phone buzzes with a text. I know it'll be Paisley, his wife. The pair seem to have some sort of telepathy or intuition going on. 'You're done, too,' he says without looking at me but rather still looking down at his phone. Looking at it. Smirking at it. Sliding it into his pocket with a satisfied air.

That, in front of me, is a man on a promise—a promise of a good shag. And you can call that intuition if you like, too.

'Tomorrow,' he says, shutting his computer down. 'Just be a good lad and turn up at three. Bring a decent bottle of wine that I'll pretend you haven't already charged to my credit card.'

'The company credit card.' One of the perks of the job. I don't use it often—I don't need to—and I only usually do so to wind Keir up. And occasionally to send a "thanks for last night's fuck" flowers. And when I do that, I always make sure flowers are also sent to Keir's house. His house is overrun with women. Paisley, his wife, Sorcha, his daughter, and Agnes, Sorcha's stand-in granny. I love all three of them. I don't think it's conceitedness to think the sentiment is returned.

'Is it a bring a date kind of thing?'

'You can,' he replies, grabbing his suit jacket. 'But Chastity will be there.'

My heart does one of those cartoon thumps. *Ba-dum!* Though, unlike a cartoon, it's not exactly my heart that springs forth through my clothing. My heart isn't straining from my chest, but my dick might be feeling a bit lively.

Chastity . . . fuck me. Now there's a handful. *And a little bit more.* I've never had a thing for posh girls before—in fact, I've actively avoided them—and though she pretends to hate my guts, she sure was fun to fuck.

Sun, sea, the Seychelles, and Chastity. That was a killer combination right there. I'd met her before Keir and Paisley's wedding. At her house, in fact. Let's just say sparks didn't so much fly as ignite into a bush fire. *She was so hot—the dangerous kind.* She somehow got the idea I was a journalist and after some juicy gossip from her friend, so she threatened to impale me in the nastiest of ways. Grabbing an umbrella from an antique-looking umbrella stand, she suggested she'd shove it up my arse. Then she insulted my balls. It was the liveliest bit of foreplay I'd ever taken part in. So I reciprocated by telling her if she came any closer, I'd teabag her.

Her face. My balls. A date.

She wasn't impressed. Seems the foreplay idea was a bit one-sided. So by the time the wedding rolled around, she'd made it abundantly clear that as far as she was concerned, me and her weren't ever going to happen. To cement the point, she brought a parasol to the beach service—a white floaty thing I overheard her telling Sorcha was to protect her English rose skin.

Nah, she brought it to make a point. And that point was: I should keep my distance or else she'd make good on her threat. But I've always liked a challenge. And Chastity was certainly that. And though she might look like an angel, it's a total ruse. She's petite and sort of sweet looking. Blonde ringlets, peachy skin, and she has an accent a bit like the Queen. But beneath her sweet beauty and those warm chocolate eyes, she's fierce, feisty and fiery. And she runs a porn company, of all things.

My dad once jokingly said he'd aspired to marry a nymphomaniac with her own pub. I think an angelic looking pornographer is something more along my fantasy lines.

Jesus, how she burned in my arms—flayed the skin from my limbs. Because, despite her apparent disinterest in any activity that didn't involve some kind of disfigurement of me, we spent the night together, fucking until dawn. I've never had a night like it. And probably never will again. At least, not until the next time I get to work my charms on her ...

'Was the question too hard for you?' Keir's voice brings me back to the moment. The office. The dreary London spring.

'What?'

'I asked you if you were still bringing someone. You know, seeing as how Chas will be there?'

I try not to wince. As an Australian, it's in my DNA to shorten everything. We Aussies love a good yarn, or chat, but we like to abbreviate where we can and are the kings of brevity when it comes to renaming things. Service station? Servo. Breakfast? Brekkie. Afternoon? Arvo. Australia? Straya. John? Jonno. Okay, so the last one didn't quite work, but you get what I mean. But I hate—*hate*—how Chastity's friends shorten her name to Chas. She so isn't a Chas. A Chas is a Charles or a Charlotte, but never a Chastity. At least, not my Chastity. Not in my eyes. Not from my tongue.

Come to think of it, maybe that's because her name has the word titty in it? And as far as tits go, she has the best fucking—

'You're doing it again.' When I look up, Keir has this weird half-smirk on his face.

'Have you got wind?' I ask with an aggressive tip of my head. 'It's not like you to smile so much. That must be, what? Three times today?' That's not true. Keir is a solid bloke, as well as a good boss, but I shake my head in fake exasperation anyway. 'It must be Paisley's influence.'

'My smile is a reflection of how good my life is.'

'You've become an evangelist. Next thing we know, you'll be banging on doors to spread the word.'

'I don't need to. See, I'm also smiling because of what I see in your face when I mention a certain blonde cine-matographer. Looks like you're about to be clued in.'

'Clued in? Mate, stop talking in riddles.'

'Flynn,' he says, clearing his desk to clamp his hand on my shoulder. 'Women are good news. Relationships are good news. Embrace it. And get your arse to my house tomorrow afternoon. Bring wine but not a date.'

'It was just a thought,' I say with a shrug. 'My mate Sorch is all I need for entertainment.'

'And do yourself a favour,' he replies with an air of long suffering. 'Don't keep shortening my daughter's name in front of Agnes. Or one of these days, you'll get a nasty surprise. Most likely via delivery of her rolling pin.'

What is it with women threatening me with long or sharp objects lately? A question for the ages, though not one for Keir.

'Nah, me and Agnes, we're like that.' I cross my middle finger over my index one, holding them between us so he can see. 'Tight.'

'Yeah, 'cause everyone loves Flynn.'

'Too fucking right. And you especially.'

His hand slips from my shoulder as he makes for the door. 'You keep tellin' yourself that. And don't forget to lock up when you leave. See you tomorrow.'

'You do know it's March, don't you?' I call after him. 'It's fucking freezing—not barbecue weather.'

Keir doesn't turn. He's adept enough to shoot me the bird without breaking his stride, multitasker that he is.

3

CHASTITY

IT'S true that I don't have a lot of friends, but those I do have, I consider more like family. Paisley is the sister I never had, which is odd, considering I haven't known her all that long. But I love her all the same. And I love hanging out with her and Keir, her new husband. I even like his friends. Well, most of them. I refuse to include Flynn Phillips, though it's strange that my body seems to know the minute he walks into their kitchen. A brush of anticipation dances from the nape of my neck down, causing me to turn at the same moment as he enters the room. Our eyes meet, electricity humming between the space. It really is the most shocking of things until I let my eyes wander over him . . . and I'm met by the most ridiculous outfit I've ever seen.

'I don't remember saying today was fancy dress.' Keir sounds wearily amused as he relieves him of a bottle of red wine and a very decent bottle of champagne.

'Mate, you invited me to a barbie.' I'd forgotten how much his voice affects me. There's something about that drawn-out, lazy speech pattern of his coupled with his deep tone. 'This,' he says, plucking at his shirt, 'is suitable attire.' *Ah-tie-ahh*. 'Boardies, thongs, and my sunnies.'

One arm wrapped around my waist, I bring my glass to my lips to hide my snigger. Sunnies, I guess, are sunglasses. Boardies, board shorts, and while I know thongs are what Australians call flip-flops, here in England, they're flimsy bits of underwear that get stuck between the cheeks of your bum.

'What are you laughing at?' Flynn asks. Despite his relaxed demeanour, I can almost physically feel the touch of his gaze. 'I suppose if a bloke comes to a barbecue at your place, he's expected to wear a tux.'

Immediately, the prickling hairs on my neck turn to bristling spines. Spines that I tamp down, though I can't help my vinegary reply. 'Oh, that's right.' My tone is heavy with false sympathy. 'You wouldn't know, would you? You've never been invited?'

'I'll just go open this and, er, let it breathe,' Keir says, tactically raising the bottle of red. As he pulls open one of the French doors, a gust of cold air sweeps through the room before he steps out, closing the door behind him. The room falls quiet, and I begin to feel mean. I shouldn't be so unfriendly, only—

'That's true.' My attention snaps to Flynn once again. 'I haven't been invited to your home.' I don't fail to notice his eyes travelling over me blatantly this time. It's definitely not a casual glance, more like a thorough inventory. And the bastard knows—does it on purpose, even. All to draw a reaction. A reaction I'm not in charge of, it seems. My throat is dry, and my nipples are hard enough to poke out an eye, and let's not talk about the reaction currently dancing between my legs.

He steps closer. Close enough to make my nerve

endings erratic. Close enough to make my fingers twitch with the desire to pull him to me by the front of his ridiculous tropical print shirt.

'I might never have been invited into your house, duchess,' he repeats in a husky whisper, bending his mouth to my ear. 'But I was lucky enough to receive an invitation into your underwear.'

The absolute bastard.

Instinctively, I unwrap my hand from my waist and press it to his chest. I think if it weren't for the recent presence of Keir, I might use it to push him up against the wall to see if I can discover where he's hidden my orgasm. Because I'm suddenly sure it'll be on him somewhere. Say, on his fingers, his tongue, or maybe his dick . . . Instead, my brain sends a barrage of cock-blocking words tumbling from my mouth, clit-oference, if you will.

'I thought we agreed not to mention that night.'

It's not surprising I'm sabotaging my own plans. For one, I don't like him very much. *I don't think.* Even if he smells so divine.

'Did we?' His forehead creases as though deep in thought before his eyes rise to mine, his gaze full of daring. *Full of mischief.* Somehow, I know he's going to say something provocative, yet I'm still unprepared for how his words make me feel.

'Nah, that's not right.' His accent renders the words into a drawl with a serve of taunt. *Not roi-t.* 'I think what was said was that *you'd* prefer to pretend it didn't happen. To forget. But I haven't.' His eyes make another shameless sweep of my body. 'I haven't forgotten one bit of it.'

Oh. My. God.

I came here today with a plan. A plan to get my orgasm back. Well, maybe it wasn't so much a plan as it was a demand—a demand for a second go on the Flynn ride. See, I've decided the blockage is all in my head. I've made too much out of the night we spent together—it can't really have been that good.

So I'd decided a do-over would work. A one-time deal —okay, another one-time deal—here on my own turf, where the tropical setting wouldn't seduce me, or I wouldn't be drinking the wedding-romance-y Kool-Aid. But it's not going to work if he keeps looking at me like that, not if he keeps speaking to me in a tone that reminds me of rum cocktails, sunshine, and mind-blowing sex.

'Flynn!' The man staggers back as Keir's daughter comes barrelling into the room. Flinging her arms around his waist, she squeezes him tight. 'Why are you dressed for the beach?' she asks. Stumbling back, she's prevented from falling by Keir's hands as he catches her.

'Watch it, Sorch.' His voice trembles with laughter. 'You'll have Agnes coming after me with her rolling pin, or so your dad says. And I'm not dressed for the beach; I'm dressed for a barbecue. So the question should be, why are you dressed for a patrol of the arctic?'

'Because it's cold in the garden, silly!' Sorcha replies, giggling as she feeds her small hand into his. 'And now you're going to freeze.'

'What? You mean your dad hasn't opened the barbecue lid and brought summer alive?'

'You know that's not the way it happens.' She giggles, pulling on his arm. 'My dad's not magic.'

'Not like me, you mean.' With that, he pulls a bright shiny coin out from behind her ear.

'A two-pound coin! How did you get *that* out of my ear?!' she exclaims, clearly delighted.

My God. If as if being annoyingly attractive wasn't

enough, it suddenly hits me that Flynn is also good with kids. Fuck. Why does he have to be good with kids? I love kids . . . even if they don't seem to like me very much. *He'll be one of those hot, fun dads someday. A total DILF.* I shut the thought down immediately, taking a sip from my glass and ignoring the sudden stinging of my eyes.

'He must be trying to impress someone. Doubling the stakes, huh, Flynn?' Paisley shoots me a sly wink as she enters the room, *thank the Lord.* She pulls open the door to a commercial-size fridge, hiding her smile in the depths of it. 'Watch out for bankruptcy.'

'You may laugh,' he replies, patting the little girl's head. 'But Sorcha here is building herself a nice little nest egg.'

'What?' Paisley's response comes out as a tinkling laugh. 'She hasn't told you she spends it on candy?'

'Sorch,' he says, drawing her name out even as he shortens it. 'Sorcha, Sorch, So.' He shakes his head disparagingly. 'How are you going to pay for all the things a dog needs?'

'I've decided I don't want a dog,' she replies quite seriously. 'Princess Kitty wouldn't like it. Besides,' she adds, pulling her hand from his, 'I like sweeties.' And as though to prove the existence of her sweet tooth, she skips off to follow Paisley and what looked like a large chocolate cake.

'What are you smiling at?' Flynn asks once we're alone again.

'I was just enjoying the cuteness factor. You've got hidden depths.' I take a sip of my drink to hide my surprise at my compliment. We don't compliment each other. We snipe and argue. Apart from that one time we fucked.

'Seeing another side to me, were you?'

19

I am. And I don't want to.

'I'll admit, I'm a little jealous,' I say, my tone turning snarky once again. 'You never performed magic for me.'

'Huh.' He steps closer—so close I can smell his after-shave. It's spicy and woodsy and all kinds of yum. He smells like holidays and the best kinds of memories. Or maybe he would if I closed my eyes. But even looking at him reminds me of all kinds of things. Like how we'd snuck away from the wedding party. How we'd stumbled into my hotel room. How we hadn't even stripped out of our clothes the first time he sank into me. How his eyes had rolled closed as I'd clenched around him and moaned.

'I disagree.' I shiver as his deep voice rumbles across my skin. 'Because I seem to recall making your knickers disappear.'

4

FLYNN

'LIFE IS LIKE . . . it's like arse. I'm telling you, man.'

'Hang on,' Keir states, holding up his beer bottle and his free hand. 'I sense Flynn has something important to impart—something of note. Peel your fuckin' ears back, lads.' With a flourish of his hand, he indicates I should go on. *Keir. My boss, and mate, and a colossal piss-taker.*

'I wasn't making an announcement,' I protest.

'I feel otherwise,' he replies with a slightly drunken, though very smug grin.

'Come on, out with it,' Mac, the big fucker, adds merrily, wrapping his arm around my shoulder. And he is a big fucker. I mean, at six-foot-two, I'm not exactly small.

'You're a bunch of tossers,' I complain cheerfully to the faux grumbles of the small garden crowd. Pushing the meaty arm off my shoulder, I make the inappropriately appropriate gesture with my hand.

We're in the garden, and it's cold enough to freeze the balls off a brass monkey, though at least Keir has a state-of-the-art setup—outdoor heaters and a fireplace—plus I've put on street clothes since. Jeans. Boots. A jacket—the lot. *Spring has arrived, my arse.* We're not eating outside in the frigid weather, just standing around with beers like men, critiquing Keir's cooking skills while dishing out innuendo.

Keir's mates, Mac and Will, can hold their own pretty well, chucking food-based puns around and basically taking the piss. How does Keir like his salad tossed? How does he pull his pork? I know, juvenile, but it's a manly kind of bonding. And I'm in good company. Australians, as a rule, are a sweary lot, but this lot match me curse for curse.

'Go on; life is like arse,' Will, aka Dr Pussy, prompts. And that's not my name for him. Nope, that's his wife's name, and I'm not arguing with a newborn wielding woman for no one.

'Yep.' I nod. 'The way I see it, you're either kicking it, kissing it, busting it, or trying to get a piece of it.'

'Aye, and we know which one you're doing tonight,' taunts Mac.

'I don't kiss Keir's arse,' I retort. 'I already got my pay raise this year.'

'If you're not kissing my arse, you're not busting it for me, either.'

'Mr McLain, I've told you, I don't swing that way, no matter the price.' I clutch a set of invisible pearls. 'Talk about harassment in the workplace.'

'What workplace?' someone jeers.

'You know, this one,' Keir continues, hooking a thumb in my direction, 'wouldn't work if his arse was on fire.'

'You employ him.' Will laughs. 'So which of you is the stupid fucker, eh?'

'Piss off,' Keir retorts before turning back to face me. 'According to my calculations, that leaves kicking it, and I don't fancy your chances,' he says, comically flexing his shoulders. 'Or trying to get a piece of it.'

'And we're all spoken for, y'ken,' roars Mac, clearly delighted by his own half-drunken wit.

'All spoken for out here, but not in there.'

We all turn to the bank of windows at the back of the house where the sensible people sit. And that would be the female contingent. And of more interest to me, where Chastity sits. I know I was a bit of a cock to her in the kitchen, but she seems to bring out that side of me. I want to pull her pigtails and snap her bra strap just so she'll look at me. And when she does look—really look—I see the real her. The shit she can't hide as her breath hitches and her pupils dilate, her fingers flexing like she wants to pull me closer rather than push me the fuck away.

Beyond the glass, the fire is lit and the lights are low, Chastity is curled against the arm of the sectional sofa, holding a glass of something pale in her hand. She throws back her head, laughing at something one of her companions has said, and the light from the fireplace catches the gold in her softly curling hair, giving her a goddamned halo. Fuck a duck, I want to storm inside and chuck her over my shoulder. Drag her back to my lair and screw her for weeks. I've been avoiding thinking about her and that night for six long months, yet I still wake some mornings to the spectre of her curls dragging across my chest. And the smell of her floral perfume lingers on sheets she's never lain in. It's the most bizarre thing, but I think I might be formulating a plan to get my life back, especially after hearing what the *ladies* were discussing when I stepped inside earlier to syphon the python.

See, I reckon these feelings I have are like a holiday hangover, and that's why I can't get her out of my head. It's like, I had the greatest holiday—only substitute holiday for sex—and I can't get the fun of the experience out of my head. So what do you do when you come back from a fabulous break to grey skies and normality? You start planning your next little trip. And I think I might just have a plan . . .

'I think you missed one.' Keir pulls me from my thoughts, my gaze turning from the window at the sound of his voice.

'Missed one what?' I ask, my mind a step behind my mouth.

'Life is like arse; you're either kicking it, kissing it, busting it, trying to get a piece of it, or in your case, acting like a total arse.' He tips his bottle towards the window again. 'Any fool with eyes can see she's got you tied up in knots. Question is, what are you gonna do about it?'

Well, that's for me to know, and Chastity to find out.

5

CHASTITY

My phone buzzes with a text.

Aunt Cam: *What's new on the website?*
Me: *I loaded a new sequence yesterday called Anal Adore?*
Aunt Cam: *Darling, anal doesn't interest me. Not since my first husband left me for a man.*

I look up from my phone, my pink running shoes almost screeching to a halt at my garden gate. Not that I've been running. I don't. Run, that is, unless I'm being chased. But I do like chocolate biscuits, so I walk most mornings, weather permitting. And that's where I've been this morning, and I come back to . . . this. To him.

Flynn bloody Phillips.

'What are you doing here?'

Is it not enough that he taunted me at Paisley's barbecue last week—that he made comments and poorly veiled references to the night we'd shared at the wedding?

That afternoon, I had a plan to play nice—to not bite —to invite him back to my house and make him give me a good seeing-to. A night where he could return my orgasm to me, proving that the problem was all in my head. That it was nothing to do with his stellar bedroom skills.

But *nooo*. It was too much trouble for him to behave nicely—I couldn't bring myself to suggest a hookup. Not when I'd spent the night glowering at him. Not when *he'd* spent the night getting on my tits. So like a scaredy cat, I'd left. Left before my wave of wine bravery swept me away. *Or threw me at him.* He was still in the garden when I snuck out, so I didn't even say goodbye.

And now he's here. In *my* garden, if you can call this postage stamp of space such a thing. Sweat slicking his black hair back, he's holding a garden spade in his hand. At my exclamation, he smiles, slices the spade once more into the barren flower bed, then props one foot on the metal and his weight on the handle.

'G'day, duchess.'

'Flynn, are you having some kind of psychotic break-down?' He laughs but doesn't answer. 'What on earth are you doing digging up the flower beds?'

And be still my beating heart. Did he hear Paisley last week tell her new friends about our *Lady Chatterley's Lover* segment? My aunt Camilla loaned us the woods and gardens of her place—a large manor home an hour out of the city—where we'd spent the day filming Sophia, a lovely Spanish adult actress, being banged all over the potting shed and wheelbarrow by our very own Mellors. Whose name is actually Alan.

One conversation flowed to another, and before long, we were discussing what our likes and turn-ons were. From a business perspective, it was a useful conversation. And I might have been a little forthright about my own likes, too. But Flynn couldn't have heard us. Could he? I dismiss the thought because . . . God, no. The world isn't that cruel, surely.

I'm not a fan of alfresco sex, especially not when the weather is a little biting. However, I am a fan of classic literature. I might've said that, too. I also happen to be a fan of a Henry Cavill lookalike standing in my garden in honest-to-goodness biker boots and a thin t-shirt, sweat and use moulding it to his body. Add the authentic smudge of muck on his forehead, and I'm afraid I might be a little too much into this.

'This do it for you, does it?' My mouth works silently, though I prevent myself from looking down to my crotch to see if my leggings are wet. Because, yes, Flynn bloody Phillips does indeed do it for me.

Every. Fucking. Time.

'D-does getting my weeding done turn me on?' I stutter, ending with something just as smooth. 'I usually just get a man in.'

At least, in my dreams I do.

His deep burst of laughter is startling, and like God himself is trying to save me from the extra mortification, he sends a deluge of rain from the clouds above.

'Fuck!' I put my hands over my head—because rain and my curly hair don't get along—and jog up my short garden path. Jog, not run. Hair emergencies and all. I pull the key from my pocket and shove it in the lock before I realise he's behind me.

The door falls open, and I stumble in with Flynn directly behind me.

'You weren't going to leave me in the rain, were you, duchess?'

'I . . . I . . . ' Fuck. 'Yes.' I nod, feeling just a pinprick of shame.

'That's harsh.' He chuckles a low dark sound as he pushes a slick of damp hair from his head. Biceps. Flynn Phillips has biceps for days. He takes a step closer, and I take a step away.

'Yes, because I found you in my flower beds and, quite frankly, I think you might need help.'

He nods as though considering my point of view, still stalking slowly towards me, forcing me deeper into the room. 'Connie let Mellors fuck her on the forest floor.'

'W-what?' My body tightens through shock. Or through something else entirely.

'What was it you said last week? Everyone has their own fantasy, their own perfect moment in their head.'

'You were eavesdropping!' *Oh, fuck.*

'Guilty as charged.'

'But not very well,' I crow. 'Lady Chatterley's lover wasn't my thing!' And just when I think I've got the upper hand . . .

'I'm aware. That was the thing you last filmed. At your aunt's house, I think you said. It was an interesting conversation, but not as interesting as listening to you describe your fantasy.'

'You eavesdropping bastard, you!'

Ignoring my outburst, his eyes shine bright as he carries on. 'The library scene in *Atonement*, you bad, dirty girl. Though, the way you described it, it sounded more like the movie than the book.' So. Busted. But that scene is a work of art! 'And while I thought about it, I reckoned you wouldn't fancy meeting me in Chelsea public library, let alone be up for me throwing you against the stacks.' His lips curve in a show of wickedness. 'This was the next best thing. 'Especially after hearing you describe *your* set. In detail.'

Oh my God. Flynn Phillips heard me say I want to be dominated in a library. And heard me describe the potting shed sex. And, ohmygod, Flynn Phillips has been thinking of ways to fulfil my fantasies!

In a bare minute, he's pressed up against me, weaving his hands in my scarcely damp hair. 'Tell me I'm reading the signals wrong.'

Heat spreads through me, crawling through my veins, all thoughts are drowned by a wave of want. I shake my head slowly and watch the dawning of his devilish smile.

Well, it looks like I'm getting my orgasm back today.

6

FLYNN

'I've been thinking about you.'

My words are more growl than anything, and for the first time, I notice our surroundings. We're at the dining end of an open kitchen. Modern, bright, and with older accents. A whitewashed table, a matching cabinet, and a window seat looking out over a garden. The space is stylish enough to feature in a home magazine but still homey. I slot away the little insights for examination later as I push her up against the island bench.

'Have you thought about me since that night?'

'No,' she whispers, holding her chin a fraction higher. 'Not one bit.'

'You're a terrible liar.' I chuckle through my accusation as I begin loosening her hair from the bun she's wearing it in, ready for exercise. But she still looks fucking pristine. I work the hair tie loose, and blond ringlets spring every-where. It looks the same as it did in the Seychelles, so much wilder than the way she wears it usually.

'And you are delusional,' she whispers, one hand reaching for the curls almost self-consciously. 'You were in my garden, digging up weeds. Maybe I should call some kind of mental health crisis team.'

'So I just imagine the way you look at me?' My voice is raspy, my fingers on the zipper of her jacket.

'I've no idea what you mean,' she says as I pull slowly.

'No? It's the same way as I look at you.'

'Which is?' Her expression suddenly reads like she hates asking. She bites her lip as though biting back words as I slide the jacket from her shoulders. As it hits the floor, she's already toeing her feet out of her running shoes. Game fucking on.

'Like I'm imagining you without your clothes.'

Her head in my hands, I lower my mouth to hers, all soft lips and sweeping tongue. At least for a moment, because our kiss suddenly becomes sweet music fast reaching a crescendo. Lips pressing hard, all growling, and sucking, and fucking tongues. I don't even realise it's happening, but my fingers are on the hem of her t-shirt and I'm pulling it over her head as her fingers fumble with the zipper of my jeans.

I push off my boots, trying hard not to make a fool of myself in my haste as I swipe my wallet from my jeans. Slamming it down on the worktop, I pull out a condom with one hand, then pull back a few inches as she wiggles her fantastic self out of her running leggings.

I don't move after that, I just freeze, smiling down at her like a fucking idiot. It takes her a moment to realise I'm watching, her complexion flushed as her gaze darts up to mine. Her lips are slightly swollen and kiss-pink. Her hair is an mess from where I'd threaded my fingers, curls springing in all directions, tumbling across her shoulders. Her undies and bra are cute but functional, though nothing like the lace I tore her out of when we snuck away from the wedding.

My hands at the back of her thighs, I lift her onto the island, putting her pussy at optimal *Flynn-dick-height*, then I pull her against me, sliding my fingers in her hair.

'Want to know what my favourite part of your book is?' My question is just a rasp of air, my lips on her neck as I press my cock harder against the soft cotton layer—just a fraction away from where I want to slam myself.

'The library fuck,' she answers, all breathless and desperate, pulling on the waistband of my boxer briefs.

'No.' I growl the word into her mouth, whispering my answer along her jaw. 'When he writes her the letter.'

'Oh . . .'

It could be that she remembers, or it could be the real-isation that I'm sheathing myself with a condom, my fingers and cock so close to her pussy. Whatever the reason, she melts into me as my mouth reaches her ear.

'I can sympathise because I dream of kissing your cunt, too.'

It's such a dirty word, even if this time it was pulled from honest-to-goodness literature. And it's gratifying to get such a visceral reaction as she spreads her legs wider, wrapping her hand around my cock and pulling it between her legs with a breathy, 'Yes!'

'You in a hurry, duchess?' I span my hands across the pale skin of her ribcage, rubbing soft circles over the fabric of her running bra. Her nipples stand to attention, and I can't wait to get my mouth on them. But I might have to as Chastity lets out a frustrated breath.

'Flynn Phillips, stop talking and just fuck me.'

Never let it be said I can't take a cue.

My heart beats like a drum—though it could be the

pulse in my cock that's deafening—as I hook her knickers to the side, and she feeds me between her soft thighs.

'Holy fuck.'

The heat of her against my tip.

The soft slickness of her as I push in.

The hot grip of her walls.

I dip my knees to prevent my legs from giving out.

'Holy fuck!' This time, the reaction is hers, just a short hiss as she arches her back, her mouth falling open with the plea.

I push into her, as close as two bodies could be, my hilt rubbing her clit as the nails of her left hand dig into my shoulder so sharply I hiss myself. As I pull out almost to the tip, Chastity's eyes are so blue and so clear, and she lets out the best fucking sound. It's somewhere between a breath and a moan as her insides clench around my retreat as though desperate to keep me there.

'That's it,' I growl. 'That's fucking perfect.' Grasping the back of her knee, I lift it over my thigh, and with a snap of my hips, I slam back in.

'Oh, my God!'

This time, I'm not sure if she said it or me, but all I know is as she wraps her legs around my waist, my brain shuts down. I begin to fuck and rut, her arse in my hands, my body curling into hers as though I could crawl right inside.

'Oh, o . . . there it is!' she cries. 'There. It. Is!' If I'd thought the exclamation weird, the thought is lost as she punctuates the words with a thrust of her hips.

My cognisance is shot. I'm deaf, dumb, and blind to anything but the feel of her underneath me. I slide out a little. Slam back in. Rotate slowly. Repeat at speed. Pound into her, again and again, not able to get close enough for full satisfaction, yet no longer capable of restraint. Her arse feels fantastic in my hands, her breathy moans in my ear fucking sublime—I both feel and hear when the moment arrives, the moment she reaches her peak. She goes rigid, her pussy grinding against me, her body taut. Taut and tight and at risk of making me blow my fucking mind. *And my fucking load.*

I want to devour every soft inch of her. Fuck her until there's nothing left of me. Eat her pussy, then kiss her mouth. Bite and suck every inch of her flesh.

My thoughts are wild and my movements frantic as I try to fuck my thoughts into her. I want to be in her deeper, harder. Leave my mark inside and out. And then in one brilliant moment, everything freezes, blurring around the edges like the best kind of special effect. I feel nothing but the pound of my heart and the throb of my release, and the latent pulse of hers.

I place my head against her shoulder as the white noise retreats, the sense of satisfaction almost overwhelming as I feel her throbbing around me.

'Oh, Flynn,' she pants, her palm on my head.

I'm a bright bloke, but just after I come, my brains are a bit like pancake batter. Still, it doesn't take much to realise she's trying to push me away.

'Not so quick, duchess,' I growl. 'What's your fucking hurry?' I place my hands on her thighs, the backs tanned against the pale of her skin.

'My brother is staying with me.'

Shit. Does that mean no second round?

'Pizza delivery.' My voice is still a little hoarse, though my wits are beginning to return.

'W-what? You're hungry?' I look down at her wet pussy. I could go for a bit of that. *Dessert.* 'I have some

34

chicken,' she says, her tone perplexed. 'Would you like a sandwich? I suppose it's the least I could offer after you . . .'

'Ploughed?' I wink. 'I ploughed you good.' Her eyes narrow, and if I'm not mistaken, she's about to start shouting, so I make it quick. 'Pizza delivery. That's my fantasy; that's what comes next.' Literally.

'What?'

'Or I can meet you at the public library. I'm game.'

'What?'

'You already said that, duchess.' I grin. I can't help it. I'm fond of smiling in general, but I also know this kind of attitude pisses people off. Which just makes me smile all the more.

'I'm not letting you fuck me in a library,' she says, lifting my hands from her thighs. So I place them on the benchtop on either side of her, caging her in.

'Next time we fuck, I get to choose the fantasy.'

And by now, I'm pretty sure the chance of her brother walking is bullshit, or else why would she still be talking? And naked.

'Eyes up here, mister,' she says, her fingers on my chin. 'I'm not saying we will revisit this t-topic again.'

'The topic of fucking?' I lift my hand, pushing a bunch of her wild curls behind her ear. *Jeez, would you look at that. Fucking makes her ears go bright pink.* 'I'm pretty sure we will visit the topic. Again and again.' Why the fuck did I leave it this long? I'm sure as shit not gonna wait six months until I'm inside her again.

'Ridiculous . . . this conversation is ridiculous,' she says, moving her hand from my chin to smooth the curls back over her ears. 'This isn't happening again, Flynn.

Besides, I refuse to believe your fantasy is the most basic of porn plots.'

'That's where you're wrong,' I say, my eyes flicking from her face down. 'Sometime soon, you're ordering pizza. And I'm delivering . . . all over these perky tits.'

7

CHASTITY

THE THIRD SUNDAY of every month, Paisley and I meet for brunch. Initially, it had started as a way for me to get her out of the house after her breakup. When I say house, I mean *my* house as she was staying with me after her fiancé did the dirty deed with another woman. It's odd to think I barely knew her at the time. Odder still to realise how close we've become. This has been a strange year, not bad exactly. I've certainly gained a lot from it. Paisley, for one, and, of course, my business, which has gone from strength to strength. *Thank goodness for pervy people.* I can't quite put my finger on what it is, but I feel . . . restless. Sort of unfulfilled. Even as I think these thoughts, I'm chasing them up with how ridiculous it is to admit to them because I have a good life. I own my own home in one of the most expensive cities in the world. I have a thriving business. I have my brother, Max, and Paisley, and by extension, Paisley's lovely new family, who involve me in their lives greatly. Yet, at times, I still feel like something's missing.

Maybe it's my looming thirtieth birthday. Maybe it's

the shock of finding Flynn standing on my doorstep. Or maybe it's my screwing him again. *Why is it, even when he's not speaking, I feel like he's teasing me?* I'm so not going to think about him. I'm not going to remember how shocking it felt to be reminded how big he is. How manly. In an age where men are waxed from the scrotum up, Flynn is a welcome anomaly. And when he runs a hand across the stubble on his jaw, I can literally hear knickers in a five-mile radius dropping to the floor.

Maybe Max isn't the only one suffering a quarter life crisis, even if that can't quite be mathematically correct in my case. *I'm more like a third.*

'Am I late?'

I look down at the latte glass in my hands, my mind a beat behind Paisley's words. 'No,' I answer with a slight dazed shake of my head. 'I was at a loose end, so I came early.'

I watch as she unfurls a lengthy floral scarf from her neck before sliding onto the banquette opposite me. Her complexion is rosy, and though the weather is a little brisk, I know the flush in her cheeks has nothing to do with the weather.

'That's not like you. You're never not busy. And coffee?' With a slight frown, she looks down at my almost empty glass.

'I wasn't going to start on the booze without you.'

She shrugs off my response, pausing for a beat to examine me. 'Why are you looking at me like that?' In answer, I raise one brow as I lower my now empty glass to the saucer. 'You saw,' she says, her soft American accent tinged with accusation.

'Sweets, the whole restaurant saw.' I wouldn't be able

to bite back my smile even if I wanted to. 'That was some kiss. And when I say kiss, I mean—'

'A mauling.' Her shoulders hunch as though anticipating a blow.

'I was going to say a fantastic display of frottage but mauling also works.'

'Oh, my God. I can't believe I let him do that.' Hands on her heated cheeks, there isn't a hint of regret in her words. Just a little embarrassment.

'Let him? It looked to me like you were pretty complicit in that whole bump and grind.' Maybe that's what has me in a funk, watching Paisley and Keir be so into each other, they forgot about the passing world. 'It looked like a precursor to sex—an appetiser course before the main meal.'

'Actually, it was more like a palate cleanser between courses.' Her eyes sparkle with the admission. 'And I plan on returning to the buffet table many, many times over the course of today.'

'Someone has a child-free Sunday,' I tease. Paisley married Keir, the serious Scotsman who swept her off her feet last year—totally unfazed by the fact he has sole custody of his daughter. Sorcha must be eight or nine years old and a bit of a livewire. I do wonder if my best friend will be as chill when her stepdaughter hits her teen years.

'Sorcha's with her grandparents. All. Day.' She comically widens her eyes.

'You should've said. We could've met for brunch another weekend.'

'No way. A plan is a plan. Besides, it's just business as usual, if you know what I mean. We just get to be a little more creative and a little less furtive when Sorcha isn't around.'

'Tell me more,' I reply, propping my elbow on the table between us, my palm cupping my jaw. I might flutter my lashes innocently for good measure. Anyone who knows me knows that I'm always on the hunt for new material. That the things they say and do, the stories they tell, are fair game in front of me. I imagine it must be the same as being an author. We all have to get our material from somewhere.

'No way,' she repeats, this time her words wavery with a barely suppressed giggle. 'Get your sexy scenarios some-place else. It's bad enough that a dozen people saw my husband dry hump me against the side of the car.'

'After he helped you from it,' I supply. Keir is a man who takes care of those he loves, and he loves Paisley a whole lot. 'He was every inch the gallant until . . .' I allow my words to trail off, thinking better of mentioning the fact that the restaurant and I got a glimpse of her stocking tops as her husband trailed his hand up her outer thigh, dragging her woollen dress higher as it travelled. Not that I'd be complaining were I in her stockings, not that I have a thing for Keir. But to have someone look at you like that —need you like that—must be heavenly.

I've no idea why my mind seems to think it's appro-priate to remind me of Flynn's wicked sapphire gaze at this moment. *The persuasion and the challenge.* Probably because of the fact that any climax I've reached recently, while few and far between, has been down to him. I feel myself frown as I push the thought away. I thought yesterday might've reset the blip in my system. Unfortu-nately, it has *not*.

'That's Keir.' Paisley's words bring me back to the

moment with a snap. 'He's always a gentleman. Until he isn't.'

'If it helps, this place is quiet today. Not to mention, you looked like you were enjoying it.'

'If I find this as the basis of one of your films . . .' Paisley points a warning finger in my direction. 'I'll be very unhappy.'

'You should be so lucky,' I reply, which is pretty much bullshit. I've already slipped the sexy little snippet into my work bank. Not to be confused with my wank bank.

'Speaking of being lucky,' she says, 'What's going on with Flynn?'

At the mention of his name, my stomach does an anticipatory flip, though outwardly, I project something a little like an iceberg. Serene. Reflective. Cool. 'Going on?' I manage to say, though as a response, it's not very genuine. When I think of Flynn—see afore mentioned wank bank —the things that go through my head are a little more like.

Hard. Glorious.

Absolutely annoying.

A little bit too full of himself.

And a little bit too much length to fill me.

See point one re: hard and glorious.

Yep, Flynn is a big boy. If he was to star in one of my films, I could meta-tag it as *hung*. Not very inventive, but as a description, it's pretty apt. I could also use *cocky* and *annoying* and *needs a slap*, but that wouldn't help my subscribers find their joy.

Or course, I don't say any of this. Just like I don't tell her that Flynn has stolen my ability to orgasm. Because that would just be mad, even if it feels true. I thought yesterday's gardener shenanigans had put an end to my drought, but it seems like it was only a temporary reprieve. Because this morning, when I'd attempted to play back his visit, a sort of Flynn/*Atonement* mashup, accompanied by a little two-fingered knuckle shuffle, frustration struck again.

At this rate, I'm going to need therapy.

'Don't play innocent with me.' Paisley interrupts my thoughts sounding a little *too* happy. 'You two are like . . . explosive. *Ka-pow!*' I recoil as she slaps her palms together before doing a weird sort or jazz-hand thing when she pulls them apart. 'Sparks and fireworks and all that sort of stuff.' I'd forgotten how you were at the wedding, but it all came flooding back on Saturday afternoon.'

'Oh, that.' I nod. 'You're right. We're highly combustible on account of not being able to stand each other. We're not a good idea. Like dynamite and a match.'

'Apart from that one time,' she taunts as she slides the menu onto her open palm.

'I thought we agreed that what happened in the Seychelles, stayed in the Seychelles. Wedding hookups are almost inevitable.' I'm not going to tell her about yesterday—I'm not!

'Even with people you don't like?'

'Apparently so.'

Start with a romantic beach wedding, add a little sun, a lot of rum, and a whole heap of hot looks and dangerous chemistry, and the result is the hottest one-night stand I've ever experienced. *The same hot one-night stand that has damaged my solo sex life, it seems.*

'Stop looking at me like that,' I add blandly.

'You mean, like I'm not sure who you're trying to fool?'

I fold my arms on the table and lean forward, my

denial hitting the air in a rush. 'He just rubs me up the wrong way.'

'I'll bet he'd just love to rub you up in *all* the ways,' she answers, sniggering.

'Ew. Bad pun alert.' Ella's amused tone pulls both of our attentions to where she stands at the edge of our table. 'Do me a favour and never pun again in my presence.' Pulling her denim jacket from her arms, she slides onto the banquette next to Paisley. 'Shove up, skinny butt.'

'Like your ass is big,' Paisley grumbles good-naturedly.

'It needs more space than yours. This place looks nice,' she says, glancing around at the industrial chic interior of pale floors, exposed brick and steel beams.

Londoner Ella is someone pretty new to my social circle. As the wife of Mac, one of Keir's best friends, she was bound to become an acquaintance of Paisley's at least. But she's become more than that, the sweetheart that she is, and I'm only surprised her friendship extended to me. Not that I'm unfriendly—quite the opposite. I have lots of acquaintances, just not many friends.

'You've escaped without your brood, too, I see.' My words are a touch droll, maybe to hide my disappointment. Ella's daughter, Juno, is the most adorable toddler and Louis, her stepson, is four-foot-three inches of pure inquisitiveness, and his French accent is as adorable as his gap-toothed grin. Broody, me? Absolutely. Though that's not up for discussion today, either.

Ella nods enthusiastically, taking the drinks menu from Paisley's hand. 'Mac's parents are down from Scotland, and they've taken our tribe for the day, thankfully. The addition of children does not improve a girly brunch. Besides, Mac seemed very excited when I told him I'd be making the most of the afternoon by drinking lots of cocktails.'

Paisley snorts. 'Like he needs to get your ass drunk to get you naked.'

'Maybe cocktails make me a little more compliant.'

'And by that, she means all hot and bendy,' Paisley interjects, sniggering again.

Mac is a great bear of a man who owns a chain of gyms, but somehow, when Paisley suggests "hot and bendy" I don't think she's talking about Bikram yoga.

'Maybe,' Ella answers. 'But what I do know is talking about cocktails won't *get* us cocktails. Ladies, let's get this show on the road!'

As though summoned by her enthusiasm, the waiter appears.

'What can I get you gorgeous creatures this fine afternoon?'

An address like this would normally dial my irritation meter sky high. I'm not a raging feminist—I like a compliment as much as the next woman. Or man. However, I'm not a fan of flirty waitstaff in search of a bigger tip. Or twenty-year-old's using overly friendly terms of address. But as I turn to the waiter, my mouth closes with a snap. Dark hair and dark chocolate eyes, he's pretty. And on the right side of thirty. Which would be the *plus* side of thirty. *I'm so over boys.*

He looks familiar. So, of course, I imagine him with his clothes off—for professional purposes—but come up blank. He's not someone I've used in one of my films before. *I don't think.* And not someone I've sought out from the Adult Actors Guild. I can't shake the thought of his familiarity, though. Or the way he's looking at me.

Paisley takes charge of our order—seems we're all getting mimosas to begin.

'He was totally into you, babe,' she says as the waiter leaves.

I watch his retreating form and note the ease and confidence in his stride—okay, his broad shoulders and tight arse—and my mind goes to where it usually does.

I wonder if he has good swimmers? As though a girl can tell just by looking. And yes, I totally mean sperm. *I bet Flynn has good swimmers.* What a pity a child of his would be Satan's spawn.

'What do you think?'

'I think I'm a little too old to be screwing the waiter in the bathroom.'

Paisley gives me the look—the *why you got to be so cynical* look. 'I'm not suggesting you screw him. I'm suggesting you get his number.'

'Why?'

'Companionship. Friendship. And maybe, okay, a chance to get laid.'

'I have you two, don't I?'

'Sorry, babe, neither of us swing that way.'

'Besides, we haven't a dick between us!' exclaims Ella . . . just as the hot waiter passes by, his footsteps faltering and bringing him to a stop.

'They really don't,' I say, peering over the table as though to make sure there isn't an actual dick sitting on the velvet banquette between them. I raise my gaze to his stunned expression. 'Which is a pity, to be honest.'

'Really?' he says with a half-smile. 'A disembodied dick is really no dick at all.'

'Oh, I don't know,' Paisley interjects. 'Chastity here could probably tell you a thing or two about the phallus.'

45

I'll credit her as trying not to snigger. Again. And I suppose she's referring to the dildos and all manner of sex toys available for sale on my website.

'Is that so?'

I nod reasonably. I'm told my appearance is misleading. I have the look of an angel which hides the tenacity of a terrier. I can be very persuasive when I want to.

'I'm a history professor,' I say with a very straight face. I'm not lying because I'm ashamed of what I do. I just happen to have an aversion to being asked a million questions and becoming elevated to the oddity of the day. 'Yes, Priapus, the Greek god of fertility is a particular speciality of mine.' I know a little about him. Enough, at least, to shoot a scene around him. If you plan on googling him, just prepare for an eyeful.

'Beautiful and smart.' Oh, man. This guy is slick as well as easy on the old eyeballs. 'The son of Aphrodite, wasn't he?' Slick and good looking and, apparently, well-read.

'Fun factoid,' I supply. 'Priapus the origin of the term priapism.'

'What's priapism?' Ella asks.

'A pain in the dick,' I reply. 'Literally.'

Ella turns pink as our waiter throws back his head as he laughs, flashing a mouthful of pearly white teeth. Strangely, it does nothing for me, not that I'm not a fan of oral hygiene—who isn't?—I just mean I'm not interested in general. The pretty man doesn't make me fluttery where it counts, I realise. Sure, I can objectively appreciate his handsomeness, but that's as far as it goes. If I were to cast him in a ménage, he would be the second guy.

Oh, God, I suddenly think. *Maybe this is early onset of menopause? Losing my orgasm and a lack of interest in the opposite sex?* But then I'm assailed by another image of Flynn—a sensory memory this time—of his body pressed against mine, his short, choppy breaths in my ear. The sounds he made as he'd come.

The fine hairs on my arms stand to attention, my insides suddenly pulsing emptily. I release a long breath. It's definitely not menopause or the waiter that has left me a little wet.

'Ah, here's Sam with your mimosas.' Our waiter, who I suddenly realise isn't dressed like the rest of the waitstaff, begins lifting our drinks from a young blond's tray. As he places mine in front, our eyes connect. 'Priapus was also the son of Dionysus. Now there's a god who knew who to have a good time.' He winks. 'I'm Tate, by the way.'

'Orgies are your thing, are they?'

'If you're offering, I'm in.' And with that, he takes his confident self back in the direction of the kitchen.

'Oh my God, he was so flirting with you. Hard!'

'Agreed,' Ella adds.

'Which makes him so your type!'

'Thank you for that insight, dating guru. Maybe I just bring out the competitiveness in men?'

Ignoring my snark, Paisley turns to Ella. 'She digs an alpha.'

'Oh, me, too,' answers a nodding Ella.

'Yeah, but she likes the whole push and pull. Sparks and insults flying, that kind of deal.'

'Really? Since when?' But apparently, I'm not part of this discussion, just the topic.

'Maybe Tate isn't *captain of industry* enough?' Ella suggests.

'No, that's not it. It's all in the attitude, not the suit. Or wallet. I know she sounds like the queen, but don't let the accent fool you. She's an equal opportunities woman. The hating thing is just like foreplay to her, as far as I can tell.'

'That is not true!'

'Tell the truth and shame the devil.' Ella giggles. 'I saw you and Flynn interacting at the wedding. And can I just say, I almost needed a cigarette afterwards—and I don't even smoke!'

'But she's suffered a bit of a drought since their hookup.'

Ella's head whips from Paisley to me, then back again. 'You mean, she slept with him?' And back to me again. 'You slept with him? At the wedding?'

'Oh, there wasn't much sleeping going on.'

I take a mouthful of my drink, unsure how I'd forgotten it was there, its sweetness and bubbles rolling across my tongue. I clear my throat. 'Something tells me I'll be needing a few more of these today.'

'If mimosas will make you spill, I say bring them on!' Ella raises her glass. 'Cheers, lovelies. May all our ups and downs be between the sheets!'

8

CHASTITY

Two more mimosas, a generous portion of eggs benny, and a sharing jug of Long Island Iced Tea later, things have begun to get personal. Very personal.

'She's afraid of commitment,' says Paisley. 'Her last proper relationship was years ago.'

She's right, but I won't allow the conversation down this painful path.

'It's hard to meet men in my line of work,' I protest.

'Aren't all the men hard in your line of work?' asks a giggling Ella.

'I hate to burst your porn bubble, but that's not always true.' Unfortunately. 'Sometimes they need a little help.'

'Like a fluffer?' she asks, her voice almost pitched high enough for only dogs to hear.

'No, like Viagra.'

'That's disappointing.'

'I'll say.' Though my perspective is a little different. A leading man with a lack of functioning equipment often results in costly delays. 'Do you watch much porn?' I ask

Ella. I know Paisley has a subscription because it's part of her employment package.

'Well . . . I . . . ' She ducks her head, not that it hides her embarrassment.

'Don't answer that,' I say quickly. 'Being in my line of work sometimes removes my brain to mouth filter. Sorry.' I think I'm largely desensitised to things that should ordinarily shock.

'No, it's fine,' she says, raising her head again. 'I'm just a little shy, I suppose. I, that is to say, we—Mac and I—do have a subscription to Fast Girls.' She hides her nervous smile behind the rim of her glass. 'We like it. Quite a bit, actually.'

'That's so fab to hear! Can I just take this opportunity to say I'm also open to suggestions.'

'Fishing for information,' interjects a laughing Paisley.

'Absolutely. I'm all about the customer experience.'

'Well, this customer,' replies Ella, her cheeks still pink, 'is very satisfied.'

'I'm sure you are.' I lift my glass, chinking it against hers. 'Mac clearly adores you, and you have two of the cutest children known to woman.'

'I am . . .' She inhales, pushing out a deep breath which ends in a wide smile and, if I'm not mistaken, tear-filled eyes. 'The luckiest, not to mention, the happiest a girl could ever be. And to think, it wasn't all that long ago I was poised to move back into my parents' house. Not to mention, a virgin.'

Cola and hard liquor don't feel so great coming out of your nose, let me tell you.

'Oh, God, I'm sorry,' I say, mopping up the spray from my chin. 'Excuse me but how—*how*—could that be possible?' Ella looks like a young Sophia Loren; all soft curves and olive skin. Her wavy dark hair is always stylish, and while I don't go for girls, even a straight girl like me feels the urge to touch her fabulous boobs.

'I had no confidence,' she says with a short shrug. 'I was also, unwittingly, a fag hag to my long-term boyfriend. And obviously a bit stupid.' Both Paisley and I begin to protest. 'It's true,' she continues with a rueful laugh. 'God, I was such a disaster. And then I met Mac, and I discovered love.' I can't help the wistful sigh that escapes. 'Along with the joys of sex.'

'I think that's a book,' replies Paisley. 'Pretty sure I discovered it under my parents' bed when I was a kid.'

My *ahhh* turns to an *ewww* before morphing into a giggle. A giggle that's infectious, it seems, as I cast my eyes to the other side of the table.

'Imagine going from being a virgin to Mac.' Paisley brings a hand to her mouth, but it doesn't hide her laughter. 'Lord, that man looks like he could break you in two.'

'No comment,' titters Ella.

'No comment needed. I've seen him in his rugby shorts. The man needs a cup before he hurts himself. Sorry, Ella,' she adds. 'I haven't been perving purposely. It's just kind of hard *not* to see.'

'Oh my God, this is so funny!' Ella responds, her chest heaving with laughter as she wraps an arm around her friend. 'I've told him he needs to strap that down, but he prefers a bit of free running!' The end of her sentence ends in a bit of a screech, tears beginning to roll down her face.

'Seriously, babe, he'll put himself out of commission,' Paisley advises, composing herself and straightening the wide neckline of her dress. 'You've got to protect your own interests. If it was Keir—'

'Keir is too much the gentleman,' protests Ella.

'That's not what you would've said this morning,' I quickly add.

'He was a little handsy when he dropped me off,' Paisley adds a little shyly. 'And not very gentlemanly at all.'

'Even the good ones have a naughty side.' At Ella's words, both sets of eyes turn to me.

'What?'

'The sentiment totally fits you.' Paisley's mouth hitches in one corner as the pair continue to examine me. 'You look like butter wouldn't melt in your mouth—like an angel—but you absolutely have a naughty side.' It's not an insult or even teasing as she leans across the table, her hand raised, inviting a high five.

'I wouldn't mind, but I don't even get the benefit of naughty,' I say as my palm meets hers. 'Not very often, at least.'

'I don't get it,' Ella says. 'You must meet lots of fit men in your line of business.'

'Call me old fashioned, a hypocrite, or whatever'—I shake my head and the thought away—'but I prefer monogamy. I know some adult actors consider themselves faithful to their partners and sex at work is exactly that—just work—but I can't think like that. I'm not wired that way, maybe. I'd be too jealous. I'd be the crazy girlfriend, and no one wants to deal with that.'

'I hadn't thought about it that way,' she adds. 'But there must be other men you meet.'

'Not ones I want to date.'

'Not true. What about the guy you introduced me to last year? The one who looked like Clark Kent? God, what was his name again?'

'Troy,' I supply. 'And I can't believe I went to the trouble of introducing you to a completely nice, not to mention hot, man when you were already in love with Keir. Sneaky much?'

'What can I say? I thought I was protecting my heart.'

'More like fooling yourself. We've all been there,' Ella says.

'Why don't you ask him out? Or get hot Tate's number?' Paisley's eyes slide to the bar, her eyes sparkling with mischief and her fingernails twirling the straw in her glass.

'Don't even think about it.' I'm not looking for a boyfriend. I just want my orgasm back. And maybe a baby sometime in the not too distant future. There, I said it. Admitted it to myself. Time is a-ticking, and I'm tired of waiting for the right man to come along. Besides, the right man is a unicorn—a mythical beast. 'Who'd want to marry someone who does what I do for a living?

'Who said anything about marriage?' *Oops. A slight Freudian slip.* 'We're talking dating here. And if porn stars can find partners, you sure as hell can.'

'Really? Then why make me sound as appealing as a tin of Spam.'

'What about online dating?' Ella suggests.

'Tried it.' I shrug. 'It's like that adage; the odds are good, but the goods are odd. Or married.' Yep, that happened one time.

'When did you try online dating?' Paisley seems surprised.

'Before we met. In fact, I found Jesus there.' Both women laugh as I slip my clutch onto the table from the empty space on the booth next to me. 'It's true.' I pull out my phone to show them the snapshot of the profile of a

53

Spanish model I'd dated early last year. I say *dated* but banged for three days straight would be a better description. *It was a three-day weekend.* 'His name is pronounced *Jesús*, but whatever.'

'*Swipe right if you need Jesus in you*,' Ella reads from the snapshot. 'Oh my God, talk about talking yourself up. What a chancer!'

'I can't say I found redemption, but he nailed me well and good.'

'Oh, the puns!' Ella cries, clutching the blouse covering her ample chest. 'The puns!'

'He's seriously hot.' Paisley looks up from my phone. 'What happened with him?'

'I decided I couldn't date a man who uses more hair product than I do.' And that's saying something because curly locks are no joke. Unimpressed, she shoots me her *bullshit* look. 'He was just a bit of fun,' I add with a light shrug. 'We found we weren't really compatible on our next date. Young, dumb, and full of . . .'

'*Eww!*' Paisley protests.

'I was going to say *fun*.' My words are a touch smug as I pick up my glass. Ours was hardly a meaningful connection.

'Sure, you were,' she responds, using the same superior tone. 'But why is this just a screenshot? I can't see the app on your phone?'

'*Jesús, María y José!*' I exclaim, taking my phone from her hand. 'Nosy much? I no longer have the app because I no longer date online. I deleted it after getting this close'—I bring my forefinger and thumb together, leaving a tiny space between—'to screwing a married man.'

I take a fortifying sip of my drink. I've never really had close girlfriends before. Not the kind to confide in, anyway. My friendships pre-Paisley were shallow and consisted of coffee dates and evenings out. Certainly not the sharing and emotional kind. But maybe that's just me. Maybe those are the friendships I've sought. Whatever the reason, I still sometimes feel a little strange admitting to my own problems and fears. To the mistakes I've made or, in the case of the married man, almost made. Though my biggest mistake of all I'll always keep to myself.

'God,' Paisley replies in horrified tone. 'But that's on him, not you. You can't let one asshole, one bad experience, put you off.'

'Oh, that was only one of a number of bad experiences.' My tone is dry as I recall the date who invited me to slip into the bathroom with him to do a line of coke from his dick, and at least four others who misrepresented everything on their profiles from jobs to heights and hairlines. 'Online dating is not for me.'

In fact, I've found that dating full stop isn't for me. I've had one serious relationship in my life, and that was enough to put me off ever getting involved again, but I persevered. Like the family motto on our crest says, *Virtute et labore.* By valour or exertion. Let it not be said that I haven't tried, because I have, but it just hasn't worked. Quite frankly, I'm done. And in fact, as I approach my milestone birthday, I'm beginning to form other plans. Big plans. Exciting plans. Plans that prove that I don't need a man. *With the exception of the one little issue I'm currently dealing with.* With that thought, I open my clutch to return my phone at the same moment it *bings* with a text.

'It's not a question of needing,' Paisley protests, but I'm not listening. *I might not need a man, but it seems my body wants one*, I consider as I stare down at the phone in my

55

frozen hand. Unfortunately, my hand is the only frozen part of me as the rest—from brain to body—turns to goo.

'Flynn?' My God, Paisley has the vision of a hawk. 'Does that say Flynn?' Her words are like little bullets of excitement as she tries to swipe the phone from my hand. But I'm quicker.

'It's him, isn't it?' she demands as I move the phone from her reach. 'You sneaky sneak! How long has this been going on? Don't need a man, my ass,' she adds gleefully. 'Could that be because you've already got one?'

'Don't be ridiculous.' I slip my phone into my clutch, steadfastly ignoring how my face has begun to heat.

'Have you been holding out on me? Because if you tell me you've been seeing him since the wedding—'

'Don't be ridiculous. That was just one night. I told you.' And since then, I've just been thinking about him. And cursing him. Him *and* his magic penis. 'Do you honestly think I could've hidden that sort of secret from you for months? I couldn't even keep it from you for a day.'

She smiles like the cat that got the cream—no, the cat that bathed in the cream, like some superior Cleopatra of cats. 'Am I to understand this happened last Saturday? After the barbecue?'

'No,' I say again. 'I came home from my walk yesterday morning to find him in my garden.'

'That sounds a little sinister,' Ella says. 'I hope he wasn't wearing camo and hiding in the long grass with binoculars.'

Paisley snorts. 'Flynn is more likely to be found dressed as a garden gnome or something equally ridiculous.'

'You're both wrong, though he *was* in costume, I

suppose.' My heart pitter-pats at the recollection. The bulge of his bicep as he'd swept a lock of hair from his face, the bloom of lust deep in my belly as I'd watched his thin T-shirt ride up, flashing me a peek of those washboard abs.

'Come on, then. Don't keep us in suspense.'

'He was in my garden. Gardening.'

'Why?' Paisley asks. 'Altruism seems a little farfetched. Besides, you're not a pensioner . . .' I feel a little smug as the realisations dawns across her face. 'He overheard you talking about the potting shed shoot at the barbecue.'

I incline my head. 'And the rest. What else did we talk about on Saturday, hmm?' I've no idea if Flynn caught only my smutty confessions. It's not the kind of question I'm likely to ask. It's not the kind of question any of us are likely to ask.

'Oh!' she exclaims, her hands flying to cover her cheeks. 'No! He was eavesdropping on our conversation?'

'Now who's holding out, hmm?' With a sniggering laugh, I take a sip of my drink.

'Holding out? More like holding potentially embarrassing material. The total sneak!'

'So he heard our slightly drunken conversation—our very *smutty* conversation. So what?' As a description, I'd have gone with "insightful conversation", especially from a business standpoint. But no matter. And strangely, while Paisley looks shocked, Ella looks rather serene.

'What are you smiling about?' Paisley begins. 'Aren't you worried?'

'Why would I be? Mac already knows all my fantasies.' She inhales deeply, her next words girlish and giggly. 'And he already calls me his little girl.'

Daddy kink. It should be absurd—the pair are

57

married and have children. Technically, Mac is already a daddy. But I can totally see how it might appeal to the pair. While Ella doesn't appear the least bit submissive, I can see the appeal in someone taking care of you. Taking care of your needs. But can I see myself calling a man daddy? Probably not. But I can foresee others being into it, so slot away the idea for further *professional* examination later.

'*Fuckkk . . .*' Paisley's curse hits the air like an exhaled breath. 'It's okay for you,' she says, 'but I see Flynn on the regular. How am I going to be able to look him in the eye now?'

'Please.' I snort. 'You and Keir can barely keep your clothes on in public.' Tactile doesn't even cover it, as seen in their display earlier today. 'I'm sure Flynn is already privy to, if not the details of your sex life, then the frequency.'

'Breadth, if not depth!' Ella giggles. Maybe someone really ought to stop her drinking.

'Are you attempting to sexually shame me?'

'If the ball gag fits,' I retort, smiling.

'No dice, ladies, because Keir likes me loud.' She cackles as she brings her glass to her mouth.

'What man doesn't,' titters Ella.

'A common theme, maybe, but men all have their *thing*. The thing that tickles their pickle, so to speak, big time. I think it's only fair we know something of Flynn's secrets, wouldn't you say?' I frown. Is she talking to me? How would I know his thing? He might like being pegged by aubergines for all I know. Our kind of acquaintance doesn't extend to those kinds of details.

'Come on, babe, pick a side. You have to restore the balance. Tell us a little of Flynn's peccadilloes.'

'No, no, no, no, *no!*' Ella slaps the surface of the table with her palm before draining her drink. 'Flynn can't have a little pecker or a little dildo because life is too short to deal with mean penises and little men. Wait!' she adds, almost visibly playing her words back. 'Life is too short to deal with mean men and little penises. Because mean penises aren't really a thing.'

'I dunno,' begins Paisley. 'I've known a few mean dicks in my time. Mean dicks with small dicks. Robin,' she fake-coughs her ex's name into her hand.

'I thought you said you were a virgin pre-Mac?'

'Closeted gay boyfriends also have dicks,' Ella says with a one-shouldered shrug. 'They're just a little mean with it. Still, I suppose I have him to thank for my awesome blow job technique.'

I begin to laugh, doubly so as she makes a lewd gesture involving her hand, cheek, and tongue, right at the moment Tate choses to approach the table again. My first thought is that we're being a little rowdy, that maybe his other customers are sending our table a lot of dirty looks, but his open, smiling expression seems to say otherwise.

'Enjoying yourselves, ladies?'

'Very much so,' Ella says, her head moving like a nodding dog. 'Brunch was delicious. A visit to this beautiful and very respectable establishment has made for a perfect Sunday.'

'Respectable,' Tate repeats, cocking a teasing brow in my direction, a strange sort of gleam in his eye. 'Maybe Miss Landry would care to visit after closing hours. We're not so respectable then.'

He doesn't wait for me to reply, which is just as well given that my jaw is on the table.

'He surnamed you,' Paisley crows, 'I thought you

didn't know him?' I don't, but he does look familiar. *From where, though?*

'More importantly, he delivered an invitation to a disreputable experience.' Ella giggles, all comic wide-eyed.

'That's not what I heard,' I reply, the tips of my ears fiery again.

'Then you need your hearing tested,' Paisley retorts.

'Not interested in men, huh? Good for you it doesn't work the other way around.'

9

FLYNN

I SEND HER A TEXT. I get no answer, my expression twisting when I note it's been almost immediately read. *She might be busy*, I reason, so I chuck my phone down on the couch cushion, telling myself I'll leave it a while. I flick on the TV, a little fucked off.

Two one-night stands months apart is hardly the foundation of an addiction, but maybe I should be examining this. Is my eagerness a warning? Bad enough that I've been thinking about her since the wedding. What's that about? We fucked, and while I was sleeping, she fucked off. That should've been that. End of. Her prerogative to leave, and certainly no skin off my nose. Only, it wasn't like that. Not then and not since. At the wedding, I was frustrated that she wasn't there the next morning, but I shrugged it off. Ate my brekkie under an endless blue sky that reminded me of home, then boarded a plane back to London, my second home. And then . . . I might've thought about her a little. Usually with my cock in my hand. But I haven't obsessed. No way.

But yesterday—what the fuck was I thinking? I sure as

shit wasn't thinking with my big head. Yesterday was *all* little head thinking. I didn't consider the consequences of planning some half-cocked seduction, only that the ingenuity or the cuteness factor might get me laid again. If I'd thought about it properly, I might've realised I was running the risk of feeling like this again. Used. Not good enough. Because despite saying all was hunky-dory waking in an empty hotel room, I was still left with a sense I'd been dumped like a used cock sock—a used condom.

It gives the adage "treat 'em mean, keep 'em keen" a whole new meaning. I mean, I've never had that mindset with women *personally*, but I can tell you it feels pretty shithouse being on the receiving end. The reverse psychology has totally worked on me because I feel like I need to see her again real soon. And what the fuck! I didn't even get a full night out of it this time before she had me pulling up my jeans, saying her brother might walk in. She couldn't get rid of me quick enough. So why am I so eager to get into her knickers again?

With a huff, I chuck my head back against the sofa, ignoring the itch in my fingers to pick up the phone. Until, what do you know, it rings.

'How do you have my number?'

No *hello*, no *I'm just returning your call.* No après sex coyness or seduction. All the same, I'm still smiling.

'Magic.'

'No, really,' Chastity huffs.

'I should've been called Mike,' I say with a happy sigh. 'Magic Flynn just doesn't have the same ring to it.'

'Oh, I don't know.' Her words run together a little too easily, which makes me think she might've been drinking. 'Something tells me you've got moves Mike couldn't compete with.'

'Was that a compliment?' Alert the press!

'It might be,' she says, all teasing tone. She's definitely been drinking. The only compliments she's ever paid me were in the throes of sex.

'Duchess, I've got moves you wouldn't believe.'

'I'm always suspicious when a man needs to blow his own horn . . .'

'Have you met me?' I say, pointing at my bare chest like she can see. 'I don't need to blow myself.'

'You probably could if you tried.' Her words are an equal weight of titillation and taunt. *This woman.* I find myself laughing, a deep burst of laughter springing from the depths of my chest.

'Two compliments in one minute? Watch yourself, you'll get a nosebleed.'

'You still haven't answered my question,' she says crisply, her tone all business. Chastity is the kind of woman who can cut you down from the knees with a look or a sharp word. *I wonder if I'm turning into a bit of a masochist?* It's hard to reconcile her with the girl telling me she's imagining me with my lips around my own dick.

Note to self: Find out her favourite tipple for next time we're in touching distance. Tipsy chicks are fun.

'I'll tell you what,' I respond. 'I'll answer your question if you answer mine.'

'Are you going to ask me what I'm wearing? What colour lingerie I have on?' Before I have a chance to protest or correct her, she carries on. 'Pink. And lacy.'

I close my eyes and tip back my head, my mind going exactly to there. *Pale pink . . . no, dusky. Same as her nipples.*

'Right, my turn.'

'Sorry, duchess. While that was good to hear and imagine, it wasn't what I wanted to ask.'

A frustrated noise rattles down the line before she adds, 'Oh, go on, then.'

'On a scale of smashed to just tipsy enough to legally consent to me coming around and fucking you senseless, exactly how drunk are you?'

'Probably the latter.'

'Right, I'm putting my boots on.'

'You're funny, But that's not happening. Again, I mean.'

'That's cute.'

'I mean it, Flynn. We can't keep doing this.'

'What, you mean we can't fuck more than once every six months?' I say, trying to get a rise out of her. A man's got to get his kicks somewhere.

'No,' she answers softly, not taking the bait.

'Then I guess you're never gonna know if I can blow myself.'

I find my smile widening at the sound of her snort-giggle and *not* at the thought of blowing myself. I'm not interested in the taste of my own dick, unless it's a part of some kind of girl-to-Flynn transference. Plus, I'm pretty fit but not a fuckin' yogi.

'You can't stop a girl's imagination, Flynn.'

My reply? Just a groan. A carnal groan. God bless this petite blonde purveyor of porn.

'My turn,' she demands, all business again. 'How'd you get my number?'

'Chastity, I've been inside you twice. Don't tell me you feel violated by me being able to call you once in a while.'

She sighs. 'No, that's not exactly it. I'm just trying to work out who the snake is. The Judas in our mutual social circle.'

'We have a mutual social circle?' That's news to me.

'It's more like an oval—imagine a Venn diagram.' I'd

rather imagine her tits in or out of pink lace. *I'm not fussy.* Sadly, I sense she's on a roll, and as such, probably not receptive to my preferred topic currently. 'That little overlap between my circle and yours is pretty small, but someone inhabiting that tiny space is trying to make you and me a thing.'

'By giving me your phone number?'

'Exactly!'

'I don't know how to break it to you,' I reply, rubbing a knuckle against the corner of my eye, 'but no one's trying to fix us up.' Though Keir seems to think some kind of relationship between us is inevitable. *A man can't live by one-nighters alone.* I've done pretty good so far—two for two with Chastity—so it shows what he knows.

'Then how did you get my number? *No one* has my number,' she repeats in a slightly panicked tone. What the fuck!

'That can't be true,' I half say, half laugh. 'How else would people contact you? Is there some kind of bat signal I'm supposed to use? A big light I have to install on the roof with a secret sign?'

'Flynn,' she says gravely. 'You remember what I do for a living?'

'It's not the kind of thing you forget.'

'My business is exactly the reason few people have my number. I have a business number too, but I pay an answering service to screen those calls. Do you get what I'm saying?'

'That you get all kinds of fucked-up calls.' All levity disappears, my molars suddenly clenched tight as her words settle in my gut like a lead weight.

'Well, that's the least of it,' she answers softly.

Fuck. 'What else?'

'This is not a conversation I want to have on a Sunday afternoon. A Sunday afternoon following a delicious brunch and some good company.'

'Don't forget the decent flow of cocktails?'

'Yes. Those, too.'

'Some other time then?' I press, suddenly needing to know exactly what it is she means as all kinds of bullshit runs through my head. Dirty phone calls? A stalker? Threats?

'Maybe, if you tell me which of them gave you my number. My money's on Keir, by the way. Paisley's just not that good of an actress.'

'It wasn't one of our friends, but you're not gonna like it all the same. And just so you know, I like brunch, too.'

'Jealous much?'

'I'm always jealous of people who get to spend time with you.' Shit. Talk about over-reaching.

'Flynn . . .' The way she says my name? It's like disappointment, but it's a ruse because I can hear the smile in her voice, too. 'You're not supposed to say things like that,' she says softly.

I sigh as though anticipating a brush-off, but my sigh is also a ruse because what I say next is nowhere near beaten down or overcome. Quite the opposite.

'I took your phone,' I admit.

'When?'

'When you waddled your way to the bathroom. You know, after we'd fucked.'

Boy, did we fuck. I'd picked her running leggings from the floor, chucking them on the kitchen bench. Turns out, her phone was in a concealed pocket and the way it hit the worktop didn't sound too healthy. So I unravelled the fabric and pulled out her phone, just to check that it wasn't busted.

'Waddled? Are you suggesting I'm duck-like in some sense?'

'Don't you want to know how I got into your phone?'

'Right now, I'm more concerned what you mean about me waddling.'

'Remember, you'd been well and truly *ducked* at that point.'

'You're such an odd man,' she says so softly, I wonder if she's talking to herself. 'Was it my gait? My wobbling bottom? What?'

I groan like I'm in pain. 'Chastity, you can't tell me about your lacy pink undies, then remind me about your fantastic arse. Not unless you really want me to put my boots on and come around there to make you waddle again.'

'*Oh* . . . so you were the *cause* of my waddle.' Her answer is sort of scornful, like I'm talking myself up or something. For the record, I don't need to. And she knows it. We both do.

With the meat of my palm, I palm my meat. 'You were wet.' Unexpectedly, my voice sounds rough as I recall the kitchen. Her bare arse on the bench and my forehead propped on her shoulder, I'd felt content to stay there forever, cocooned in the warmth of her body. Plus, I happened to be staring down at her tits. But she'd stirred beneath me, so I'd stepped back, sad for the loss of her immediately. Her pussy was pink. Wet. Glistening. *Fucking perfect.* But I didn't have long to appreciate the view as she'd hopped down from the worktop. 'I expect you were waddling because you were trying to stop cum from running down your legs.'

It's wrong, but I want to do her bare. Paint her in my cum. Watch the stuff seep out of her and run down her legs.

'Oh, well. I-I'm glad we've had a little chat. That we've cleared up some things. It was nice chatting with you,' she says quickly and through gritted teeth, if I'm not mistaken. 'So . . . goodbye!'

I'm left with a hard-on, a smile, and a phone beeping emptily in my hand.

10

CHASTITY

If anything is going to sort out mixed emotions, it's a Monday morning. Working for myself is a joy. My hours are mostly my own, but sometimes, I still have to drag myself out of bed early. Like today, for instance when we're shooting a scene in a five-star city hotel. I'd tell you which one, but I don't want to get kicked out of the place before we've filmed today's actors, Sasha Savage and Nathan Cox, screwing against a wall of windows, the dramatic backdrop of the city beyond.

I take pride in the beauty of my work. There's the obvious beauty in sex, yes, but I also like to make sure my sets are top-notch. I have a small studio, but I much prefer filming on location; Prague, Barcelona, Ibiza, and places closer to home. *Like my aunt Camilla's potting shed.*

Travel cup in hand, I place it on the roof of my Mini Cooper. Yes, I suppose in some ways I am that clichéd city girl. But not only is my car adorable, she's also very cool. For instance, she has a fabulous name. None of this *Mini* or *Cooper* business. It's Minerva, like the Roman Goddess of warfare. Which is pretty apt as driving in London *is* a battle.

I pull open the rear passenger side door to throw in my bag, when a deep voice calls out in greeting from the other side of the road.

'Beautiful morning, isn't it?'

Is that . . . the waiter from the restaurant? What was his name again?

'Yes, it is, isn't it?' I reply, looking up momentarily into the clear blue sky. This is the song of my people—British people. We're all about the weather. It's so erratic, it's probably been ingrained into our psyche somehow. But it's also a safe conversation starter. Polite, I suppose. *Bugger it. What was his name again?* Throwing my bag on the back seat, I close the door.

'How's your head this morning?' Now *that* wasn't so polite, and neither is the way he's looking at me, or the way his mouth hitches up in one corner.

Hmph. I refrain from swapping him a judge-y look for his judge-y comment, though I glance across at him again. The bastard is chuckling and from his garden gate, it seems. Someone new moved in recently. So he's my new neighbour and not some random out running. Pity because I could've told him to *jog the fuck on.*

On any other day, I might take a moment to appreciate the sight of a fit bloke dressed for the gym, especially one as easy on the eyes as him. But not today. Today, my head is a mess from my conversation yesterday with Flynn. We aren't supposed to be building a friendship. He was just a means to get my orgasm back. Which brings me to another sore point in my day. Quite literally sore, from overwork, because my orgasm hasn't returned. So fucking much for that plan.

'Perfectly fine, thank you.' My answer is crisp, if not a little belated, as I clear the back of the car on my way to the driver's side. *I am fine, if I discount the fact that I almost gave myself friction burns this morning.*

'Have a good day in the stacks,' he calls. His words almost cause me to falter mid step. How in the hell does he know about . . . *Ohhh.* It dawns on me that he's referring to my fictious career as a historian—a historian of the phallus—and *not* my fantasy of *Atonement's* library scene. Bloody Flynn Phillips dominating my bloody thoughts. He has single-handedly spoiled the start to my day, and he's not even here!

With a weak wave and an equally weak smile, I open the driver's side door and slip into the seat before pulling away from the kerb. In my rear-view mirror, his assessing eyes follow me down the street.

'Come on, you. Shove up.'

'Oh, you are in such a crabby mood this morning,' Hillary, my latest hire, moves along the love seat at the end of the bed. Just the two of us are here at the moment, though Paisley is due soon, along with the two stars of the show. 'Here,' Hills says, shoving a banana in my hand. 'Your blood sugar must be low.'

I murmur my thanks as I take it, peel it savagely, and bite a whacking great piece off the end. 'What?'

'You're making my puddings feel all queer,' he says with a shivery wince. I've no idea what his "puddings" are, and I know better than to ask. And despite the misleading name, Hillary isn't actually a girl, but one Christopher Hillary.

'Darling,' I say, one brow raised. 'You are every inch the queer.'

'You say the nicest things,' he responds, fluffing imaginary hair. Not that he doesn't have hair—he has plenty. Red and wiry, it covers both his face and his head. Stylishly so. He's quite the hipster. And as camp as a row of pink tents—pink tents festooned with floral bunting. He's also a film student, which makes him super useful and a bit of a love.

As you can imagine, in my line of work, it can be pretty difficult getting suitable staff. I don't have a huge budget because Fast Girls doesn't produce films for the mainstream porn market. My customers are subscribers to my website, and mainly women, though sometimes couples, and are interested in something other than mass-marketed porn. They want tasteful. They want seduction. They want fucking from something other than the perspective of a man deep-throating the equivalent of a Barbie doll. *Because that's not really sexy at all.*

But it is hard hiring suitable crew. I'm told there's a certain awkwardness in the job. Whether you're dealing with lighting or running errands, it can be strange lurking in a room fully clothed while trying to look like you're *not* watching naked people getting it on. Once the initial worry of being turned on, and worse still, the possibility of being called out for it, is lost (which doesn't take long because, believe me, there's nothing sexy in the production of porn) I'm told it still makes people seriously question their life choices.

But not me. I make a good living out of this, and I'd say the same goes for the adult actors. And while they themselves always look like they're enjoying themselves, I know that's not necessarily the case. It's part of the fantasy, and they deliver because they're professionals. And if they didn't like it, I'm sure they'd find some other form of work.

'Shitty morning?' Hills asks, who is officially my part-time production assistant while he studies film at a local university.

'How can you tell?'

'I'm a sensitive soul. An empath. Not to mention your aura,' he adds, waving his hand in the general direction of my head, 'is sort of the colour of . . . fucked off.'

'Then my aura speaks the truth.' I pause for a beat. 'What colour is your aura today?'

'Pink fairy dust,' he answers with a straight face. 'What did your gorgeous brother do to piss on your cornflakes this morning?' Hills has a crush on Max, one that I tease him about mercilessly, but I'm not in the mood today.

'Max has gone to Goa.'

Hillary pulls an expression of emphatic disapproval. 'It's all right for some.'

'Isn't it just. My mother probably paid for him to go just to get him out from under my influence.'

'Families,' he says with a shrug. 'So are you going to tell me why your face is as long as an undertaker's tape measure?'

'I left my travel mug on the roof of my car and drove off.'

But that's not the only reason. In this morning's mail, I discovered a brochure I'd recently sent for when I arrived at the hotel. Not shoes or pretty underwear, but a brochure of men. Statistic of men, anyway.

Last week, I'd been invited to Ella's little boy's birthday party, which was less than fun. Not because it was filled with children and noise, but rather I was the only woman there without a child of her own. Paisley was there, of course, and technically, she doesn't have a child. Sorcha is Keir's daughter, but I feel like Paisley doesn't count that, given that she isn't heading rapidly towards her thirtieth birthday.

To cut a long story short, I got home late afternoon and opened a bottle of red almost as soon as I'd stepped through the door. One glass led to two and two led to a third. And a third led to a website for a fertility clinic. Hence, my brochure of sperm donor details.

I thought I'd feel more excited about it. I'm not going to think about it. I mean it. It's not like I'm thirty yet!

'Fuck's sake,' he huffs. 'That's not worth getting your knickers in a knot over. You could've stopped at Starbucks.' Now it's my turn to pull a face. Starbucks, bleurgh. 'What am I saying?' he adds, slapping his forehead. 'We're in a hotel!'

Note to self: Never go apply for MI5. Espionage isn't for you.

'*Ohhh!* Hillary said knickers,' Paisley says, breezing into the room. 'Careful. Say it ten more times and you'll turn hetero.'

'It's so unfair, isn't it?' His gaze flicks to me, then back to Paisley as he makes a show of giving her a thorough inspection, up then down.

'What?' Paisley trills, her own gaze following his as though expecting to find something wrong with her outfit.

'You had *sex* this weekend. Lots and lots of sex.'

'What's wrong with that?' She straightens, all smiles and bright eyes. 'And what's wrong with you two?'

'Because we haven't.'

'Speak for yourself,' I reply.

74

'Right!' he scoffs, crossing one leg over. 'Is that not a face of extreme sexual frustration?' Hills points a finger in my direction but directs his words at my friend.

'I'm keeping out of this,' she says, laughing as she slips out of her coat and hangs it in the open closet. 'I have something for you.' As a grumbling Hillary moves from the love seat to begin unpacking our gear in the other room, Paisley slides in next to me. 'Give me that,' she says, taking the flaccid banana skin from my hand. 'When I paid the bill at brunch, that waiter guy asked me to give you this.' She slides a business card into my hand.

'Tate Peters,' I read aloud. 'I saw him today.'

'Where?'

'Looks like he's my neighbour.' I shrug, not really wanting to get into this. Since Paisley paired off with Keir, she's been a little militant about these sorts of things.

'Maybe that's how he knew your name!'

'How do you work that out?'

'Maybe he's taken a parcel in for you, or maybe your mail was delivered there by mistake? But at least we now know he's solvent and not a waiter squatting on million-aire row.' Looking up, I frown.

'What has that got anything to do with it?' It's nothing to be fabulously impressed over. I live in Chelsea. You can't buy a spot on a park bench for a million.

'Because I know you. And a starving artist *isn't your cup of tea*.' The latter she delivers in a terrible rendition of a British accent.

'You sound like Dick Van Dyke, even if you are right.' I want a man ready to settle down, not one who needs babying.

'Thank'e gov'nor.' She doffs an invisible cap.

'Careful, someone will steal you and shove you up a chimney.'

'Are you two talking about lesbian porn in there?'

'No!' we yell simultaneously.

'Good looking, solvent, owns his own business, according to that card.' She pauses from counting off on her fingers, pointing at the business card that speaks of quality and expense. *Tate Peters, Owner.* 'Appears sane,' she adds, continuing with her count, 'and he likes you.' Her smile is a touch indulgent in response to my scrunched expression. 'At least you won't have to travel far in your walk of shame?'

'And if he turns out to be a terrible person, I'll have to move or spend the rest of my life sneaking around to avoid him.'

'For fuck's sake,' she grumbles.

'That's what I said,' yells Hills.

'Just go for a drink with the man before you decide he's giving out *Fatal Attraction* vibes. Unless there's something or *someone* keeping you from dating?'

I make a noncommittal noise, our conversation halting as Hillary appears rather dramatically. Framed by the connecting double doors, he throws his head back, his hands clasped at his chest.

'Very Gloria Swanson,' Paisley teases.

'Don't tell me,' I add, 'you're ready for your close-up now.'

'It's the kind of close-up that worries me,' she continues. 'I'm not holding the pussy light up for him.' And yes, that is an actual thing. For close-ups and I'm saying no more.

'Are you two quite finished?' he asks. Paisley and I look at each other. I nod, and she shrugs. 'You've totally stolen my dramatic effect,' he grumbles, one hand now on his cocked hip.

'A do-over?' I suggest. Hills shrugs before making a show of theatrically "centring himself".

'Ladies and straight people, as Fast Girl Media's official cock-ficionado, I'd like to announce that your stars are here.'

'Sasha's arrived?' I ask. She's not the best time keeper, I've found, though she is a lovely girl. Really sweet.

'She has. As has Nathan. He's currently in the bathroom preparing. You know.' Hills ducks his head an inch, the small movement speaking volumes. Not that it matters as he makes a swift rude gesture with his hand.

'I'm surprised you haven't offered to help him with that,' Paisley says, picking up her hefty makeup bag.

'Nathan doesn't even go gay for pay,' Hills pouts. 'But it's just as well I work on straight shoots, really. All those hetero pheromones flying around keep me in line and stop me from the pet shop dilemma.'

'What's a pet shop dilemma?' she asks, slinging the bag over her arm.

'Let's just say my flatmates wouldn't be impressed with me coming home with handfuls of irresistible and adorably cute merchandise.' Paisley sniggers. 'And boss lady here wouldn't like me coming *on* the cute merchandise.'

As the three of us make our way into the other room, I slap Hillary's butt.

'Sexual harassment in the workplace!' he trills.

'You should be so lucky.'

'Don't I know it, babe.'

11

CHASTITY

SATURDAY AFTERNOON, I'm working in my home office, which doubles as my editing suite, when my phone rings. Still concentrating on the screen, I answer it without looking at the screen.

'G'day, duchess.'

Flynn. Was his tone always so seductive? As if his accent wasn't hard enough to resist. As if *he* isn't hard enough to resist.

'Flynn,' I reply, surprised my words sounds so even, almost serene, because it feels like a flock of small birds are beating their wings against my chest. *Okay, knickers.* 'So nice of you to call.'

'That's me—that's *nice* Flynn Phillips, not to be confused with *bloody Flynn Phillips.*'

'Oh,' I answer, biting back a grin. 'I wonder who refers to you that way.'

'I heard this cute blonde chick telling her mates I annoyed the shit out of her at a barbecue recently.'

'A barbecue, you say? I have to wonder what kind of company you're keeping. It's hardly the weather for standing around outdoors. You must be hanging out with a strange crowd.' He laughs softly, which makes me feel all kinds of warm and satisfied.

'Nah, they weren't all weird. Only the idiots stood outside. The sensible ones were indoors, sharing secrets.'

'If you tell me there were pyjamas and feathery pillows involved, I'm afraid I'll have to spoil it for you by telling you I've already seen that film.'

'Fuck, you must be *the* perfect woman.' I sort of snort and laugh at the same time at such a ridiculous notion, and even though this is just a silly, joking conversation, his words still warm my insides. 'Smart, sexy as fuck, and you like porn.'

'What makes you say I like it?'

'Babe,' he answers solemnly. 'Are you tryin' to make me cry? Please don't say otherwise because that'd be like telling a kid there's no Santa Clause.'

'I do watch a lot of it,' I admit. 'Mostly in a professional capacity.' I consider turning the volume up on the ménage clip playing out on my screen but decide against encouraging him.

'I feel like this could be a marriage made in heaven.'

'What a pity that I don't take proposals over the phone.'

'Get a lot of them, do you? Proposals?'

Once. I've been proposed to once in my life. *And look how that turned out*, my mind pipes up. I push the thoughts away, matching Flynn's enquiry with a taunt. 'Well, you did just say yourself I'm perfect.'

'Yeah, apart from that mouth of yours.'

'I don't remember any complaints from our time in the Seychelles.' Why did I say that? I don't have long to process the thought as he groans—yes, that kind of groan

—the kind that hits me right where it shouldn't. It's the kind of noise a man might make while being tortured. *By a tongue.* 'Sorry,' I add quickly. 'Don't answer that.'

'Jesus, duchess, I can't. All the blood from my brain has drained to my crotch.'

'Sorry,' I say again, without feeling sorry at all. It's hard to feel any sort of contrition when imagining his erection. *While imagining Flynn Phillips with his erection in his hand.*

So not sorry.

'Actually . . . ' He draws the word out like a taunt, all smoky and sort of sexy. 'You might say I'm currently watching a poor interpretation of exactly that thing.'

It takes me a moment to work out exactly what he means, his tone a spike of heat to my bloodstream. 'Exactly what thing?'

'She doesn't have your technique, but I like the way she stares up at him with his balls in her mouth.'

'You're . . . watching porn while talking to me? God, you are such a bloke,' I huff, the heat in my veins now fuelled by something else.

'Nah, not really. It's just playing in the background. Nothing could be more interesting than spending time with you, even if I have to make do with the sound of your voice.' I do *not* feel placated. 'Say something sexy to me,' he adds, humour colouring his tone.

'Next time I see you, I'm going to kick you in the balls.'

'Calm down, killer.' *Kill-ah.* 'I'm just yanking your chain. But you and me? We could make a beautiful team.'

'If you and I were the last people on the planet, the world would go extinct.'

'Nah. You wouldn't be able to keep your hands off me.'

'From around your neck, maybe.'

'I know I wouldn't be able to keep my hands off you.'

'Well . . . that's probably a little closer to the truth,' I reply snippily. Even though I feel slightly mollified, it doesn't hurt to hear he finds me desirable. 'I have to get back to work.' *Before I say anything else ridiculous.*

'I could come around and help?'

'Oh, tempting,' I reply even though I sound like I mean the opposite.

'I'm a connoisseur of porn—I could consult.'

'All for a small fee?'

'I'm sure we could come to some arrangement,' he replies, his tone back to smoky. 'We could make it mutually beneficial. What do you say?'

'I'd say you're pushing your luck, and I'm hanging up now.'

'You don't know what you're missing.'

'Goodbye, Flynn,' I reply right before I hit *end*.

———

Sometime later, the doorbell rings, which is strange enough. I don't get many callers, not without a prior arrangement, at any rate. I glance at the clock on my screen and realise three hours have passed since Flynn called. But it's not quite eight yet, so maybe it's a package. Or, as has happened before, a takeaway delivery to the wrong address.

When I open the door, I discover its none of those things. Except, I suppose it's the kind of package I want, even if I seldom admit it to myself, because Flynn Phillips *is* the full package.

Standing on my doorstep, a black leather jacket coats

his broad shoulder, dark denim clinging to long legs, the same boots from his *Mellors* gig completing the rugged look. I don't know whether it's the sight of him standing there or his cocky grin, but the words that fall from my mouth aren't exactly sane.

'You really don't miss a trick, do you?' I push the door wider, one hand on the door handle, the other on my hip. And then I realise what a state I must look. Boyfriend jeans turned up at the ankle to hide the ragged seams, though there's no concealing the holes in the knees. *I didn't buy them like this. They're just old.* As is the tatty man's shirt I'm wearing. Pink, of all colours—my complexion doesn't like pink.

'What . . .' I stop myself from continuing as I notice he appears to be holding something behind his back. Do I *really* want to know? 'What are you hiding?' Apparently, the answer to that is yes.

'Duchess,' he says, his mouth curved in his perma-cheeky grin. 'This is where you've got to play along—be a little creative. I know you've got it in you, or at least you will have, if things go to plan.'

'I'm not having sex with you today,' I blurt out.

'But we're good for tomorrow, right?' In the absence of trusting my own words, I just shake my head. 'Hang on, we're gonna start again.'

'Start what again?' I ask, exasperated. This is the Flynn Phillips' effect. One minute, I want to kiss him, and the next, slap him across the face.

'Play along. Look—I'm ringing your bell.'

'You're—' Apparently, he's a man of his word, though why he's ringing my doorbell when I'm right *here* and the door is *open*, I don't know.

'Oh, whoever can that be?' I ask, deadpan.

Flynn stares at me with a playful kind of intensity, the kind of look that makes my heart skip a beat, sending the pulse elsewhere. And then I notice his arms moving as though to reveal what's behind his back. A motorbike helmet. *Jesús, María y José,* the man rides a motorbike. *Of course, he does*, my consciousness cries because apparently, God is laughing at you today!

Definitely laughing as his other hand reveals a pizza box emblazed with the name of my local Italian joint.

'Pizza delivery.' The words sound like a taunt as I bring a hand to my mouth and begin to chuckle. A chuckle that turns to the kind of laughter that has me clutching my sides

'Surprised?' Flynn asks, his gaze still filled with the same kind of confidence, the same kind of daring. I notice the skin around his eyes is creased in the outer corners, as though he'd spent his childhood laughing and running around in the sun.

'Just a little.'

'None of that,' he cautions. 'Back into character. I'm about to start my lines.'

'You can't be serious,' I begin.

'As serious as turning up to dig your flower beds.'

It all comes back to me in a flood of heat and sensation —the image of Flynn in my kitchen, his tanned and toned body over mine. The feeling of the cold kitchen counter under me, and the fiery brilliance of my well overdue release building between my thighs. I swallow and ignore the pulsing sensory memory. That day, he might not have been able to conjure a library for me, but he did channel a little bit of rough in the guise of Mellors. Truthfully, I'd never had sex like that before, so urgent and frantic, and it resulted in the best orgasm I've ever had. *But that could be the result of not having come since the last—the first—time we'd had sex.* Then to cap it all, Flynn above me, with his perpetual cocky gleam in his eye, told me about his pizza plot. And his expectation that we do things his way next time.

This is madness.

'Dug my flower beds,' I repeat with a touch of asperity. 'There's a euphemism if I ever heard one.'

'That would be ploughed, babe.'

'Are you always this . . . happy?' I'd wanted to say *annoying*, but the truth somehow falls from my mouth instead.

'Happiness is a choice. It's also a result of being around you.' He doesn't give me a moment to process that little vignette. There's not time to be irritated or flattered or to call him out. 'Come on, play along. I told you it would be my turn next.'

'I chose *Atonement*—a wonderful piece of literature, and your fantasy is pizza delivery porn?'

'Porn shaming is beneath you, Chastity,' he says with a pout. 'That's not what you're doing right now, is it?' Damn him and his infuriatingly sexy grin.

'No, absolutely not,' I answer. 'But I'm still not having sex with you.'

'See this,' he says, holding the box aloft. 'This is the next best thing to sex. And if you're a good girl, I might give you some.'

Oh, the innuendo! I shake my head not quite believing that, despite my words, he's winning me over—that I'm about to play along. But I suppose that's the thing about this man. He's persuasive. And irritating. And has a magic dick, which apparently, makes me easy.

'Oh, mister pizza delivery boy,' I begin, aiming to channel some breathless, sultry coquette.

'That's mister pizza delivery *man*.' His lips twitch, belying his deep, sombre tone.

'Okay, Mister pizza delivery man. I ordered a pizza and now I can't find my purse to pay you.' I flutter my lashes dramatically, pleased my front door is concealed from my neighbour's view by a large hedge.

'Jeez, lady. That's too bad, lady.' He makes to turn, and I can't believe he's trying to make me work for this, the total git!

'Wait!' I say, reaching out to grasp his strong forearm. 'I'm hungry. Really . . . hungry.' *Rawrr!* 'Is there a way we can come to some kind of deal?' Never mind the hedge, I hope my neighbours can't hear this.

'Deal?' Flynn's gaze falls to where my hand touches his jacket, and when his eyes rise to mine, pure blue heat burns there.

'It would be such a shame to let this go to waste,' I purr, pulling my hand away and accidentally brushing my knuckles against the hardness of his dick.

'Wasted sausage is never right.'

'Is that what you have for me there?' I ask as Flynn takes a step forward, backing me into the house.

'Yeah, I got sausage for you. And it's extra-large.' *Extra-laaj.*

'Flynn, no one likes sausage pizza.' I gasp, trying to tamp down my giggling.

'Come on,' he cajoles. 'I was almost there!'

'So soon?' I say, resuming my role. 'You came awfully fast.'

'Now who's adlibbing?' he responds, pushing the front door closed with his foot.

'Well, it's such a lazy plot device. Is there extra cheese?' I add, sniggering still as he continues to back me farther into the house.

'You've seen my dick. You know it's cut.'

This time, I laugh loudly. 'Maybe you *could* consult.' God knows he's open enough.

'Truthfully, duchess, the only consulting I'm interested in is with your pussy.'

'I have a confession to make.'

'Go on.' Flynn drops the pizza box on the console table and his bike helmet to a chair.

'I'm afraid I ate earlier.' My heel meets with the wall at the base of the stairs, Flynn taking two steps closer until our bodies almost touch. But almost isn't good enough, it seems, as my hand slips between the halves of his open jacket to find his solid chest. It isn't there long as he takes it between his larger ones to bring it to his mouth where he presses his lips against my palm.

His eyes are full of mischief and desire, his tongue darting out to lick my palm. The action obscene, the sensation echoing between my legs.

'Doesn't matter,' his deep voice rumbles, 'I'm gonna stuff you full anyway.'

12

CHASTITY

WE COME TOGETHER in a rush of heat and need. His hands grip my hair as mine clutch the cotton of his T-shirt, something greedy and grasping driving us on. It's a kiss full of longing and need—the kind of kiss that steals both breath and sense.

A bruising kiss, I think as he pulls back, watching me with those hungry blue eyes, his ragged breath matching mine. *God, I want to be bruised by him, want to feel his touch on my body into next week.*

'The things I want to do to you,' Flynn rasps as he presses his lips to my neck.

'I'm not eating pizza from your dick.' Despite being more turned on than I have been since I was last in his arms, it seems nervous ridiculousness is still capable of spewing from my mouth.

'Ah, you've seen that movie, too,' he replies, pulling back and pushing the curls from my face, a look of indulgent amusement curling in the corner of his mouth. 'Shame I already ordered a pizza with a hole in the middle.'

'You're ridiculous,' I murmur, realising the mess I've made of his T-shirt. Unfurling my hands, I smooth away the creases with my palms, then slip them higher up his ridiculously defined pecs. I'm surrounded almost daily by near perfect bodies, so why is his so hard to resist?

'I'm ridiculously fucking hard.' My eyes slip down between our bodies to where the strong, proud length of him is pressed against the fabric of his jeans. I swallow deeply, my teeth digging into my lip to prevent the words on my tongue.

Give it to me. Fuck me. Fuck my mouth.

'You want it.' His voice seems lower, harder, all levity gone. 'It's all for you, Chastity. I'm so fucking hard for you.'

Without speaking, I slide my hands higher, tipping onto my toes to push the leather from his shoulders. His jacket hits the wooden floor with a surprisingly solid *thunk*. 'Looks like I'm staying,' he says with a crooked grin.

'It would appear so.'

'I'm not fucking you in the kitchen this time,' he says, his grin replaced by something else. 'So you'd better get your arse up those stairs.'

Oh, my. Commanding looks good on Flynn Phillips.

I turn swiftly, excitement building in my chest like a kid on Christmas morning. I reach the first stair, and the absolute exhilaration of Flynn's body so close behind me has me bolting to the top of the stairs. I can't explain it. It must be my fight or flight reactions kicking in. I'm light-headed with anticipation and feel as desperate as a doe on the escape. Each *clunk* of his boots on the stairs behind me has my heart pounding in my chest until, at the second to last stair from the top, my excitement hits fever pitch when solid hands find my hips.

I raise my head, catching a glimpse of myself in the

large mirror at the top of the stairs. My complexion is flushed and my hair a mess, and it's no wonder I'm running—no wonder my body thinks it might be under attack—because as I look at the reflection of Flynn behind me, he looks like the devil himself. *Dark. Wicked. Self-satisfied.*

'Not so fast, duchess.' Strong arms loop my waist, his body enveloping mine as his hands reach for the fly of my jeans.

'What are you doing?' I whisper as he flicks the button open. My gaze falls to the sinew in the tanned arms curling around my waist, and I think I might actually moan. Or whimper. It's a little hard to tell when the man you want so desperately is taking his own time spelling out his plans. I lift my head to the mirror again to try to gauge what he's thinking by his expression—to see what plans he has in store for me. Standing one stair above him reduces the disparity in our heights, but I don't feel any bigger or stronger. If anything, I still feel like prey. The willing kind.

'Patience is the key to paradise.' His deep voice rumbles against my cheek, his face pressed against mine. *He really is breathtaking.*

'Those are some lofty goals there. You sure you're going to be able to deliver?'

'I didn't hear any complaints last time.' In the mirror, my expression twists. 'It's a proverb, duchess,' he says softly, a lock of his dark hair falling across his forehead as he presses his lips to my cheek. His eyes gleam wickedly as he moves the collar of my shirt to test the soft skin of my neck with his teeth. 'Read a fuckin' book.'

'Patience is also apparently a virtue—'

'One you weren't blessed with.'

'You can't have everything.' Why did that sound like a purr?

'Wrong.' His tongue licks away the sting of his teeth as he begins delivering soft open-mouthed kisses to the space behind my ear. 'You've got the lot, and I'm tasting it all tonight.'

'Oh, God, is there anything as unravelling as kisses there?'

'Was that a rhetorical question?' he murmurs. I huff a short laugh, not realising my breathless words were fully audible. 'Because if not, I'd have to disagree. There's nothing quite like a good hard fuck.'

I'd have to agree . . .

In the mirror, Flynn's expression is the embodiment of wickedness as he lifts his hands to the buttons on my shirt, managing to loosen each tiny hinderance without touching me once. Never before would I have imagined the art of undressing would be so erotic, but it leaves my body trembling as the much-washed cotton brushes my skin.

As he flips the final one from the placket, his large hands push the sides wider, revealing the ruffled trim of my blue bra.

'Fucking heavenly.' How can a guttural curse sound so reverent? If I had the answer, it's lost as he trails the back of his fingers against the soft swell of my breast, before slipping his hand inside. I gasp at the contact, and as he brushes my nipple, my body arches on instinct, chasing his touch. 'You like that.' The coarse pads of his fingers rub my nipples. 'So rosy and delicious.'

I whimper as his hand slips away, my body sagging against his, but as his fingers find the button of my jeans and work it loose, my attention is dialled once more to ten.

No longer fastened to my waist, my baggy jeans hit the stairs as every fibre of my being hums for his touch. I watch as he flattens his hand on my belly, dragging it down my skin, my breath hitching as his long fingers disappear under the elastic of my mismatched pink cotton underwear.

'What are we doing?' I rasp, rolling my head back, giving him access to more of my neck. My nipples ache as between my legs pounds, and while there's something erotic about being covered yet exposed, I long for him to touch me everywhere. I long for him to fuck me now.

'I would've thought that was obvious,' his deep voice rumbles. If I had anything else to ask, the words turn to dust as his finger finds the wet ribbon of flesh between my legs.

'Fuck,' he grunts, pressing his erection so solidly against me, it wedges the cotton of my knickers between my butt cheeks, his large body curving around mine like an embrace.

'My bedroom's just . . . there, oh, God, *just there.*' My hips jerk as the pad of his index finger finds my clit, presses it, toys with it, then slips away, leaving me a pulsing, twitching mess. But I don't have time to object or complain as his full hand cups me. Rocking my body against his, he sandwiches me between his cock and hand.

'That's it, duchess, ride my hand. Find your relief.'

'Doesn't work that way,' I whimper as he rotates his palm. 'Let me step out of my jeans, at least.'

'I kind of like you trapped like this.'

Instantly, my mind goes to a recent shoot at a local hotel. Sophia was strung willingly between the base posts of a four-poster bed, tortured and teased in the best kind of way until her orgasm, and subsequently her legs, gave out. What would it feel like to be tethered by Flynn? Brought to the brink again and again until both my body and mind are limp?

'You're so fuckin' hot,' he rasps. Grasping my chin with his free hand, he turns my mouth to his. It's a fierce kiss, one that swiftly becomes a battle of teeth and probing tongues. He tastes of toothpaste and temptation as I grind myself against his hand, and he grinds into me from behind.

With one last bite of my lip, he twists my face back to the mirror again, my chin still in his hand.

A moment later, I cry out as his fingers thrust expertly between my legs—I spread out my arms, one hand grabbing the bannister, the other flattened against the wall, whimpering as he gathers wetness from my seam, dragging those long fingers back to my clit.

'Please, Flynn.' I find myself whimpering as I writhe. 'Please touch me harder. Please make me come.'

His answer is a low groan and whispered husky, '*Fuck.*'

I try once more to widen my stance, my hips moving and chasing his fingers as I chant my litany of need— *please, please, please!*—as an intensity, white hot and fluid, begins to build in my extremities. The rhythm of his fingertips is sublime, and as he slips his fingers into the cup of my bra again, palming my breast, I cry out.

'*Oh my. Oh, f-fuck!*' My knees buckle from an overload of sensations, his fingers sliding fast and wet across my clit, my nipple hard and aching between his fingertips. His sucking bite at my neck, and the look of us in the mirror— my desperation and his absolute determination to draw me to the edge at his will.

'You're so fucking beautiful,' he rasps. 'So fucking slick.' But I can't . . . can't concentrate on anything but the feeling between my legs, my eyes glued to our reflection, flicking back and forth between his expression and where his hand disappears under the soft pink cotton of my knickers. Between his sucking and licking and dirty encouragement, I can barely make sense of it all. All I know is I need this connection, this orgasm, like others need air.

From fast finger work to barely there, Flynn teases me with a bare swipe. I'm up on my toes immediately, chasing his touch, rewarded as he thrusts two fingers into my depths. Two fingers, then three, his thumb pressing my clit.

'That's it, beautiful. Come for me. Come all over my fucking hand.'

I buck. Cry out. Fall. Come apart. And when cognisance returns, I'm held up only by his arms.

13

FLYNN

I CARRY her into the bedroom, the one she points to with a leisurely wave of her arm. Seems to be the right one, though with dove grey walls and a huge bed in the centre of a velvet covered wall. The place looks like a hotel room. *A hotel room with an unmade bed.*

'I can see you're a bit of a slob on the quiet.' I kick the door closed, just in case her brother is about, though we've left her jeans on the landing. But I doubt she'd have let me finger fuck her on the stairs if he was. It wasn't a conscious decision on my part. I saw the mirror and thought, *what the fuck?* Seemed like a good idea to strip her there and watch her blush deepen, then make her walk naked into her room. An arse like hers should be available to view. Not universally, of course. I'm not a complete fuckwit Neanderthal, but there's something about her that makes me want to keep her to myself.

Jesus, I hope she's not going to sleep, I think when she doesn't answer, but it doesn't seem so as I lay her down on the bed. Her hair splayed out against the mass of pillows like a halo around her head, her body languid and

94

submissive as she stretches out along the bed. What is it about women and pillows and cushions? The attraction, I mean. Beds and sofas worldwide are infected with the fuckers.

I'm surprised she'd let me carry her at all, intense orgasm or no. Chastity is a rare bird, and I don't even think she knows it. Keir's told me what she did for Paisley by taking her in, and how she looks after her brother. How good she is to her employees and her friends, and how she threatened to find a lookalike of Paisley's ex to use him as a gimp in one of her X-rated movies. Not that, from what I've seen, they're that kind of films. She's heaps good to her mates—it's just my balls she wants to bust. But she is a good woman. A strong one, too. I like that she pushes, just the same as I like how she can take the pushback.

'Are you going to get naked or what?' *So much for submissive.* Drawing her hands under her head, she crosses her legs at the ankle, the pink painted toes of her right foot pressing against her left.

'I will if you will,' I drawl.

As quick as a flash, she sits up and starts pulling the shirt from her shoulders. It gets tangled at her wrists, and she huffs with frustration, pulling it over her head, which leaves her hair looking like a blonde nest. What in the hell do they call that shade, anyway? It isn't one colour, and I know it isn't from a bottle, unless she's in the habit of dying both collar *and* cuffs. It's like a riot of summer— flaxen curls mixed in with honey, butterscotch, and gold falling into her face as she leans forward to loosen her bra. Both items are quickly deposited on the floor, my cock harder than ever as she hooks her thumbs into the thin sides of her undies, wiggling them down over her hips. As they reach her ankles, she flicks them from her foot across the room. The woman deserves a round of applause.

'I win,' she purrs, leaning back against the pillows again like Mata fucking Hari.

'No, no, you don't.' My words are delivered with a deep, rumbling chuckle. 'The prize is all mine, duchess.'

'Flynn Phillips, are you trying to flatter me?' Something blooms inside me, satisfying and sweet.

'I'm just calling it as I see it. And what I see is pretty damn fine.' Understatement of the year right there, even if she's turned a little pink in pleasure. Fuck me, she's gorgeous. All milky skin and pink bits. *How come it gets better each time, seeing her naked? Six months I waited between the first and second time we fucked. This time around, I could barely wait a week.* 'Touch your tits for me, Chastity.'

'Did you just use my name?'

I feel my smile hitch as I move to the end of the bed. 'What? Am I supposed to call you something else? You're not one of those women who like to be demeaned in bed, are you?' She laughs a low and sultry sound but doesn't answer, and though something tells this is unlikely, I carry on. 'I can roll with that. What's your favourite? Do you like whore or slut? Daddy's little cum bucket.' She tries not to laugh but can't keep a straight face. 'I think I like Flynn's fuck doll,' I say, rubbing a considering hand across my chin. 'That one has a little something to it. The alliteration, maybe.'

'Why don't you give it a go?' she answers all silken voiced. 'Try it on for size?'

'No, thanks. I like my balls where they are. I expect it'd be a bit painful to suddenly find them in my mouth.'

'Bright boy,' she answers, her gaze making a slow

sweep of my body. 'Bright man,' she amends, her eyes suddenly glued to my crotch. 'Are we going to argue all day, or are you going to fuck me?'

Fuck me, I like this version of Chastity. I mean, I like all the versions of her, including the Chastity who looks at me like she doesn't quite know whether she wants to hit me or screw me, but I know which I prefer. A close second is her slapping me *while* screwing me so, you know, I'm not fussy.

'Depends,' I answer. 'Are you gonna touch your tits or not?' And she does. *Fuck me blind.* 'That's right. Pinch those rosy nipples. Make them hard.' Just like a posh hotel, she has one of those cushioned benches at the foot of her bed. It's in the way, but I'll need it in a while, so I nudge myself between it and the bed, pulling off my boots. Reaching behind me, I grasp my T-shirt and pull it off from the neck.

'Slowly,' she murmurs, her eyes dark and avid, her tongue darting out to wet her luscious deep pink lips. 'It's too nice a job to rush.'

'You're not at work now. I'll be the one giving directions from here on in.'

'You're spoiling all my fun.'

'You say that, yet you look to be enjoying yourself.' My eyes travel over every inch of her skin, from where her cherry-ripe nipples peek between pink fingertips to the sweetness glistening between her thighs. *All for me,* my mind roars. *Fucking perfect.* 'Has anyone ever told you you've got gorgeous tits?' *More than a handful. Full and round. I'm gonna bury myself between them,* I think as the buckle of my belt *clinks* in my haste to loosen it.

'I'm going to guess you weren't breastfed,' she murmurs.

'I'm game if you want to give it a try.'

'You really are the most . . .' Her breath hitches as her words drain away. 'You aren't wearing any underwear.'

'I'm not a fan of laundry day.' I chuckle at her expression, the mixture of scandal and delight. 'Reckon you're a fan of me going commando, though.' I slide a condom from the back pocket of my jeans, flicking it onto the bed before they hit the deck, then trail my fingers along my length before giving it a decent tug.

'Need you so bad.' My words are rougher even as things become clearer. Chastity likes the sight of my cock in my hand. She seems to like the direction, too. She might run a porn company, and she might spend her days surrounded by sex, but she wants this. Right now, she wants *me*.

'Do you shave or wax, and can I volunteer to help?'

'Were you dropped on your head as a child?' She smiles up at me, and her lips are kiss plump and her cheeks lightly flushed.

'Babe, I'm one of four boys, and in the rough and tumble of that life, I've fallen from a horse at least twice and got hit on the head by a two-by-four another time.' I hiss as I squeeze the head of my dick, but because I like the sound of her laugh, I carry on. 'I've been wiped out in the surf more times than I care to admit, and when I was a kid, Raftery, my younger brother, pushed me off the top of a slippery dip, and I might've broke my head.'

'Things are becoming so much clearer to me.'

Ah, man. Her laughter is like crack. Not that I've tried it. I drew the line at a little dope—a little cannabis—in uni back in Aus. These days, a cold beer and a hot woman are the extent of my vices. *And none have ever been hotter than this woman.*

'Nah, I'm just fuckin' with you. It was actually my arm that broke.'

While I love to make her laugh, I'm conscious of not derailing this train, so I take my cock into my hand and begin to jack it. Slowly.

'Open your legs, duchess,' I rasp. 'Remind me how pretty your pussy is.'

Her groan is one of pure need and carnality, and though she pauses, she tentatively spreads for me.

'Fuck, that is one beautiful sight. You are the most gorgeous creature alive. I've been dying to taste your cunt for six long months.'

Her hips jerk from the bed as she whispers, *'Flynn, yes!'*

Fuck, yes. 'You like the sound of that? Will you mewl and curse like you did at the beach? Will you tighten your hands in my hair and ride my face?'

'Please, Flynn . . .' She draws out my name over endless syllables.

'Is that a yes?'

'Just tell me what you want. Please.'

I want you wet on my mouth and my chin.

I want your cries in my ear and your body shaking beneath mine.

'Babe, it's like getting a glimpse into heaven watching you come, and I'm gonna make you come again and again. I'm gonna make you come so hard you won't remember your name. I'm gonna bury my head between your legs and make it my home.'

With that, I release my cock and wrap both hands around her ankles, dragging her down to the end of her bed. Unable to resist the proximity of her lush mouth, I brace my hands either side of her head and press my lips to hers.

'Oh, Flynn . . .' She wraps her fingers around my wrists and moans into my mouth, changing what was supposed to be a quick kiss into something more fierce. I push my tongue into her mouth, relishing the noises she makes as she welcomes it, sucks it, entwines it with her own. Before I change my mind and dive straight into the main course, I force myself to hook my foot around the leg of the bench, pulling it closer, ready to sit my arse down because this is a meal worth savouring.

She whimpers and murmurs my name as I pull my mouth away.

'Shush, now,' I whisper, beginning to kiss my way down the smooth column of her neck. I flick my tongue over her collarbone, ground her against the bed with my hands pressed to her hips. She groans her appreciation as I lick between the valley of her breasts, lave her nipples, bite the undersides of her tits.

'Jesus, Flynn, I can't. I just can't—'

'Yes, you can. And you will.' I push her tits together, my gaze crawling up her body, my eyes meeting hers, dark and full of want. 'You'll take it all and then some. Because you're Flynn's little fuck doll.'

Her body trembles with a mixture of laughter and need as I kiss my way down her belly, situating myself between her legs. I can't help but swallow deeply at the sight of her wetness—can't help but lick my lips as I push her thighs apart, my eyes glued to the slick flesh between her legs.

Bending forward, the smell is . . . like heaven. Not tasting her would be like walking past a bakery without going in. *Oh, Christ*. I groan as I lick the full length of her with my flat tongue, pushing between her slick lips to taste every ounce of her deliciousness.

'Jesus fuckin' Christ, duchess. I've been dreaming of this since the first time.' To reinforce the point, I lick her again—groaning again.

Chastity's hands grasp the bedding at her hips, bucking up into my face as she expels a mouthful of garbled words.

'Still sensitive, huh?' Sensitive and swollen from my fingers.

'Yes. Oh, yes!'

'Think it might help if I do this?' A rhetorical question. I know from experience that the answer is both yes and no as I slide my thumbs into her centre, pulling her apart like a ripe peach—you get the analogy; sweet, wet, and luscious—and blow a breath over her heated flesh. She squirms a little more, twisting her body away from my mouth. But that'll never do. Plus, it won't work. Not as I take her clit into my mouth.

'You're not directing this show, babe,' I growl against her flesh. She doesn't answer, which is unfortunate as I begin to lash that sweet bundle of nerves with my tongue.

'Oh, oh. My—'

'Spread your legs.' I take her arse into both hands, tilting her for better access as I would her head as I begin to kiss her. Small kisses at first, dotted along her flesh. Then deeper ones—fuller ones—until I'm making out with her pussy and her thighs are squeezing my head. Which is all fine until I need more. *Until her whimpers make me ravenous, pushing me over the edge.* My tongue still buried in her cunt, I grasp her calves, lifting her legs and planting her feet flat on the bed. Pushing her pale thighs wide, I go to town.

And we're loud—so loud. The sounds of our pleasure rebounding through the room; my animal grunts and growls, my demands that she open herself. The sound of wet flesh—of tongue and pussy. Of wet sucking and fast finger fucking and the cries of her pleasure that drive me fucking wild.

'There—yes! There it is!'

Wherever this mythical place is, it's clear I'm getting there—getting her there. But I want in on it, too. Pushing the bench back, I stand and glance down at her. She looks like an angel who's fallen from heaven, pillow soft sweetness debauched.

Well, if she has to fall, the best place for her to land is on my dick.

It's my last sentient thought, not *sensible* thought, before I slide on the condom and bury myself deep inside to feel her come undone.

14

'DUCHESS, CAN I ASK YOU SOMETHING?'

'Why won't you go to *sleep!*'

It's late, or early, depending on your perspective. The only light in the room is from the street lamp peeking through the plantation shutters at my window, the relative darkness barely concealing the fact that my bedroom is in disarray. *London is never really dark. Not really.* But the mess can wait until tomorrow because I'm comfortable. Sated. I may well have stocked up enough orgasms to get me through until the summer, courtesy of the man lying next to me. I'm on my front, naked but for the bedding tangled around my legs. I *ache* in all the right places, and I refuse to move. In fact, I don't think I can. I'm exhausted and ignoring the fact that my clothes are strewn around the room—condom wrappers, too—and that a tray of food lies abandoned on the floor on the other side of the bed, and I'm not even sure I'll get the fig juice stains out of my sheets. There are a couple of sodden towels draped over my Kurt Olsen chair from our earlier shower. That would be our shower prompted by a messy food fight that devolved into a messy fuck. Flynn's stomach had complained loudly from missing dinner, so after I reassured him that Max wouldn't be around, he bounded naked downstairs to raid my fridge. His feet sounded on the stairs not ten minutes later before he reappeared in my bedroom—*ta-da!*—holding a laden tray including several slices of reheated pizza, a piece of Chevre, a small vine of red grapes, and a few figs. Plus a bottle of champagne but no glasses.

Essentially, we'd had a naked picnic in bed, while swilling champagne from the neck of a bottle like a couple of fancy louts. In a revisit to the theme of his arrival, Flynn insisted I give him a tip. Apparently, telling him not to eat yellow snow wasn't what he was looking for, and neither was the fig I'd squashed to his lips when he said so.

Game on, apparently, and when he eventually strapped me to the bed, both of my wrists pressed in one of his hands above my head, he'd kissed me so sweetly—not just from the fig juice—and announced he'd give *me* the tip instead.

And he did.

Just the tip.

Only the tip.

And nothing else.

Using his free hand, he'd held his cock, sliding it through my wetness, nudging my swollen clit. Nudging it. Petting it. Let's call it what it is—torturing me with the frenulum and head. Making me watch him get himself off using my wetness and his fingertips.

The. Hottest. Thing.

And believe me, I'd know.

Leaving the spilt champagne and fruit pulp in my bed, we'd showered. And even that had led to sex. The man has more energy than my fully charged vibrator! I don't think I'll ever have a night like this again. He owned me body and soul . . . if only for a few hours. Owned me with his honeyed whispers, his threats, and his promises. *All delivered tenfold.* Pleasured me with his fingers and stubble, his cock and tongue.

Beside me, Flynn *tsks*, an almost convincing reproving click of teeth and tongue. I lift my head and twist to peer at him, aware of what a mess I must look. A shower and no tending to my hair makes for tight spirals rather than soft curls. *Think orphan Annie without the ginger.*

'What's with the scowl?' he asks, lips quirked in some semblance of a smile.

'You've stopped tickling my back.'

Yep. Partway during the night, he'd discovered the one thing to make me completely submissive, the one thing apart from his cock, I mean, is light twirling fingers dancing along my back.

'Because I wanted your attention.'

I try to gather the sheet from my legs to shield my modesty but give up. *Too much effort.* So I turn to face him. 'There. What?'

'Earlier, you said this thing. Actually, you kinda whimpered it. Cried. Called out.' His eyes widen comically. 'Come on, Chastity. You watch people fucking for work— you know I'm asking you why you say what you say when you come.'

'I'm certain I don't know what you mean,' I answer evenly. 'People cry out all kinds of strange stuff when they climax. Most of it nonsense.'

'Your actors don't.'

'What?' I pull my head back to better examine him. 'What's that supposed to mean?'

'I might've subscribed,' he answers with a nonchalant shrug of one shoulder.

'Oh. Well. That's . . . odd. You're not exactly our demographic.'

'Nah, odd would be asking if you've got any jobs going. What's with the funny face?'

'Max, my brother, asked exactly that.' But also, the thought of me watching Flynn—directing Flynn—having sex with someone else is enough to make me feel . . . weird. There's a tightness in my stomach that doesn't feel very nice. But unaware of my internal reactions, Flynn carries on.

'No way! Watching your brother fuck would make you never want to bone again—make you want to boil your eyeballs *and* chop off your ears.'

'Something like that,' I agree, curling a hand between the pillow and my head.

'Do you know,' he says, reaching out to slip my hair behind my ears, 'the tips of your ears go pink when I say something filthy?'

Pulling the hair back in place, I hide the evidence. 'I don't know what you're talking about. And what's wrong with the actors in my films?'

'They're not big on talking.'

'We're not making talkie films.'

'What are you making?' he asks in a low, teasing tone.

'Films where people fuck.'

'I love it when you talk dirty.'

'How's this for dirty?' I ask, breaking into the company mission statement in my best media-darling voice. 'Fast Girl Media produces women and couple-centric erotica with an emphasis on seduction, romance, and sensuality.'

'And fucking. There's definitely an emphasis on fucking, no matter the spin.'

'We provide a highly curated experience,' I continue, not allowing him to put me off my stride, 'from beautiful cinematographic sequences to sensual photographic stills. We also have a wide range of erotic literature for a different kind of stimulation.'

'I'm all about the stimulation,' he growls, the sudden husky timbre of his voice sending a shiver of anticipation across my skin.

'You can't be serious.' I didn't mean that to sound so excited, so breathless.

'Does this not look serious to you?' he responds, bringing my hand to his hardening length. 'Come on, duchess,' he growls, rolling me over to straddle him. 'Come and stimulate yourself on my cock.'

One slow, rocking fuck, a joint effort to tidy up, and two *separate* showers later, Flynn is sitting on my bed in nothing but his jeans, staring at me while slowly shaking his head.

'Just stop.' Through my dressing table mirror, I try not to smile back at him as I fasten the button at the front of my dress.

'I didn't say a word.'

'You didn't need to. Look, I'm going out and you have to go, too. Besides, my poor vagina is out of business for the foreseeable.'

'Poor? Your vagina is rich and bounteous.'

'Er, steady on,' I warn, turning to face him to ensure he sees the full weight of my words. 'My vagina is anything but generous.' The latter comes out as a mutter as I turn back, a mutter I hope he can't hear.

'Maybe you've just been seeing the wrong kinds of

blokes,' Flynn replies with a self-satisfied air. 'Anytime she, or you, need more than a helping hand, you know where to find me, yeah?'

'You're ridiculous!' I cap my mascara, throwing it back into my makeup bag and turn to face him with a flounce.

'Maybe there won't be a next time if you can't learn to keep your mouth shut.' Oh, fuck, I think I just implied I want to do this again. And I do—I'd be mad not to. But I can't afford to make this a thing. Not now. Not with him. As I stand, I grab his T-shirt from the floor and throw it in his general direction, I hope, because I can't look at him now. Not without him reading all the thoughts from my face.

'Hurry up and dress. I need to leave soon.'

'Does this mean I don't have to bring pizza next time?'

'I didn't say there was going to *be* a next time,' I reply, studiously avoiding looking at him as I gather wet towels and other sexual detritus.

'Yeah, love, you kinda did.' He stands, dropping his T-shirt to the bed. In two languid steps, he takes the towels from me, dropping them back on the chair, and my traitorous body loves it as he takes my hips in his hands.

'I want to do this again,' he says, sort of shimmying my body between his fingertips. 'Look at me, Chastity.' So I do. It's hard not to when he uses that tone. Smooth, confident, and uniquely him. *Flynn Phillips, why are you so irresistible?* 'I'm just puttin' it out there,' he says. 'No pressure. I want to see you again, and I don't want to have to wait six months this time.'

'Flynn . . .' His name sounds ridiculously long as I sigh. *And not for effect.*

'We don't have to give it a name or make it a thing unless that would help.' He ducks his head to catch my reluctant gaze. 'Would it help? You wanna call this a friends with benefits deal?'

'How can we be friends,' I mumble, 'when we don't even like each other?'

'Duchess, how can you say that! I like you,' he says, his hands falling to grip mine. 'How can you not like me?'

'Well, you're very annoying. And you have terrible taste in porn.' The latter is mumbled against the coarse hairs of his chest as he pulls me in, banding my back with his strong arms.

'Next time, we'll compare. How about that?'

'I didn't say there was even going to *be* a next time yet.'

'No, but you will.' He kisses the top of my head, pulling away. 'Gonna see if I can rinse the fig juice out of my T-shirt.'

'Did you get the bus here?'

At the door to my bathroom, Flynn turns with a quizzical expression. 'Are you asking if I got the bus, holding a pizza? And a motorbike helmet?' His mouth twitches, presumably to restrain his smile.

'Who's going to see the stain on your T-shirt if you're riding a bike?'

'The way I ride? No one. But I'm also going out.'

He doesn't elaborate, and he looks totally suspect as he turns, walking into the bathroom. I can't help but feel annoyed. Men can be such twats. I'm sure women can, too, but given the fact that I've never dated a woman, the point is moot. I stomp out of my bedroom, my mood having taken a slide, but at the top of the stairs, I note my jeans slung over the bannister, and I remember I'm *not* dating Flynn. He doesn't need to tell me . . . *things*.

15

CHASTITY

WHILE I MEET the girls once a month for brunch, we also get together for a slap-up Sunday lunch. This one is usually a family affair with partners and children and whoever else might be around. I don't think my friends really know how much I appreciate being involved. But family isn't always blood, I feel. Unlike my own family, these people accept me for who I am, quirks and all. There's no favouritism, no sniping, and no underhandedness. Just friendship and acceptance.

'Where are the menfolk?' Slipping my jacket from my shoulders, I take my seat at the long table at the back of The Drunken Duck, an old English pub that's a firm favourite of my friends due to the outdoor play area. It keeps the children amused, especially on days like today. Though it's chilly, spring seems to have sprung overnight. Or maybe that's because I'm wearing rose-tinted orgasm glasses today.

I thoroughly recommend!

'The rugby season is just around the corner,' Ella says, looking up from the menu. I've no idea why she's looking at it because she always orders the same thing. *Roast beef and Yorkshire puddings with lashings of horseradish. Yum.* 'Training started up this weekend,' she adds.

Both Mac and Keir, along with their friend Will, play for the Dissenters, an amateur weekend rugby team, though they seem to take their commitment very seriously.

'No Sadie today?' Sadie is Will's wife, and the pair are new parents to a beautiful baby boy.

'They've gone to Scotland to visit that draughty old castle,' Ella explains.

Will recently inherited his father's Scottish lands and titles, making him Lord Travers and a peer of the realm. Not that you'd know it to speak with him. The man is irreverent above everything else.

I keep my disappointment to myself as Paisley slides me a pre-poured glass of fairly decent red. Sadie and Will are a lovely couple, but I was mostly looking forward to my Sunday lunch quota of heavenly newborn baby cuddles. I know my friends wouldn't guess in a million years that spending time with them sometimes leaves me with an empty feeling for the next day or two. It *is* wonderful to see Paisley and Keir so in love, and by exten-sion, their friends, but it does make me all the more aware of what they have, and I don't. *Love. Partnerships. Children.*

'Here's to the merry rugby widows,' I say, holding my glass aloft. I'm not wishing ill on their men. The name is one my friends have coined themselves.

I turn and glance out of the French doors to where Ella's son, Louis, and Sorcha, Paisley's stepdaughter, are running around the play area, enjoying the unexpected sunshine. Meanwhile, little Juno, Ella's toddler daughter, sleeps soundly in her stroller in the corner.

'Isn't it amazing how nothing keeps Juno awake,' I ponder aloud.

'Poor thing had to get used to it. Ours is hardly a quiet house, what with Louis and Mac and the dog running about. Boys are such noisy creatures. It's just as well my girl can sleep on a washing line.' Ella turns, smiling serenely at her sleeping child. 'Still, let's make the most of the quiet before the little monster awakes and spoils our wine time.'

'She doesn't spoil it. She enhances it,' I say.

Ella snorts delicately. 'She keeps the calories off my hips at least.' Juno is at the age where she doesn't seem to know that her bottom can be used for sitting on. 'Although you seem to do the lion's share of chasing her around the playground when we're here.'

'I like to pitch in,' I respond. *And I like to snatch my chubby baby cuddle time where I can*, I admit silently as I take a sip of my wine.

'Have you had a nice weekend?' Paisley asks. I put my glass down on the table as I begin to cough.

'Went down the wrong way,' I say, thumbing my chest. 'S-same as usual, I suppose. And yours?' She doesn't know about Flynn, does she? How could she? Unless he told. And if he told, someone's about to get butt hurt. *With my umbrella.*

'You didn't see anyone . . . go out for dinner. Maybe sign up to any dating sites . . . ?'

'You missed your calling. You should've been an archaeologist.'

'Digging? *Moi*?' She touches her chest lightly, faux offended.

'Hey, what's a yoni?' Ella asks no one in particular, making me cough-choke my wine again.

'Honey,' Paisley begins, amused. 'Do you want to ask that a little louder. I think some of the people standing at the bar didn't hear you.'

'Oh, God. I take it it's something unpleasant.'

'I wouldn't be without mine.' Paisley snorts. 'I think the word is Hindi. For your bits.' Brows raised, I lower my eyes to my lap. 'You know?'

'That was very circumspect coming from you, fast girl.'

'Watch it, you,' I respond, pointing a finger in Paisley's direction. 'Fast Girl is responsible for your pay check as well as mine.'

'But where did that come from?' Paisley asks, turning to Ella. 'And how the hell do you not know?'

'It's not really a *thing* over here,' I interject on Ella's behalf. Still, she must be a little sheltered. Or I'm a little too knowledgeable in such things.

'I read it in a magazine,' Ella replies. 'It sort of came back to me just then, so I thought I'd ask.'

'Most people use Google,' Paisley replies.

'Can you imagine what results that search would've yielded? Google will literally make me blind one of these days.' Unfortunately, this will probably happen.

'That's on account of you being a dirty pervert,' Paisley replies with a chuckle. 'In a totally professional sense.'

Can a person be classed as perverted when they can only orgasm with one person? Not even with themselves? That sounds more like broken than depraved. And that was a bullet dodged earlier this morning. I can't help that I can't censor my orgasm outpourings no more than I can my *come face*. It's just a shame, and a little bit weird, that they appear to sound so directional.

Oh, there it is . . .

Imagine if I told Flynn this morning he's the only one

that can "find" my orgasm. As if he's not already full enough of himself.

'Oh, God, I have to tell you something funny before Keir turns up!' Paisley is suddenly super animated. 'So there have been a couple of break-ins in the neighbourhood, and Keir decided it would be a good idea to beef up security, like we really need it,' she adds, rolling her eyes.

'We were going out last weekend for dinner. I called a cab, it arrived, but as Keir was coming out of our bedroom, the damn cat ran inside. Princess Kitty should be called princess pain in my ass because the last time she was allowed in our room, she left a calling card in the bathtub, if you know what I mean.'

'Kids and animals,' commiserates Ella, indelicately screwing up her nose. 'Poo.'

'Exactly. So I did what any sensible woman would do—'

'You got the hell out of dodge?'

'Exactly. I got into the cab, but the cabbie seemed a little skeevy. He made a couple of comments on the house, and I don't know. Something felt a little off. It's silly really, but I was kind of conscious of not telling him the house was going to be empty for a few hours. Sorcha was at her grandparents, and Agnes wasn't home. So I tell him my husband's coming, that he was just saying good night to my mother.'

'Sensible,' Ella adds.

'Up until that point, maybe.' Paisley's lips twitch as though holding a laugh. 'Anyway, Keir comes out and gets into the cab next to me with a face like thunder. The cab pulls away and Keir is still silently fuming. So I ask him what's up and he answers, *Jesus,*' Paisley says, trying to imitate Keir's Scots brogue. '*What a pain in the arse she is!*

He sort of explodes, just as the cabbie caught my eye, his expression aghast. But Keir was on a roll. *The wily bitch ,'* Paisley continues with her impersonation, *'was hiding under the bed. I had to poke her arse with a coat hanger to get her to come out. She tried to scarper, but I wasn't havin' it, so I grabbed her by the scruff of the neck and held her out of the way so she couldn't scratch me like last time—I've still got the scars!'* By now, Paisley's trying very hard to get her words out. *'Then I carried her fat arse down the stairs and chucked her into the laundry room. She can stay there all night for all I care. She'd just better not shit in the tub again.* Oh my God,' she adds in her own voice now, tears streaming down her face, 'that cabbie's horrified expression will haunt me for the rest of my days!'

'You can bet your house isn't going to be burglarised.' Ella giggles. 'Imagine their fate if mothers-in-law's are kept in a dungeon!'

'Who keeps their mother-in-law in the dungeon?' Mac's broad Scots accent carries across the space. Placing his hand on the back of her chair, he leans in towards Ella, bringing with him the scent of soap and clean man.

'Did you win?' she asks, tipping her face to meet his lips.

'It was just a practice, darlin'.' Their lips meet briefly, but the love is obvious there.

'If it was just a practice, why does he look like that?' asks Keir, bringing up the rear as he hooks a thumb over his shoulder.

' 'Cause the man can'nae keep his trap shut,' Mac grumbles, pulling out a chair next to Ella. 'We brought a straggler with us,' he says, tipping his head.

I feel my expression twist, instinctively knowing who is sliding into the leather chair next to mine before I even turn my head. It's a strange kind of awareness, almost as though my body recognises his. The shape of him in the air. I know, it sounds ridiculous, but it's hard to explain. Whatever it is, every inch of my skin seems to be aware of him.

'G'day, everyone.' Much like Mac, Flynn smells of freshly showered man, but the smell of his cologne hits me almost viscerally as heat radiates deep in my belly at the familiar low timbre of his tone.

'Flynn!' Paisley exclaims, her expression turning to one of delight, though her pleasure doesn't completely hide the way her gaze flicks almost questioningly between him and I. Maybe she's wondering why he took the chair next to me, or maybe it's more than that—maybe I'm not the only one sensing things in the air between us? Actually, she's more than likely wondering why I'm acting so weird and sitting so rigidly in my chair. Wondering why I haven't turned to greet him.

'I'm so glad you could make it,' she continues. 'God knows we're always inviting you.'

I still can't bring myself to look at him for fear of what he'll see on my face. Paisley, too. Sometimes I feel like I don't need to speak, like my thoughts are telegraphed to her by my expression. Though none of that stops my eyes from following his strong forearm as he reaches across the table for the carafe of water and pours himself a glass.

Muscles engaging, extending, contracting, reminding me of last night. *Damn.*

'And this time you said yes.' I aim for a tone of barely masked disdain—our go-to interaction—as I finally turn my gaze to him. Other than his perma-smirk, it's hard to tell what he's thinking, given the blue-framed wayfarer glasses he's wearing. 'You must've had a heavy night last night if you still can't cope with a little sun at'—I make a show of turning my wrist to look at my watch—'one fifteen?'

'A heavenly night more like,' he murmurs from behind his glass. 'It's surprising,' he continues, setting down his glass, 'how well pizza and champagne mix.' *Bastard.*

'You can't help being a bit of a philistine,' I reply as though bored. 'I take it your dazzling wit and personality are too much for even you today.'

A low chuckle travels around the table, but Flynn doesn't speak. Rather, he reaches out, leaning his long arm across the back of my chair as, with his other hand, he slowly lowers the sunglasses from his face.

I gasp. Then I see blood red.

'What the fuck happened to your face?' I almost clap my hand over my mouth, my eyes making a quick sweep of the surrounding area. Thankfully, there are no children nearby. However, for anyone caring enough to pay a little attention, that was far too passionate an enquiry from someone who isn't supposed to care.

'You should see the other guy.' *Otha guy.* Gah! This man and his stupid but irresistible accent.

'Arsehole.' Keir chuckles from across the table, his gaze flicking to Mac. 'I see him, and he looks just fine.'

My head turns to the bulk of Mac who doesn't appear entirely comfortable. He folds his arms as his deep voice rumbles, 'It's what you get for being on the other side.'

'It was a friendly game, you fucker,' Flynn responds on a chuckle.

'Aye, well, Mac doesn't take kindly to loud-mouthed taunts.' This from Keir. 'They're not all as good-natured as me.'

'Now you tell me,' Flynn retorts, making everyone laugh. Except me. I'm still staring daggers at Mac.

The waitress comes to take our orders, but my blood pressure refuses to come down. So I drink—great mouthfuls of wine. I drink to keep my mouth occupied, and I drink to keep the thoughts at bay.

'Duchess, chill out,' Flynn murmurs as more wine and beers are delivered to the table. 'You look like you're about to go off like a cat in a wheelie bin.' I turn my head to him and blink as I try to process his words. 'Stop plotting Mac's murder. I'm big enough to take care of myself.' My eyes roam to the swelling under his right eye, the discolouration and swelling, though I refrain from pointing out his injury points to the opposite. *Rugby is a violent game,* I silently remind myself. Not that it has any effect on how I feel. And how I feel is . . . unwelcome. I don't want to care about him any more than I would a stranger in the street. No, that's not fair. I do care. I care in general about a lot of things and a lot of people, but it doesn't alter the fact that I don't want to feel this way about *him.*

'I was on the opposition, and I might've let my mouth run a bit.'

I turn my head swiftly. '*That* doesn't surprise me one bit. But,' I carry on, my words a quiet hiss as my glare cuts to Mac, who's currently bouncing a delighted Louis on his knee as the little boy relays some story about a snail he found outside in the playground. 'It's supposed to be a game, not a boxing match.'

Unfortunately, my hiss is a little loud, and all eyes turn to our side of the table.

'Y'ken, it's like this,' Mac begins with a wry expression. 'Due to the presence of women and wee ones at this table, I can't tell you what he said to provoke such a tackle. And it was a tackle. I did'nae elbow him in the face or anything.'

'He's right,' Flynn says, beginning to shuck out of his coat. A navy overcoat this time, the kind that city gents wear over suits. Hitting mid-thigh and teamed with jeans and those rugged boots, he looks every bit as good. *Okay, infinitely better.*

Hooking his coat over the back of the chair, he shoots me a wink. 'I deserved it for the way I spoke about Mac's balls.'

Our tablemates start to chuckle, doubly so as Louis pipes up, 'Yes, because my daddy has funny shaped balls.' His gaze flicks around the table, his little face scrunched in a frown. *'Tu ne me crois pas?'* he asks, slipping into French.

'*Si,*' Ella answers, wiping away an escaped tear. 'Of course, we all believe you, Louis.'

'*Bon.* Because my daddy does have very funny shaped balls—rugby balls.'

'Louis, you cheated!' Sorcha, Paisley's stepdaughter, appears at the end of the table. Fists curled, she stamps her foot. 'Inside was out of bounds.'

Louis theatrically slaps his head. 'I forgot we were playing hide and go seek.'

She isn't cross long as her gaze falls to Flynn. 'You came!' she exclaims, dodging between our chairs and throwing herself into his arms, narrowly missing his swollen eye.

'Ratbag!' he says, ruffling her blonde hair.

'Scumbag!' she responds with equal delight.

'Looks like I've graduated.' He chuckles, covering her ears with his hands. 'One step up from bawbag,' he says, looking directly at Keir.

DONNA ALAM

'Why'd you cover my ears.' Sorcha pulls away with a stern look. 'I heard you anyway. And I heard my daddy call you that naughty name over the phone.'

'Thank you, Sorch,' Flynn answers, holding out his hand for a high five. 'I'm adding that to my nice little blackmail file 'cause I'm pretty sure your dad doesn't want to end up in an employment tribunal.'

'What's a tribunal?' she asks, reciprocating as his gaze cuts to Keir.

'About twenty grand,' her father deadpans.

'Oh, good.' Sorcha bounces up onto Flynn's splayed knees. 'Half of twenty is ten. I'm going to be rich!'

'Sorch is collecting the evidence.'

'Yes, because Flynn said he would split his payout with me.'

The table erupts into laughter again.

16

FLYNN

'You know what I don't understand?'

I lean my body close to Chastity's, though keep my hands in my pocket and, therefore, to myself. I know she likes me touching her in general; back strokes, and cuddles, and my fingers tight on her hips. She's tactile. But right now, I'm not so sure she'd appreciate the contact given that we seem to be a source of fascination for the gawkers pretending not to look. Yeah, that lot just beyond the window.

Cock-blocking bastards.

Fuck me. I'm the pornographer's dirty secret.

'What don't you understand?' she repeats with an air of inconsequence. 'The scope in that question is so wide.' Stepping away from me, she takes with her the smell of her floral perfume while also giving me a lovely view of her arse. *Chastity giveth, and Chastity taketh away.* 'What are you doing out here, anyway?' She crouches in front of little Juno, the movement making her dress bloom around her, blessing me with a glimpse of her stocking covered legs. It makes me wonder what else under that dress as she pulls Juno's little pink pompom hat more solidly over her ears.

'Same as you. I've come to play with the kids.'

'Ah, your intellectual counterparts.'

Hands still in my pocket, I dig my toe into the spongey child-friendly surface. 'You got me there.' Her soulful brown eyes meet mine, mischief burning there. The connection is broken as Juno wraps four pudgy fingers around Chasity's index ones, pulling her in the direction of one of those springy rocking horses.

'Horsey!' she exclaims, making grabby starfishes with her hands.

'You want to ride the horsey, sweetheart?'

'I know what I want to ride,' I say quietly, coming up behind her again.

'Stop,' she whispers. 'People will see.'

'Fuck 'em,' I counter, frowning, though moving slightly away. For her, not me.

'Flynn, come and show Louis how you make a pound coin disappear.' Sorcha pulls on my arm, pulling my hand from my pocket.

'That's easy,' I say, looking down at her pleading gaze. 'Take him to the lolly shop. It'd disappear quick there.'

'How many times do I have to tell you,' Sorcha's says in a singsong reprimanding tune I recognise from my childhood. 'We don't have lolly shops. They're called sweetie shops, unless you're from 'merica, like Paisley, then sweeties are called candy. But lollies come on sticks, not in bags. And *that's* the same everywhere.'

'Not in Australia, it's not. We eat red frogs and call them lollies.'

'You're so funny, Flynn,' she says, giggling, her fingers

digging into my arm as she lifts her feet from the ground. My bicep strain from the weight of her, but I'd keep her balanced there for hours just to see Chastity look at me like that.

'Push me on the swings, Flynn. Please! *Please!*'

'All right, ratbag. Race you there.'

Sorcha takes off like a shot, allowing me another look, or ten, at Chastity's arse. At least until she stands. When she turns, she's holding Juno in her arms.

Ever had your breath taken away? Me, too. It happened earlier on the field when Mac decided to wipe me out and blacken my eye in the process.

But this? This is different. *Whoosh!*

'Go on,' she says with a resigned sigh. 'Say whatever witticism it is you're clearly dying to say.'

'Say?' The word is more like an intake of breath. 'Nah, not me. I've got nothin' to say.' I stick my hands in my pockets again, my shoulders up around my ears. I am *not* going to tell her that she looks like . . . like an angel holding a smaller angel or something. A cherub? And I'm not gonna tell her that the little cherub— 'Juno looks at home there.' *Fuck me.*

'Does she?' It's such a small compliment, yet she looks stoked. Tickled pink. 'Well, I'm very happy to have you here, too,' she says to the baby, not me, as she bounces her in her arms.

'Flynn, we're *read-y!*'

'Looks like you've got double the work.' Chastity's smiling gaze travels to the other side of the playground to the swing set where Sorcha and Louis sit, happily dangling their legs.

'I'll cope.' I don't miss the way her eyes travel across my chest before touching my exposed biceps.

Feet planted wide, I tighten my hands into fists, not that she could tell. And not that it stops my desire to reach out. Pull her to me. Kiss the snark right out of her mouth.

Jesus, but it's fucking cold out here. I'd only meant to step out for a minute so hadn't brought my jacket. No. I'm lying. Chastity had offered to take Juno for a toddle in the playground following lunch, and I'd thought I'd play it cool by drinking my beer and lounging back in my chair. That had lasted about two minutes before I'd followed, trotting behind her like a little dog happy for scraps and a pat on the head. Or penis, in my case. A man has to have aspirations.

But she's still looking at my pecs, so that's a good thing, right?

She steps closer. 'What does your T-shirt say?'

'What?' I look down and remember the barely discernible image of a koala bear, just a black outline over navy cotton, the words a little washed out. 'It says I'm not a bear. I don't have the koala-fictations. Marsupial humour.'

Rafferty, my brother and I, have this sort of competition going. We regularly send each other T-shirts with asinine or offensive slogans. The idea is to take a photograph while wearing the T-shirt you've been sent, kinda like a dare. And wearing it at home doesn't count; you have to be out. Raff sent this one when the trade first started. It's a little tame compared to his most recent delivery. Although it's a T-shirt encouraging Aussie tourism in the Northern Territories, it's not one for the kiddie crowd as it states:

CU (in the) NT.

Juno wriggles as Chastity snorts, so she sets her down, stepping closer still, her arms folded across her chest. *This is all on her*, I think, keeping my hands firmly in place. Still in my fucking pockets.

'Have you been a fan of the ridiculous T-shirt long?' she asks mildly. Her eyes smile though her mouth stays the same, those full lips slightly parted. *As though she'd like to taste me.*

'Lifelong fan,' I answer. 'I might own one or ten a little too risqué for this crowd.' I gesture to the kids on the swings and their impatient wiggling legs, my poor heart stuttering in shock as she places her palm flat in the middle of my chest. The connection is … everything.

'Risqué? Flynn?' She sort of pouts. 'That can't be so.'

'I'm afraid it is. When I decided I was coming to lunch, I grabbed the first one out of the drawer to change. Besides, this one is Sorcha's favourite.'

'Why did you decide to come today of all days?'

'Thought that would be obvious, duchess.' She looks down at her hand as a crease forms between her perfect brows.

'If my nipples were any harder, they'd give Chuck Norris a run for his money.'

She doesn't laugh, just stares at my chest, but then her little finger stretches out, grazing my right nipple. I ball my fists tighter. *Jesus fuck.*

'And I can sympathise,' she whispers.

'What are we doing here, duchess?'

Her eyes slide to the window and the people inside. 'They can't see.'

My heart sinks. 'Are you worried about being seen with the help?'

'Just when I thought you couldn't get any more ridiculous,' she murmurs, pulling her hand away. 'For what it's worth, Flynn,' she says over her shoulder, 'you look good with the kids. You ever think you'll have some of your own?'

'Fuck, no.' It's a rote answer delivered without much thought. 'I'm strictly uncle material, me.'

'Yeah. That's what I thought.'

17

CHASTITY

I PULL out my phone for about the tenth time today, the hundredth time this week, and put it away.

I will not call Flynn and ask how his face is.

I will not call Flynn with an invitation to my bed.

This week has been hectic and not in the fun way. I've barely moved from my studio office all week, catching up on all the horrible admin jobs I always postpone until the last minute, add to that the plans I need to make for the quarter ahead. In other words, burying my head in the Flynn free sand.

I can't afford to get involved with Flynn Phillips. We're just not compatible. We're not in the same place. Okay, physically, we may be in the same place sometimes—and those times are fun—but we're not in the same place in our lives. I need to write that shit down a hundred times daily. Maybe make a mantra of it. Chant *that* a hundred times.

Lord, his reaction when I suggested he might make a good dad—yes, I know, a slip from the vault that is my subconscious—anyone would think it was contagious. But

I stand by my opinion because he will make a good dad. Though he'll probably be one of those first time geriatric fathers, pushing the stroller from his wheelchair, because it'll take him that long to grow up.

No, that's just my bitter lack of orgasm talking. Because my O? It's still not turning up for solo flight.

Thursday, I get back home around six, having grabbed takeaway from my local Italian joint. I'm just about to spoon the carb-y, garlicky pasta goodness into bowl when my front doorbell rings. Twice in two weeks? No one in Chelsea knocks on a door without issuing some fore-warning that they're about to. *That's what phones are for.* Flynn gets a pass for not being a Londoner. Okay, Flynn gets a pass for bringing orgasmic gifts, and while I glance regretfully at my dinner and my stomach rumbles in protest as I make my way to the front door, I'm still hoping it's Flynn.

'There's only so long a man can wait before taking things into his own hands,' says a large bunch of flowers. Or, at least, the voice behind a large bunch of peach-coloured cabbage roses.

'Erm . . . okay?' My voice wavers as I try not to laugh, mainly from embarrassment. When was the last time a man gave me flowers? I can't even remember. I can't even get excited either because these flowers aren't from Flynn.

'I gave your friend my business card.' My neighbour, Tate, lowers the hand-tied bouquet. While beautiful and expensive-looking, it isn't some extravagant display but rather tasteful. 'I thought you might give me a call. Maybe say hello in the street . . . knock on my door to welcome me into the neighbourhood?'

'Oh.' Really? Because he gave Paisley a business card?

What am I? Mayor of Whacky town? 'I'm sorry'—*I am so not sorry*— 'I've been very preoccupied with work.'

'Apology accepted and reinforced if you'll have dinner with me,' he says, passing the flowers into my hand.

'Dinner?' That sounded . . . like I thought he doesn't have a chance. *But flowers—really?* Is that not a huge presumption?

'Not because I brought you flowers,' he adds quickly, almost as though reading my thoughts. 'A coffee, then. Nothing nefarious, Professor. I promise.' He holds up his right hand in a boy scout salute, something I recognise. Max was a cub scout for a while.

And, fuck it. Why do I get myself into these scrapes? Flowers at the door and a fictitious career?

'I'm not *actually* a professor,' I begin, unravelling myself from this knot. Oh, what a tangled web we weave . . .

'I know,' Tate replies quite happily.

'Well, then. I suppose that begs the question *how*?' My stalker senses are tingling. Not that I've been stalked especially, but in my line of business, I've had to create a wall between myself and the crazies in this world. Plus, who wouldn't be slightly concerned to learn that someone who isn't even a blip on your radar claims to know details about you?

'Courtesy of Royal Mail.'

'The postal service? I'm not sure I follow.' My gaze slides over his shoulder and across the street to his door.

'The postman delivered a piece of your mail to the wrong address,' he explains, hiking a thumb in the same direction. 'It wasn't addressed to a professor or else I wouldn't have spent the last couple of months calling you something else in my head. That is, at least, until you turned up in my restaurant when I introduced myself.'

'I am . . . unsure how to process this information.' Calling me what in his head? The neighbour who looks like she doesn't want to be your friend? And if so, why are you on my doorstep?

'Ah, I can see I've overplayed my hand. I'm a bit nervous. Can you tell?' He laughs nervously. 'I only mean that I might've seen you in passing and taken a bit of a shine to you.'

'As far as anyone can when they don't really *know* that person.' I feel my eyebrows draw in. Am I being a judgmental bitch?

'Exactly!' He laughs, so obliviously unconcerned. So maybe I'm not as bad as I think I am, or maybe he's hard to offend? 'I'll admit it. I'd seen you about and, as juvenile as it sounds, fancied you a bit.'

'You fancied me?' I repeat, my words quivering with just an edge of laughter.

'I'm man enough to take your scorn,' he responds happily. 'I fancy you. Deal with it.'

I let my gaze fall to the flowers, no longer sure how to proceed. 'It's been a while since anyone admitted to fancying me.' Firstly, I haven't heard that word for at least a decade. Secondly, I think I intimidate most men.

'Now that I don't believe.'

'So this name of mine, the one you've been calling me in your head. Care to share it with me?'

'Let me take you for a coffee, and I'll tell you.'

'Blackmail rarely works,' I reply, my voice holding a suggestion of *schoolmarm*.

'I wonder if the Metropolitan police would disagree.'

'I imagine that would be bad for business,' I retort.

'Come on,' he cajoles. 'Aren't you at least a little curious?'

'What you call me? Yes!' My words hit the air as a chuckle. But other than that, not so much because I'm pretty sure that's what killed the cat. That or frustration. And that cat will probably be me.

Here lies Chastity Lenore Landry.

Died from sexual frustration aged just twenty-nine.

'In absence of your bantering answer, I'm going to take it as a yes.' Are we bantering? Maybe I'm a little rusty at this whole thing.

'It's a free country. You can take it however you like,' I respond evenly.

'I love it when a woman says things like that.' Shocked, I open my mouth to respond when he holds up a fore-stalling hand. 'Sorry, that was absolutely *not* what I should've said, but the longer I stand here, the bigger arse I'll make of myself. How about you put me out of my misery?'

'It's still called murder even if you asked for it.'

'I deserved that, but I'd like to blame the glass of wine I drank before I came over here. Dutch courage and all.' Unsure if that was a blatant ploy or a genuine admission, I look down at the flowers and take a deep breath.

'Look,' I begin, 'I work a lot. In fact, I'll be working most of this evening.' *Hint-hint.* 'How about we leave it to fate?' His expression falters as though not quite catching my meaning. 'One afternoon in the not too distant future, I may well pop into the restaurant for a coffee. Maybe if you're there, we could have that coffee together?'

'You're likely to make a workaholic of me.'

'Think of it as me protecting your business. I hear the mortality rate of new restaurants is pretty high.'

'It's a good job I own two more then, isn't it?' In man-speak, I think that's Tate's way of telling me how successful he is. 'Well, I'll leave you to put those in water.' We glance at the flowers in my hand almost simultaneously.

'They're really lovely,' I demure. A man brought me flowers. Maybe I should've been nicer to him.

'Just think of me when you look at them,' he says, stepping back onto the garden path. 'I'll be waiting . . .'

I smile as I close the door and mutter, 'Then you'd best not hold your breath.'

When I return to my pasta dinner, it looks like congealed snails, but I do have a lengthy text.

Aunt Cam: *Darling, I did so enjoy yesterday's new inclusion. One note of criticism if I may. While girl-on-girl is always mildly enjoyable, this craze with waxing all the hair from one's body is a little much. I'm all for avoiding the horror of the seventies bush, but what you youngsters don't seem to understand is when you get my age, it all falls out anyway. And believe me, you really could do with the coverage!*

Me: *Thanks for the feedback and the horror story. I may well not sleep tonight.*

'Why are you staring at Stephen?'

Friday morning and we have a session in the studio. Stephen is fairly new to the industry, and he's doing a solo shoot, excuse the pun. I'm shooting him solo while he, ahem, shoots solo. Meanwhile, Hillary seems a little . . . distracted as Stephen undresses. We have a changing area, but the young blond says it's no big deal. I think I've become immune to nakedness and Paisley meanwhile has eyes for no one by Keir. Which leaves Hillary. And his lolling tongue.

'Hey.'

'Hmm?'

'You remind me of a fat kid in a bakery.'

'I don't know what you mean.' Tearing his eyes away, he slides me a blank look.

'She means you look like you want to cram him into your mouth,' Paisley reiterates. 'Like he's cake.'

'Hmm. Someone didn't spill their coffee this morning, I see,' he says testily, immediately reminding me of our last shoot and the brochure full of sperm I have in my home office. That is—sperm donors, I mean. Not actual jizz.

But I'm not thirty yet, so I don't have to think about it.

'By coffee, do you mean sex?' asks a slightly confused Paisley.

'Why does it always come back to sex with you?' Hillary replies with a slight flounce. 'I thought I recognised him.'

'What, by his ass?' Paisley asks.

'Don't answer that,' I add quickly.

'It looked to me like you were trying to recognise him *real* hard,' Paisley then adds.

'Honestly, you two,' Hills huffs. 'I'm off to get the coconut oil.'

'Is that for you or him or for you both?' she calls after him.

'You really shouldn't tease him like that,' I say, rifling in my bag for my notebook.

'Me?' Paisley squeaks. 'You're the one who likened him

to a fat kid. If he sulks about anything, it'll be the insult to his waistline.' She's right. When Paisley and I grab a wrap or sandwich for lunch, Hills always has a salad. Always. I'm not sure whether to believe him or not when he says he hasn't had carbs since 2009.

'So . . . ' Paisley's change of tone in that one word is enough to make me turn and run. 'You and Flynn, huh?'

'Me and Flynn what?'

'Don't play coy with me. I saw how you were on Sunday. I thought for at least one minute I might need to intervene. I mean, Mac is a big guy, but you know my money will always be on you in any sort of conflict.'

'What are you talking about?' I ask, abandoning my quest and moving to fiddle with one of the lights, which is Hillary's job, not mine. But something tells me this should be a conversation we *don't* have face to face. But at least she didn't mention seeing me touching his chest.

'I'm talking about the way you looked at Mac. Let's just say we were all pleased we weren't him. You looked pissed!'

'I think you need glasses,' I murmur, moving to adjust the settings on the other light.

'Or not,' she says, following me.

'Don't you have makeup brushes or something to wash?'

'You're like the quintessential momma bear when it comes to your friends. Fiercely protective and ready to throw down in defence of them. But what I don't know is, has Flynn been moved into the stable as a temporary guest, like a lover? Or for good, like a friend. Or something else.'

Taking her by the arm, I pull her to the other side of the room. 'What do you want me to tell you?' I ask quietly.

'That we slept together again? Because we did. But we are not a thing. Not by any stretch of the imagination.'

'That's what we all say. Look at Keir and me,' she says with a grin.

'That's different,' I reply, a hint of pleading in my voice.

'Is it? I don't see how.'

'We're not compatible, for a start. Not in the relation-ship sense, anyway.'

'What brought you to that conclusion?' she asks, twirling a lock of hair around her fingertip.

'Well, he's younger than me, for a start.'

'No, he isn't? Not really.'

'Not—he either is or he isn't,' I respond, matching her frown.

'Looks to me like you haven't taken the time to find out,' she responds slyly. 'Too busy, huh?'

'Just . . . don't, okay?'

'Why? What exactly have you got against him?'

On a good day? All of me. Naked and pressed up to him from the strong lines of his thighs to the comforting coarseness of the hair on his chest. Not that I say any of that.

'His age, for one thing,' I repeat.

'For God's sake, he's twenty-nine!'

'And I'll be thirty soon.' Not thinking about it. Soo not thinking about it.

'Whoopdee-frickin'-do!'

'And he must be twenty-nine years minus twenty, the way he behaves.'

'Does that not ring any bells? He likes you, so he's pulling your pigtails, trying to get your attention.'

I inhale deeply, pushing out the air super fast. 'Flynn strikes me as the kind of man who likes lots of girls.'

'I wouldn't know. I'm also going to suggest that you won't either unless you talk to him. That's assuming you want to get to know him. You know, beyond just fucking him.' Swallowing, I lift my head to look at her. 'And that's okay, too, you know.'

'If not a little awkward later.' Meeting him at social gatherings. Seeing him turn up to meet our joint friends with another woman on his arm. My dark thoughts are no doubt reflected on my face as Paisley places her hand on my arm.

'It's only awkward if you make it. Flynn is one of the nicest people I know, excluding you, of course. But as much as I like him as a person, he doesn't have to be mister right. Mister Right Now works, so long as you're both on the same page.'

'Flynn and I . . .' I halt. This isn't the time or place, but the words are suddenly stuck in my throat—though they're fighting for escape. I look across the room to where Stephen stands, now dressed in the robe we've provided. Hillary is nearby, the pair chatting amiably. Thankfully, the coconut oil is nowhere to be seen.

'Five minutes, guys,' I call across the room, then take Paisley's hand and pull her out of the studio and into my office, closing the door.

'What is it?' Her arms wrapped across her waist, she looks suddenly concerned.

'I slept with Flynn at the wedding.'

'Duh!'

'But for six months following, I haven't been able to orgasm.'

'Not at all?' She frowns. 'Not since? Do you mean he just didn't do it for you?'

'No, that's not what I mean. I did, have, with him. Lots!

Then nothing,' I reply, making a circular motion in the general vicinity of the offending equipment. 'It's like it's all broken.'

'Oh, honey. Have you seen a doctor?'

'A doct—no, of course I didn't! I'm not ill or else things wouldn't improve with the inclusion of Flynn. No, I'm not ill, just fucking . . . frustrated. Anyway, the bottom line is, sleeping with Flynn was clearly a mistake in the first place. I was fine up until that point.'

'There's no use crying over spilt jizz.'

'I'm pleased one of us is laughing,' I say snippily.

'Sorry. Sorry. But six months?' she repeats with a look of disbelief. 'That's not right, right?'

'You're telling me.'

'It's a wonder you haven't exploded.'

'Or had a stroke. Or killed someone.'

'But you're okay now, right?'

'Only with Flynn.' My shoulder lifts and falls in a shrug.

'What? How'd you know? Have you tried other things?'

'Darling, I'm surprised I haven't developed a repetitive strain injury.'

'Have you used toys? Watched movies?' The words are out of her mouth before her brain connects. 'Oh. Yeah.' Her lips twist. 'Have you tried sleeping with someone else?'

This is something that hadn't occurred to me. But no That's not happening. 'No. There was no one else before Flynn for a while. I wasn't going to sleep with Flynn, either. I want change in my life.' *I want a child*, I long to say, yet I can't bring myself to say the words.

'Then it has to be in your head. Maybe—' She stops speaking, so of course I want to hear.

'Go on.'

'Maybe if you slept with someone else, and things were fine, then you'd be, too?' I frown, not following her meaning. 'If you were fine before, and the issues started after Flynn, *and* it's all in your head, maybe if you introduce someone else into the equation and find the old pipes, so to speak, work with him, then you'll have proven to yourself it's all in your head.'

'But what if I feel the same? What if I find I have the same issues?'

'Then you need either a head doctor, a sex therapist, or maybe a yoni massage.'

'I'd like to say thanks for your help, but well, you haven't helped.'

'Have you spoken to Flynn about it?'

'What?' I say in the tone of *you must be mad.* 'What possible help could he be?'

'I'm just putting it out there, not judging or making any predictions, but you were all for murdering Mac before. And Flynn, well, he was looking at you much more intensely than Hills and cake boy out there.'

'I literally have no idea what you just said.'

'Some things happen for a reason. Maybe your reason for *coming* is Flynn.'

Is it me, or is she speaking Swahili?

18

FLYNN

'YOU'RE QUIET TODAY.'

'What?' Monday afternoon, Keir stands at the end of my desk wearing an expression I've seen plenty times before, though never directed at me.

'You look like you've lost a fiver and found a pound.'

'Sorry, I was miles away.' I take my glasses off and pinch the ache at the top of my nose, considering how my thoughts are really only figurative miles away as my mind slips to yesterday and The Drunken Duck. I'd always turned Keir down in the past when he'd invited me to lunch after a game. Both our teams play out of the same sports complex, and yesterday, we were down for a friendly game, a preseason warm-up. A friendly game that left me with this amazing black eye. In the past, I've always favoured winding down with a few beers with the lads over a meal with my boss and his mates, their wives, and families. Until yesterday.

Chastity. She's on my mind more than is healthy, and I think I'm kidding myself when I say it's because she's got *titty* in her name. My interest in her was always genuine—

I love the way she doesn't take any shit, pushing right back at me, meeting my nonsense toe to toe. If I'm honest, there was also that initial fantasy thing. Like my dad's joke that his dream woman was a nymphomaniac with her own pub, mine turned out to be this sweet-looking pornographer. And now she's pretty much all I can think about.

She looked less than impressed that I'd turned up yesterday which, at least initially, dialled my enjoyment up to a nine. Then she'd refused to look at me, and I'll admit, that left me feeling uncomfortable. As if I'd encroached on her turf. As if she didn't want me there. I felt about as welcome as a fart in a spacesuit, and the experience was about as pleasant. I began to question my read on her when faced with the waves of her almost visceral dislike. I needed to get out of there, and I needed to do it quick and began formulating a way to get myself out of a full meal situation where the woman I wanted wouldn't even look at me. Fuck if that didn't hurt—the longer she ignored me, the larger the twisting feeling her disregard created in my chest. Then she seemed to decide ignoring me wasn't enough. She had to take the piss out of my sunglasses, so I took the fuckers off.

Never in a million years—a hundred million years— would I have anticipated her reaction. Man, I thought she was going to cry for a minute, and she strikes me as the kind of woman who'd rather poke pins in her eyes to explain the flow rather than admit to crying in public. I mean, it wasn't that bad. It looks a bit funky today, and all the fucking colours of the bruise rainbow, but yesterday, it was just a bit swollen. Red and angry looking. Okay, I looked a bit like Shrek. She raised her hand as though to touch it or maybe touch me. I like to think she was going to hug me, hug away the ache. But then she'd caught herself, her hand retracting before anyone else at the table realised. But I saw. Saw the intention behind the movement. Saw the meaning behind her words. She fucking *cares*. Cares for more than the thing I have in my pants, constantly hard for her. And that twisting ache in my chest? Fuck my life, it grew tenfold. What would it be like to have her? I mean, really have her? Not just for a roll around her bed or a call now and again.

And then later, at the playground, I caught her looking at me when she thought I was preoccupied, and I got an honest look at her. For a moment, she wasn't hiding behind a façade of ambivalence or scorn. What I saw was stripped down and true. She's interested. And she sees *me*.

'Have those stupid glasses started to give you headaches?'

I glance down at the black-framed eye glasses lying on my desk next to Keir's Mont Blanc pen. 'Glasses stop headaches, not create them.'

'Not if you're wearing them only as a fashion statement. Also, they don't make you Superman.'

'What the fuck are you on?' I sit back in my chair, letting him enjoy his little rant. 'Because whatever it is, keep taking the pills, mate.'

'Can you strip to your skivvies in a telephone box?'

'Why? Do you wanna watch?'

'Vain fuckin' baw bag.'

'I've got a prescription,' I drawl.

'Aye, a prescription from the pretty optometrist who said they made your eyes look even bluer.' The latter he delivers several octaves higher than his usual range with a comical fluttering of his lashes.

'Doctors don't lie. Even the pretty eye doctor ones.'

'Get tae' fuck.' He half laughs, throwing up his arms.

'She was lying, anyway. You're so ugly the dog closes his eyes when he humps your leg.'

'Who the fuck pays three hundred quid for glasses they don't need?'

'The same kind of arse who paid six hundred quid for a coat. Aye, you can'nae defend yourself from that, can you?'

'It is a very nice coat,' Paisley says, appearing at the now open door. 'Dolce and Gabbana, isn't it?'

'Nah. Their stuff is made for little Italian blokes. Not for shoulders like these.'

'I'm sure David Gandy would disagree.'

Sorcha follows Paisley into the office, swinging her little blue homework bag. She gives Keir a quick hug before throwing herself on the sofa, patting the leather cushion next to her.

'How's my wee girl?' Keir asks, sliding in next to her.

'Fine,' she replies, now patting the seat cushion at her other side. 'Paisley, I want to be the ham in the sandwich.'

Chuckling softly, Paisley makes her way over to the pair, and Sorcha does indeed become the ham in a squeezing, cuddling, giggling sandwich.

Perfect. Just what I need when I want to wallow in my own misery. But they're so stinkin' fuckin' cute. So I tell them so.

'You lot are as cute as.'

'Cute as what?' pipes up the ham in the middle.

'Just what I said, Sorch; as cute as.'

'That's silly,' Sorcha replies. 'If I wrote a sentence like that, my teacher would say it was unfinished. 'As cute as . . . Paisley. That's a sentence.'

'She is pretty cute,' Kier agrees.

'Aw, right back at you,' Paisley replies, cupping his face with her hand.

'Or as cute as Princess Kitty,' Sorcha continues, but Keir doesn't look so convinced. He's not a fan of Sorcha's cat.

'As cute as you,' he says instead, kissing his daughter on the head.

'What about Chastity?' It sounds like a throwaway line, but Paisley's fishing.

'Flynn thinks she's cute,' Sorcha agrees, nodding vigorously. 'Don't you, scumbag?'

'She is pretty cute.'

'Oh, he *lurves* her.' Sorcha wraps her hands around her arms and begins making kissy faces.

'Enough of that,' Keir says, though not in reprimand. 'But now I see why he's in such a shite mood.'

'Daddy said a swear.' Sorcha glances up at Paisley with a look of heavy resignation and a heavy sigh.

'I heard,' Paisley answers. 'You know what that means.'

The little girl nods, then slides off the couch and makes her way to her school bag, pulling out a clear, plastic container full of pound coins, five and ten pound notes.

'Who put the twenty in, Sorch?'

'Uncle Will,' she says, pulling up her navy school socks. 'Agnes threatened to bash him with her rolling pin when all he did was say a—'

'Watch it.' Though Keir's voice is even, his brows are low.

'Psyched!' his daughter replies. 'Daddy,' she says, putting her hand on one cocked hip. 'Do you really think I would use bad words?'

'If you do, you've got enough money in there to pay for

a good year's worth.' I rub my hand across my jaw, trying not to laugh as Keir's displeasure is turned my way.

'You didn't take the swear jar to school, did you?' he asks his daughter even though he's still staring at me.

'Oh my goodness,' Paisley says, chuckling. 'Imagine having to explain all that.'

'They'd probably call child services, or whatever the equivalent is here.'

'I didn't take it to school. I just asked Paisley to bring it when she picked me up. There's always someone in daddy's office using bad words.'

'She's a chip off the old block, mate.'

'That jar isn't capitalism,' he replies. 'Tell Flynn what you're going to do with the money, hen.'

'Build a school in Lesotho. That's in Africa. Well, I don't think I'll get enough to build a *whole* school,' she says, tipping her jar to examine it. 'But I think I'll have enough for a library.'

'A library built on bad words. Does that mean we're cursing for a good cause?'

'Come on, you,' Keir says, standing. He holds his hand out for his daughter. 'Come help me pack up my things.'

I watch the pair walk away holding hands. Keir had a tough ride starting with parenthood. Building a business and being a single father is tough. But now he has Paisley, and those days are behind him. The pair are so in love. I never thought I'd say it, but I envy him for what he has.

I wonder if Chastity will ever have kids? I reckon she will. She'll probably marry an investment banker in a few years and shoot out a couple of kids because that's what proper couples do. They'll probably be raised by a nanny and later, be bundled off to boarding school.

What the fuck am I thinking? I rub my hand through

my hair, fucking angry with myself. What difference does it make what she does with her life? She'd made it quite clear I'm just a temporary player in it. I can't even do that properly—be a player. Not where she's concerned.

'You look like you've just had a full conversation with yourself in your head.'

I look up, a little embarrassed. I'd forgotten Paisley was still here.

'Mate, it's been one of those days.'

'This isn't like you, Flynn.' She stands and walks over to my desk, perching her arse on the very edge. 'You're always happy.'

'No one's ever always happy.' I pull my tie loose from my collar and lean back in my chair.

'Must to something in the air, then.' She picks up Keir's posh pen, then puts it down again. 'Because Chastity was in a funky mood, too.'

Now I see where this is going. 'You've been to work?'

'I had another gig elsewhere, but I popped into the studio to chat. She's not herself lately. Seems she's got a problem. Actually, she has a few, but at least one of her issues she refuses to admit to herself.'

'Yeah?' I watch her carefully as she rearranges things on my desk without once looking at me. 'You make her sound like a handful.'

'The kind you like, you mean.'

'What's the deal, then?' I ask. I'm not touching her assumption. That's between me and Chastity.

'I can't tell you about it.' Eyes lowered, she shakes her head. 'She told me in confidence.'

'Then why are you telling me, P?'

Her brow furrows for the briefest moment before she

seems to push the thought away. 'I suppose because I think you're the only one to solve it. Them?'

'What kind of problems are we talking about here?'

'The kind you'll probably have to worm out of her.'

'Sounds like a lot of effort,' I respond mildly, rubbing a finger along my eyebrow. 'A problem she doesn't want to share. A problem I'm gonna have to work for. I dunno, you're not selling it to me.'

'Well,' she begins. 'I think it's like this; sometimes, you just need someone to give you a hug. For them to pat your back and tell you everything will be okay. And sometimes you need that hug to turn into dirty sex.'

'Am I interrupting something?' My head whips around to the sound of Keir's voice. Standing in the doorway, he looks far from impressed. In fact, he looks pretty pissed.

'Keep your kilt on,' his wife says. 'I was just talking to Flynn here about Chas.'

'Fuck's sake,' he grumbles under his breath. 'You'll gi' the man a mangina!'

'A man-what?'

'We're blokes. We don't talk about problems—about that kind of stuff.'

'Really?' she says, sliding off the edge of my desk. 'So you didn't need a little push when it came to me?'

'Aye, but not from the likes of him,' he says, pointing in my direction.

'Thanks, fucker,' I say on a chuckle. Coinage chinks on glass next to my ear.

'You said a bad word,' Sorcha sings. 'Pay up.'

'Sorry, Sorch.' I slide my wallet from my back pocket. 'I forgot you were around. Sorry for starting that, too.' With a five-pound note, I point in the direction of the bickering pair.

'Don't worry, Flynn,' she replies in an air of long suffering. 'They never argue long. Besides,' she adds, watching the pair with ease. 'When they're friends again, they go upstairs to apologise in private, and I get to eat a big bowl of ice cream while watching whatever I want on TV.'

'Cool.' My reply sounds sort of strangled, but what the fuck else is there to say?

'Do you know what they're doing up there when they become friends again?'

Oh shit. I shake my head quickly because this is a job way above my paygrade. 'No idea,' I answer quickly.

'Hmm,' she says still studying the pair. 'I'm pretty sure that's when they have s-e-x.'

19

I GLANCE down at my phone.

Paisley: *How's Operation Yoni going?*
Me: *I think I'd rather stick to calling my vagina Barbara, thanks very much.*

I slide my phone away before Paisley replies with some other ridiculousness and make my way to the studio door to lock up for the day. I'm just about to set the alarm when the roar of a motorbike pulling into the carpark gives me a start. The studio isn't in a great end of town. Also, "studio" might be too lofty a title because it really isn't much more than a unit housed in an industrial estate because who wants to rent space to a company that makes dirty movies?

But I digress; the motorbike.

I pause at the doorway, one hand holding the large bundle of keys with the other wrapped around the heavy steel door. The clearly expensive machine pulls to a stop almost directly outside of the building. The powerful engine cuts out, and still I don't move. While the registered office of my company isn't this address, I still feel the slight warning edge of anxiety creeping in when I think of the weirdos I've had contact me in the past. Not that I've ever made myself the face of the company, but in the early days, certainly around Fast Girls inception, we did get quite a bit of media interest. And following that, a few strangers with even stranger requests had sought me out.

My footing is sure and my body tense as the rider dismounts and reaches for his helmet. A suit and a pocket square? This is either a man who means business or is here *on* business? Either way, I don't think anyone is murdering me today. Not in the way my imagination had sprung to because I recognise the hard body under that suit...

Chastity Leonore Landry, peddler of posh smut, killed by the sight of a man in a sharply tailored suit.

The rider lifts his hands to his helmet, the action of removing it slowing to striptease pace, eventually revealing Flynn's gorgeous, though slightly battered face.

'Are you seriously wearing Tom Ford on a motorbike?'

'G'day, Chastity.' After our awkward Sunday lunch, it does my heart good to see his almost perma-cocky grin firmly back in place.

'Well?' I ask, sounding like my aunt Camilla. Out with it, boy! *Yes, please,* pings a voice somewhere in the vicinity of my knickers.

Flynn glances down at his suit before making a show of brushing invisible dust from his shoulders. I've never seen Flynn in anything other than jeans, apart from when we were in the Seychelles, and I can't for the life of me remember what he wore then. Though I remember every inch of him without his clothes because who could forget that? Those toned abs with a happy trail leading to a lewd kind of heaven. His strong, tanned arms and lightly furred legs. The pale scar on his side he'd attributed to a surfing mishap, and the way his hair had fallen over his forehead as his body rippled above mine.

'You like the *ge-ah*?' he asks, moving closer in a confident swagger.

'The w-what? Oh, the gear—your suit. You scrub up well, I suppose. But isn't it dangerous to ride a machine like that in just good tailoring?' A dark blue suit, his white shirt unbuttoned at the neck and a tie that complements the brilliant shade of his eyes, knotted but loose from the collar. And a matching pocket square? He looks more *GQ* than Mellors the gardener.

'You think I should wear protection?'

I'm *not* touching that. 'Aren't you supposed to wear leathers or something?'

'That sounds like an invitation to star in one of your movies.' His gaze flares cheekily, and then he's in front of me, his eyes sliding over my shoulder to the darkened studio beyond. 'Aren't you going to invite me in?'

'What for? Why are you here, Flynn?'

'Maybe I've come to audition.'

'We d-don't audition. We interview. And in a public place.'

He sets off laughing. 'You have hidden depths, my tiny, dirty girl.'

I frown and bite my lip rather than spit the words my brain has supplied—*you wish*—because that would probably take us tumbling down that tempting rabbit hole. And what would be the point of that? I'd just be repeating my mistakes. And that's the definition of madness—doing the same thing over and over while expecting the results to change.

The jet black helmet dangles from his fingers of his left hand as he uses his other to loosen the single button on his suit jacket, only to slide that hand into his pants pocket.

'You spend an awful lot of time with your hands in there.' I glance down, automatically feeling the need to qualify the statement. 'In your pocket, I mean.' I continue to stare at the outline of his hand through the expensive suiting.

'You're doing it again.' His voice is almost a whole octave lower, a hint of gravel in his tone. 'You're looking at me like you're imagining me without my clothes. And I fuckin' love it.'

'Is it a comfort thing?' I ask, ignoring both his tone and his dangerous words and keeping my eyes studiously from his. On second thought, staring at his pants as though wearing X-ray specs isn't sending the right kind of message, either. As I lift my head, like a magnet, my gaze is drawn to his, my mouth running away with me again. 'Or do you just like to make sure it's still there? *Constantly.*'

'You're asking me if I like touching my own dick? Are you the masturbation police, Chastity? Feel free to say yes because I think you might need to take me prisoner.'

'I didn't remember you mentioning that you wanted to write scripts as part of the consult.' Snark. This tone of voice and I are very familiar where Flynn is concerned.

'Do you remember the rest of that statement? I'm only interested in consulting with one thing.'

I remember all right. And that particular part of my anatomy remembers, too, as it begins pulsing. Because he'd said he wanted to consult with my pussy before proceeding to convene with it in the most intimate of ways. He gave me more orgasms that night than I thought were possible, and certainly more than I'd had in the previous six months. It's like I'd been storing them just for him or something.

I clear my throat, not trusting myself to speak. Flynn Phillips is like a ninja at dirty talking and probably holds a bachelor's degree in innuendo. And this is coming from someone who makes their living by thinking up sexy, barely there plots.

'Invite me inside, duchess, and I'll refresh your memory.'

'I don't think that's a good idea.' I tighten my grip on the door even though my statement is only partially true because my body is all for letting him in . . . wherever. Wherever he'd like to go.

'Paisley tells me you've got a killer coffee machine in there.' *That accent. Kills. Me.* 'Says she's the only one who's been able to work out how to use it.'

'And that's supposed to spur me to make a decision?' I answer as I fold my arms. 'To prove to you that I can master the coffee machine?'

'You master a lot of things, including me,' I think he says, but he speaks his words so quietly and quickly, I can't be sure. He shrugs, then looks around, his hand rasping against the days' stubble on his chin as he whispers an almost inaudible, '*Fuck,*' to join his other mumblings. 'Hold that for me, would you?' he adds in a more normal tone, though just as quick, and he thrusts the helmet at me, forcing me to unfold my arms.

In the haste of the moment, I drop my keys into the bowl of the thing. And as my head comes up, I have neither the time to notice nor complain, not as Flynn takes my face in his hands to deliver the most perfect of kisses—sweet and soft but not without a delicious edge. The vibration of his groan as I open for his tongue brings my lust for this man from a simmer to a flame. But regretfully, it isn't long before he pulls away and leaves me standing there, panting and almost without breath.

'Put me out of my misery, Chastity. Let me in.' *What am I doing here?* I ask myself, even as I step to the side to allow him to pass.

I close the door, the majority of the light cutting out, and honestly, I'm still wondering what I'm doing—what *he's* doing—as I set his helmet down on a stack of boxes in the hallway.

'We're just hanging out, shooting shit. No need to worry.' His tone is mild as I turn to face him with my apparently questioning face. 'Just like mates.'

I don't for one minute think of us as friends, though it occurs to me he probably is the kind of person who makes a good friend. He's quick to laugh and to make others join in, whether with him or *at* him, and his carefree nature is almost infectious and certainly good to be around. *At least, when he's not bugging the shit out of me.* But something tells me Flynn Phillips isn't all laughs and frippery. The man has substance to him, too.

But his is all moot as I'm not in the market for new friends, especially with him. *Friends don't fuck like we have. Like we . . . do?*

'But what are you doing here—here, exactly?' I point at the industrial carpeted floor of the hallway. 'How did you even know where to find me?'

'I told you. Paisley.' I find myself narrowing my gaze as I consider the conversation the pair seem to have had. *What was said?* 'You look like that worries you, duchess.

Like you've got something to hide.' Cue a further narrowing of my eyes and add to it a little bite of the tongue. Not that I think she'll have spilled the beans on . . . on my broken bean.

Not Paisley. Not her. Not to him.

'So this is where the magic happens,' he says, turning to the entrance to the studio. Bracing his hands solidly on the frame, he gives me his strong profile and not the bruised side. Not that it's a terrible sight, especially coupled with the darkened scruff of his stubble and his impeccable suit. He still looks sexy, though in a thoroughly disreputable way.

Flynn sticks his head into the studio, and before I can tell him to stop, he steps out of the hallway and into the room. What's a girl to do but follow him?

I try to see the space like he might, wondering if it's titillation he's after, because if it is, he'll be seriously disappointed. The most visible tell in the room is a small rack of hangers containing robes. There's no St Andrew's cross, no whips or chains, or exposed dildos. On one side of the room is a set that could be a bedroom in some trendy loft—exposed brickwork and a contemporary four-poster bed dressed in pale linens. *Nothing salacious. Move along, there's nothing to see here, folks.*

'Details right down to the specs and the beside lamp.' He gestures to the nightstand, a hardback book lying open and splayed on the wood, a pair of feminine glasses folded next to it.

'Women notice the small details.' Yes, even when there's a ten-inch penis involved.

'I bet the drawer holds a treasure trove of naughty delights.'

I smile and shake my head. 'Looks like someone's been watching my stuff.'

'Someone can't take his eyes off your stuff.' As though to reinforce the point, his gaze makes a slow perusal of my body, and I have to bite my lip to halt the stuttering release of my breath.

'Sorry to disappoint,' I add swiftly, steering the topic away. 'The content of that particular treasure trove is currently being sterilised.' Not really. We haven't been filming that kind of scene today. I expect more questions —demands for particulars—when he turns away, moving to the other side of the large space housing an abandoned office set.

'Naughty secretaries?' he asks, casting a wicked glance over his shoulder, a look that makes me wonder what mischief this devil has in mind for my soul.

'Something like that.'

'And don't you look the part today.'

'So do you.' The words are out of my mouth without thought.

'Is that because you think I'm someone's glorified secretary?' His gaze hardens a touch, causing my expression to falter. I hadn't meant it like that at all.

'I don't weigh someone's worth by their job description or their title.' What kind of despicable arse would do that? 'I simply meant you look like a boss this secretary wouldn't mind being bent under.' *Jesús, María y José!* Talk about inappropriateness and oversharing.

He laughs, a perfect burst of honesty—delight at the escape of mine. Maybe my reddening cheeks stop him from taking advantage of the fact, but I suddenly don't know whether to be pleased or disappointed that he doesn't latch onto my statement.

'Do you always dress like that for work?' he asks instead.

I look down at my outfit; black pencil skirt and white blouse. 'Jeans normally,' I answer, 'but I had an appointment at the bank. Why do you ask?'

'I'd have thought it was obvious. You look like a wet fucking dream.'

'This is perfectly acceptable office attire,' I reply testily.

'Dunno what kind of office you've been workin' in. You look hot, like some sexy librarian, your blouse hinting at the lace of your bra and your skirt hugging those curves. And those shoes . . . '

He glances down at my black heels, and I concede he might have a point here. I don't own a lot of heels, and those that I do own were bought for nights out, not to complement day outfits. Still, they're just shoes.

'All buttoned up and wholesome on the surface with just a hint of the girl down for dirty fucking.'

'Flynn . . . ' His name sounds like plea, though for more or for a halt, I'm not sure either of us can tell.

'Seriously. I can't imagine your actors lasting long being filmed by you in the first place, but dressed like that? No fucking chance. And I don't remember seeing *The Two Thrust Chump* being in the title menu.'

'My actors are professionals. They're not looking at me like you would.'

'Trust me. They're men, and they have eyes. They're lookin'. Want to know what else I've noticed?'

'Please, give me the benefit of your vast knowledge.' Sarcasm travels across the space.

'Your actors, their dirty talk is weak.'

'What?' If I wasn't so shocked, I might laugh. 'I know

you've been watching, but—'

'Come on, duchess. The best kind of porn has a little nastiness in it.' His eyes flick down to my lips and back again. 'Your actors have got the beauty of sex down, but their dialogue needs work.'

'Thank you, Flynn Phillips. Thank you for that insight,' I reply with an unpleasant sounding chuckle. 'However, thousands of subscriptions say otherwise.'

'You like it. Admit it.'

This time, I don't laugh. Not as he slides the jacket from his shoulders, dropping it to the adjacent desk. Not as his long legs eat up the space between us. And not as he takes me in his hands, not his arms. This isn't an embrace.

'I want to try something.' His gaze is wide and innocent, but the man doesn't have an innocent cell in his body as far as I can tell. 'You game?' And apparently, it's not a question that really needs an answer as he crushes me to his chest. He just . . . holds me there, flush against his body, my heart hammering against his.

'Is it working yet?' His deep words rumble through me, and the idea of just letting go—of hugging him back just as tight—is so very tempting.

'Is what working?' I ask a little breathlessly, hating how I sound, hating even more that I find I have breath to squeak when his hand slides down my back to rub both cheeks of my bottom.

'I was wondering if your undies would fall off.' His chest expands against mine as he lets out a theatrical sigh. 'But they're still there.'

'With a hug? Not even you are that good.'

'No, but I am pretty good,' he answers with a gleam as he pulls back. 'And maybe a little more in tune than your best mate, Paisley.'

'What has Paisley got to do with this?'

'She reckoned you are in the need of the kind of hug that turns into dirty sex.'

'I don't believe you,' I grate out, pulling free from his strong arms. 'She wouldn't say those sorts of things. Not to you.' I find the thought of any possible conversation between the pair distressing, the idea tightening my chest.

'But I suppose we both have our theories.'

'Is that what brings you here? Theories and half-cocked plans?'

'You've got it wrong, duchess.' He grasps my flailing hand, the one I'm trying very hard not to thump him with, and brings it to the front of his jeans. He presses my palm firmly against his erection, arching into my hand. 'And this isn't what I'd call half-cocked, would you?'

'Flynn . . .' I swallow audibly, his name sounding as though dragged over rough ground. 'We can't keep doing this.'

'Doing what?' he asks using that innocent tone again. 'I dunno what you're talking about,' he says, stepping away. 'What's this chair used for?' Grasping the back of a plastic office chair, he lifts it, depositing it halfway between the desk and the other side of the room.

'It's either from my office or the break room,' I answer distractedly. To be honest, I'm not sure. The same as I'm not sure what direction this is heading.

Flynn grabs his jacket, striding to the rack of robes and hanging it there. Taking my reluctant hand, he pulls me over to the desk. 'You stay there,' he says, leaning my butt up against the edge. Then he walks back to the chair where he takes a seat.

'I've been thinking,' he begins, leaning forward to

untie the thin laces of his black oxfords. 'Something hasn't been right with you.'

'Why are you taking your shoes off?' Next off come the socks. His feet are tanned and long and rather elegant, as far as feet go.

'I tried to ask you the other morning, but you were hell-bent on going back to sleep.'

'You wore me out!' I snap my mouth shut.

If he tries not to smirk, it isn't working as he stands and loosens his tie, hanging it over the back of the chair before he begins unfastening the buttons on his shirt, top to bottom. 'You're not much of a giver are you, duchess.'

'What? What's that supposed to mean?'

'Hang on, that didn't come out right. You *are* a giver—you give to better other people—you give your time and energy. You give loads of that shit to your mates and those you love. But you don't *give* a lot of stuff away about yourself. See, to me,' he adds ponderously, pulling his shirt free of his waistband. 'There's something going on, and you just won't ask for a helping hand.'

I might argue, but my words are stolen as he strips from his shirt, exposing his sculpted torso and strong arms, but as the clink of his belt reverberates through the room, I find my words.

'Flynn, this is ridiculous,' I say quickly. 'Put your clothes on. I'm not filming you today.'

'No?'

'Please, put your clothes on.' I sound a little desperate, and if I can hear it, he can, too.

'I bet you'd like to film me, though.'

'Yes.' I swallow quickly as he folds the sides of his pants open, sliding his hand into his boxers. 'Yes,' *Christ yes*, 'I would, but—'

He tilts his head back, giving himself a concealed tug. 'What would you call my movie?'

I swallow, my heart pounding both between my ears and between my legs as I watch him touch himself, tease himself—tease me. He's groaning quietly, all languid, inviting eyes. I watch, mesmerised as his chest rises slowly, then falls, following the cording of muscles in his strong forearm as his muscles pump and flex.

'In Like Flynn,' I muse aloud.

His eyes meet mine—dark and widely dilated—but with a challenge burning there. 'I'll make you a deal. You get your camera, and I'll give you a show like you've never seen.' Lord Almighty, I think I just had a mini orgasm. I make to stand because who the hell would say no to that? Flynn Phillips touching himself—getting himself off? And all for me.

'I have conditions,' his low voice rumbles, his hand still inside his pants. 'You have to join in.' I'm already shaking my head—no way, no deal—when he speaks again. 'Off camera. But you have to give me some incentive. Be my muse.'

'Qualify *join in*,' I repeat slowly, my eyes not sure whether to watch his hand or his face.

'Just touch yourself. Let me watch. How about we have a little wager? The last one to come gets to decide what to do with the film.'

'You don't mean—'

'You can put it on the website. *If* you win.'

I wouldn't—couldn't. But I'm not telling him.

'You're going down,' I say with an evil chuckle, to which he replies, 'Ladies first.'

It takes very few adjustments to the camera for Flynn's sequence. In truth, though the camera is worth thousands, this part of the business is a pretty basic affair. I didn't go to school to study cinematography. As with most things in this business, I'm self-taught.

I move away from the setup, changing the settings for one of the lights.

'Do your hands always shake?' Flynn's voice catches me off guard. The answer is no. Not for a long time. I'm at ease being around naked people and totally at home watching them fuck. In fact, I rarely watch *them*. I'm more concerned about the scene as a whole, constantly questioning the look. Flynn being here in my studio, making his kinds of offers, has rendered my mind and my control a bust. But perhaps the best defence is an offence, so I make my way back to the desk with a sway in my step as I begin to loosen the buttons of my blouse.

Turning to face him, I prop myself against the edge, letting my fingers trail down my throat, lingering between the sides of my open blouse.

'You're a fucking tease,' he says on a deep chuckle, twisting his hand around the head of his dick. Not that I can see exactly—his trousers abandoned, he's still wearing his tight boxer briefs, his hand holding the outline of his hardness as he flexes into his palm.

'Says the man with his cock in his hand.' The beautiful man. Tanned under the lighting, his legs planted wide.

'Babe, talk dirty to me.'

'I thought you were the expert?'

'Fuck,' he hisses tightening the fabric over the outline of his substantial erection, displaying for me and the camera both girth and length. 'You know what I'm imagining? You. Naked. Squirming and soaking wet.'

'Is that the best you've got?' My retort is without conviction as he straightens his cock, pulling out the head to rest against his toned stomach. 'You're on your hands and knees with your pussy glistening and ready for me.' Despite my retort, I think I might moan a little, especially as he licks the tips of his fingers and rubs saliva over the head until it's shining and wet. 'I want to spank you until your arse gleams red and suck on your pussy until you scream.'

I gasp, blood turning molten in my veins.

'Give me your underwear, duchess,' he demands.

He rubs and squeezes his thick head, groaning as though he's in the best kind of pain, the muscles of his abs contracting as though suffering through a solid workout.

I can't . . . not do as he asks. Out of the shot of the camera, I shimmy my skirt up over my hips, hooking my thumbs into the sides of my knickers and sliding them down my legs.

'*Jesus fuck*,' he rasps. 'Thigh highs.' He rewards me and the sight of my stockings by slipping his hand under the soft cotton to release his hard cock from the confines. Tipping his head back, Flynn holds his length in both hands, yes, both hands, his thumb and forefinger teasing his engorged head, the other holding the base as he rubs.

I've never seen anything quite so explicit. Quite so erotic. And coming from someone who makes a living from sex, that's saying something.

I don't even debate the merits of my actions as I throw the balled-up scrap of lace at him, shucking out of my shirt and blouse. My skin feels alive and the fabric too heavy to bear. And I think my brain breaks a little as he catches my knickers against his chest, bringing them to his nose to deeply inhale. And all the while his other hand doesn't stop. Holding himself, he rubs hard, then soft. Fast, then slow.

Smooth skin. Wet hand. Gasping, broken breath as he begins to pant.

'You're not touching yourself,' he rasps. 'Cheat.'

Never let it be said I don't ever rise to a dare. At least, not when I'm aching and not when moisture is gathering between my bare legs. Not when something heavy and needy causes my heart to beat wildly.

Leaning back against the desk, I spread my feet and slip two fingers between my legs. My body bows at the contact, and I gasp. *When did I last feel this kind of electricity when touching myself?* Certainly not over the past six months.

'Wider,' he grunts. Images and sensations coalesce, drowning me in need as he bites the lace of my knickers, tipping his head back with a groan as he stretches the pale fabric, the colour contrasted against his darker skin. 'Let me see.'

'First—first to come gets the tape.' This from me as my slick fingers reach a place I thought I'd lost—a place I thought had abandoned me. My body arcs into my hand, almost bringing me up onto my toes as I seek a pleasure that my body has denied me for long months.

'That's it, duchess. Come here, please.' I shake my head, unable to form words. 'The tape, it's yours. Just, please. Come here.'

I was never going to make it public, anyway. And in a moment, I'm in front of him, and I'm pretty sure it has nothing to do with the tape. One hand on my hip, he brings my body over his, and as I straddle him, he tugs me down for a rough kiss. I seek to centre my body.

'No, love. You need to finish this.' He slides his fingers

through my wetness, making me to buck and hiss. Then with the gentlest of kisses to the softness of my stomach, he takes his rock-hard cock into his hand once again.

'That's it—that's it.' His eyes are glued to where my fingers move fast and slick, my body bowing forward as I support myself with my hand on the back of the chair.

'You're killin' me,' he groans, his hand moving faster as his body twists, his mouth in line with my breast. 'I'm gonna come on you.' He wraps the scrap of lace around the base of his thick length as he begins to jack in earnest now. 'Come on your sweet pussy and your tits.'

It's pure sensation overload as I bridge the gap between satisfaction and ecstasy. Flynn's face is a study in pure contrasts—of agony and ecstasy and everything in between.

I feel each nudge of his smooth head as it brushes my slickness. Feel the coarseness of the hairs on his thighs as they brush between my legs. It feels so good. Too good, and as my fingers continue their wet slide, I try not to look down. Try not to watch his expression, the dark moons of his lashes against his cheeks as he watches where we almost meet.

'I want you to suck me off,' he pants. 'I want my mouth on you.'

His breathless demands and wishes push me immediately over that invisible edge.

There is nothing else but this moment.

And my tears of relief.

And this man whispering his sweet, filthy encouragements as he bucks up into me.

There is nothing but the pulse of my body and the sight of his own climax covering me.

20

FLYNN

'THAT WAS . . . that was the hottest thing I've ever seen.' Her arms around my neck and her arse nestled into the cradle of my thighs, Chastity doesn't speak. 'Are you okay down there?'

She nods, so she's not dead, at least, though seems to rouse herself almost immediately. She stands, taking her heat from me with her as she furtively wipes tears from her face. *I hope those are tears of relief.* Talk about a one-track mind as she reaches behind me and slips my shirt from the back of the chair, her luscious tits almost in my face.

'I . . . I have stuff to say,' she mumbles, her gaze languid and her expression relaxed. Then she turns, making her way to the desk to grasp some kind of control. *Ah, the camera.* She switches the lights off, making her way back to my lap.

I like this Chastity. This unguarded girl.

'How did you know?' she whispers. She's slung her arms around my neck, hiding her face against my chest.

Ah. 'It was an educated guess, I suppose. From

watching you. When I made you come, there was something about your face.'

'Shut up,' she grumbles, swatting the back of my head. 'No one has a good come face.'

'What? Not even me?'

'No comment.'

I inhale and let the breath out along with my words. 'Surprised, babe. You looked surprised. And then there was the bit when you welcomed it while your body pulsed around me.' She twists her head to better see me, her expression quizzical. *'There it is!'* I repeat. 'Like you were surprised. Or directing it.'

'You make it sound like I was using semaphore.' God, she makes me laugh. 'I did not wave flags as I came!'

'Why not. I fucking would.' I tighten my arms around her. 'You'd be surprised the lengths I'd go to, to be around you.'

Instantly, her body goes stiff in my arms. 'Do you mean that?' Her voice is small and unsure and not like her at all. I don't like it—don't like that she'd ever doubt this.

'Duchess.' I take her face in my hands. 'I dunno how you haven't noticed, but I'm kinda into you like you wouldn't believe.'

'What does that even mean? Where are all the grown-ups?' she mutters. 'One fancies me, and one is into me?'

'Who fancies you? I mean, who wouldn't?'

'What does it matter?' she answers, standing abruptly. Before I can put my feelings into English, because apparently, Aussie English isn't working for this chick, we both hear her phone ring out in the hallway. Her heels click as she makes her way to it, her expression conflicted as she returns with the phone in her hand.

I think for a minute she might ignore it, but she only seems to contemplate this before answering.

'Hello, Mother.' I'm surprised by her address given that I got a peek of her screen which read *Caroline*. It's not only her words and diction that are stiff because her whole body is rigid.

Dressed in only my shirt, her bra, stocking and heels, she wraps her free hand around her waist, making her way to the other side of the draughty room, the lines of her body drawn tight.

'Oh, well. No. Actually, I'd made plans for that day . . . well, that's to say friends have already made plans on my behalf. A surprise, you see,' she adds coolly. 'Yes, a party. It was a *surprise*, Mother . . . No, I can't . . . You're right. It wouldn't be seemly. Yes, invitations have already gone out.' Chastity turns her head over her shoulder, shooting a regretful smile my way. 'Well, I am sorry about that. Perhaps we can catch up when Max gets back.'

Her brow furrows as she turns back to the call, so I take the opportunity to slip on my undies. The floor is frigid under my bare feet as I pad over to her, gathering the riot of her escaped hair to place my lips at her neck. Just below her pulse point I suck gently. Wrapping her in my arms seems to melt some of her tension.

She's so beautiful and so strong, and her visible discomfort makes me want to protect her. Shield her with my body. And as I can't do either of these things, I offer her my worship instead. Even if she does swat my hands away when I slide them into my open shirt to palm her breasts.

'What?' I whisper in her ear. 'It's my shirt. Maybe I want it back.' I sense rather than see her smile as I kiss her neck, feeling her swallow against my lips.

'I like you a lot, Chastity Landry.' I kiss her shoulder; my words hot in her ear. 'I want you to let me in.'

She turns her head then, her dark eyes sparkling and complicit even as she mouths the word, '*Stop.*'

'Nah.' Spinning her back to my front again, I begin kissing her ear. 'I want you in my bed, and I want you in my arms.' I've been around, travelled to a lot of places, and fucked a lot of girls, but I have never taken part in something as hot as just now. I could almost taste her wetness coating my tongue as the pulse of her orgasm beat between us like a drum. This woman is a thing of beauty when she comes. But it's more than that. This thing we have between us is more than the sum of these parts.

She swats at me ineffectually as I push my hands down her thighs, slipping them inward to drag them up again, my cock pounding against her arse.

'I want to come inside you next time. Nothing between us but skin. I want to keep you, Chastity.'

'Mother, I have to go. I'll call back soon.' And just like that, she steps out of my arms, switching off her phone.

Gears start spinning in my head, her expression one I can't make out. 'What was all that about?' I ask, gesturing to her phone.

'My mother.' She looks down at her phone, then shakes her head. 'And I'm pretty sure that was my line.'

My expression clouds. She's not dense, not by any stretch of the imagination. So I fall into default mode.

'Well, it's like this, duchess.' I step into her, taking her reluctant hips in my hands. 'When a man likes a girl, he kinda wants to . . . come inside her.'

'Oh, you!' She swats my arm. 'Why can't you be serious for just five seconds? Why must you always try to get on my last nerve?'

'The short answer is 'cause it's fun. The long answer is because, and I say again, I want to keep you.'

'That!' she exclaims, pointing her finger at me. 'That's exactly what I mean. Keep me? What am I? An ornament or a doll?'

'I thought we already established the answer to this. Didn't we already have this conversation?' She frowns, though quickly swaps the expression for something a little more irate when I say, 'You're my little fuck doll.' I probably shouldn't, given the lethal weapons she has on her feet, but I laugh. Fuck, do I ever.

'Flynn Phillips . . . Put your bastarding clothes on and g-get out of here!'

'Okay, okay,' I reply, all placating hand gestures as I back my way up to the chair.

'Serves you right if I do load your clip to the website.'

'Not my clip. It's yours,' I reply, slipping into my suit pants. 'You gonna give me my shirt back? I'll swap you for your undies,' I might taunt.

Head held high, she makes her way to the desk, slipping her skirt on under my shirt. Back still turned to me, she slides the cotton off her shoulders, substituting it for her silk blouse. She swings on her heel, making her way back over to me.

'Here.' Arm stretched out like she can't bear to be near me, she offers me my shirt from between her fingertips. 'You can keep my knickers. Call them a reminder.'

'Thanks, babe.' I slide them into my pocket, then pull on my shirt. 'I'll add them to my collection.' She makes a noise that's a little like a growl. 'You know, you're a bit of a paradox,' I say, buttoning my shirt.

'I'm surprised you know what that word means.'

'I'm not just a pretty face.' Not by any means. 'But

you're so open about a lot of shit, and I bet I could have a conversation with you about any kind of sex. Cuttlefish porn,' I say, beginning to count off my fingers. 'Female ejaculations; myth or fantasy? But, and this is a big but, the minute I pay you a compliment, I become a lying toad.'

'I must attract them.'

'That would be your swamp arse attitude!' I half yell, half say across the room. I'm not angry—I'm rarely that—but I want her fucking attention.

'Swamp arse?' she asks with the greatest disdain. And then she starts laughing. Really laughing.

So I grab her. And I kiss her. And when we come up for breath, her eyes are smiling again.

'Female ejaculation isn't a myth,' she says seriously. 'I've seen it.' I groan and mumble something about her teasing me. 'And cuttlefish porn? Sorry, but I'm not a fan.'

'Octopus, then?'

'God, yes. I'm nothing if I'm not all about the tentacle,' she says with a gurgling laugh.

'Duchess, my tentacle is the only one you're getting. If we're doing this, we're doing it right. Exclusive, all in.'

'Flynn,' she says, her eyes softening as she rests her hand on my cheek. 'I haven't had an orgasm by myself in six months. Do you really think I'm going to let you get away?'

21

CHASTITY

OVER THE LAST few weeks Flynn and I have seen quite a bit of each other, and I don't just mean in the bedroom. For the want of a better word, we're dating. It's been . . . fun. Dinners and movies, brunch after a lazy morning in bed—even an afternoon rowing on the Serpentine. Our friends reactions have been positive, but mostly circumspect, which I get. No one, least of all me, wants to get their hopes up.

However, the one thing they've all agreed on is that I'm crazy. It seems they think conjuring up a birthday party to avoid a family dinner is a little much. What they don't understand is that these evenings are painful enough without the attendance of my mother and father's companions; bitterness and younger girlfriend number twelve respectively. Usually, Max acts as a buffer for all involved. So if he's unavailable, so am I.

You only get one thirtieth birthday, after all. *Unless you're aunt Camilla.*

Flynn and my friends have had a ball suggesting ideas for my party. Because *telling* my mother I was having a party wasn't enough. Now I'm actually *having* a party. Thanks, friends. So far I've the nixed the suggestion of an inflatable bouncing castle complete with a pub and a disco ball, (Flynn) a bright pink bucking bronco penis, (Paisley) and a Margarita van (Ella). It's just a shame I don't have the space for a bouncing castle or a huge bucking dick, and I'm sure there would be licensing issues with an ice-cream van that serves liquor on the street.

So now I'm not lying about having a party. Because I'm actually *having* a party.

Well, I am turning thirty.

It's a little dramatic, and I mean no disrespect to anyone else, but it's my birthday, so I can make people wear black and white if I want to. Okay, so that's not quite how the song goes, but you get what I mean. I'm going with a stylish and tongue-in-cheek theme of black, maybe with a little white thrown in, while asking for charitable donations in lieu of gifts.

Flynn thinks the idea is "cool as" and promised he'd be a pall bearer for my youth, which, as far as I can tell, means he's game to be underneath me at some point during the evening. Over the past few weeks, Flynn and I have gotten more comfortable around each other although he insists he's always been comfortable around me. He tells me his animal magnetism was something I needed time to adjust to. That it was probably the thing putting me off. So nothing to do with the way he makes me feel like I want to wrap my hands around his throat. And not in a—*fun?*—erotic asphyxiation way.

The truth is, I can't imagine him not being around. He exasperates me, while breathing life into the empty corners of my world—spaces I didn't realise were lacking. There's more to the man than meets the eye, and while

I'm trying not to make plans to see us into retirement together, I'm enjoying my time with him. *Enjoying him. And his filthy mind.*

My mind is so caught up in the shower we took together last night. The water raining down against his body, and the way it flowed down between my fingertips, my hand splayed on the ridges of his stomach. The feeling of the coarseness under my palm as I'd slid my other hand up his thigh, my fingers drawn to the dip in his hip. The taste of him, of salt and man, as I'd tracked my lips against him and run my tongue along the head of his cock, holding the base firmly as I toyed with him. As good as he always makes me feel, I wanted to give that back, even as I'd teased and tortured, cupping him as I took his length almost to the back of my throat.

God, the sounds he'd made as I'd tasted and explored him with my mouth.

'*Babe . . . I can't. You need—*' His words were broken and made little sense. He'd slid his hand behind my head, just to hold me there, his arm travelling with the movement and bobs of my head. Had I ever made any man this senseless? Been responsible for such breathless moans echoing through the small space?

'*I can't. Fuck, yes!*' He'd thrown his head back, allowing water to cascade down his toned body. I slipped my hand between my legs, the realisation that I was responsible for this beautiful creature's ecstasy an aphrodisiac like nothing I've ever felt. I was determined to come—as determined as I was to make him come.

'*Yes! Touch yourself.*' There, crouched on the shower floor, the co-ordination had taken some mastering, but his words had served as supreme encouragement, my fingers moving faster, causing me to moan around his length.

He seemed to like the moaning. The vibration. The way I looked up at him while full of him. God, I'm such a porn cliché.

Out in the street, despite the brisk weather, my cheeks begin to heat as I recall how his words turned guttural as his hand had held my head tightly in place.

'*Yeah, that's it. Take it. Take it all.*' And I did.

His darkened eyes as he'd stared down at me, replete, made me happy—yes, I did this! I made this man look like he'd walk on hot coals to receive my attentions.

'*You amazingly dirty fucking girl.*'

He'd turned the shower off, then reached down, pulling me to my feet. My body had started to cool in the absence of the steam, the gooseflesh only deepening as he'd kissed me, kissed his essence from my lips.

'*Get your arse in that bedroom.*' His long tongue had flicked out, tasting the coating on my fingertips. '*I'm gonna make your pussy my home.*'

Damn. My purse begins to buzz, so I pull out my phone.

'Babe.' Flynn's voice travels down the line in an echo of last night. Yep, that's still happening. I'm super-hot for the man. 'Mini sausages.'

A bark of laughter breaks free. Flynn's no mini, but maybe he means, 'I'm not ordering mini sausage,' I reply, deciding this is where the conversation is heading, my heels echoing against the pavement of my local shopping precinct.

'If you loved me, you would.'

'I-I-' Don't have an answer for that, and it's not something I'm examining. Absolutely, we're monogamous, but we're also newly minted in relationship terms.

You could love him, my mind whispers. *If you just trust*

yourself. But trust isn't something I'm all that good with. So I stay in the now. Call it suspicion or experience. Call it what you like because whatever you call it, my wariness exists.

'What kind of party doesn't have snags? Mini snags for added sophistication!'

'I'm on my way to the caterers now. If you're a good boy, I'll ask them to supply you with a bowl. But only for you. And you have to eat them out of the way in the kitchen, so the rest of my buffet isn't contaminated with your lowliness.'

'You're such a snob.'

'Yet you still like me.'

'Reckon I'm some kind of masochist.'

'Oh, are we talking dirty again?'

'Not when I'm at work, babe. It makes Keir jealous.'

'I take it he's there with you?'

'He is. The inconsiderate bastard. Listening in like the perv he is.'

'It's my bloody office!' I hear Keir complain.

'Better go, love, before he cracks the shits again.' Or in English, rather than Flynn's Aussie speak; Keir's a little angry. 'See you around seven?'

'Okay,' I agree, my voice tinged with laughter.

'Great. Can't wait.'

And neither can I. I don't get much farther in my silly, soppy, smiling quest when Tate, my neighbour, appears before me. In fact, right outside of his restaurant.

'Chastity,' he says, looking genuinely pleased. 'I wondered how long it would be before you popped in for that coffee.'

Ah, hell. I did say I would, but things have changed.

But as it begins to rain, I decide to do the decent thing and have a coffee and a conversation with the man.

'I do have a little time. If you're free, we could do it now.' Not do *it*, obviously. I'm only doing it with Flynn, and that's more than enough for me. In fact, it's sometimes a little too much. The man's appetite is voracious in all the ways. If he's eating a meal, he's enjoying it. If he's eating me, then we're both pretty sweet. *That's more Flynn-speak.*

'Earth to Chastity?' Tate brings his face level with mine. 'You spaced out there.'

It's happening a lot lately and always when thinking of Flynn. Note to self: I must get a grip.

'I just have a lot on my mind. Busy, busy! But I do have time for a coffee.'

'Great. That's great. Shall we . . .' Tate holds out his arm, pushing the glass entrance door wide.

'So how're things?' he asks, setting down a latte in front of me a few moments later. He pulls out the chair opposite, sitting down himself.

'Good! I'm good.' And overly effusive, it seems. 'How's business?'

'Also good. And the renovations on the house are about to start. Plans were just given the go-ahead.'

'Oh, I didn't realise you were remodelling?' And so it goes, polite conversation as I wonder how to steer it to the important parts. I'm not unfriendly, just maybe not very good with people I don't know.

'And how's work?'

'Ah, you mean the fictitious history gig?'

'You never did tell me what you do for a living,' he asks, in the vein of someone who'd like very much to know.

'There's a reason for that.' A dirty reason.

'Oh?'

'It's top secret,' I say again, I'm not in the least bit ashamed about how I earn my crust, but there are some things I just don't talk about. Not until I know a person better, at least. 'I could tell you, but then I'd have to kill you.'

'Intriguing.'

'It's not really. I work in media.' Sort of. 'And I run my own business.' I once was asked if that made me a cam-girl. God, I laughed so hard the guy who asked must have thought I was off my rocker.

'We, er, also said we'd discuss what I've been calling you in my head.' Tate rubs his nose, maybe a little nervous. Or at least good at playing the part of someone who's self-effacing. But whatever, knowing what he calls me in his head seems like something I don't need to hear. Too intimate, perhaps. Besides, what if it's a horrid name? Like fat arse or horse face. Some things are better left unsaid *and* unheard.

'The thing is, Tate, I'm sort of seeing someone.' I wrap my hands around my latte cup, surprised that his expression doesn't change. Strange.

'Oh. Just recent, then?' He takes a sip from his own cup.

'It's new.' And exciting. 'Things are going pretty good.'

'I'm happy for you, if not a little disappointed for myself. It makes me wish I hadn't waited. But I'll be here if. Well, you know.'

Hmm. Not sure that's the way things really work.

'Tell me about your renovation,' I say, hoping to steer the conversation in another direction. And I do. Who knew remodelling a house could be so arduous. Or maybe that's just the retelling. But conversation moves along as my latte is drained. Halleluiah!

'Oh, look at the time.' I make a show of glancing at my watch. 'I'd best dash before the caterers close.'

'You're catering?'

'My birthday. I'm having a party next week. I've sort of left everything a bit late.' On account of wondering if I could get out of it, I suppose. But my friends weren't having any of that.

'We offer outside catering. You should let us cater. I'll give you my friendly neighbourhood rate.'

I'm not sure that's an actual thing, but as Tate reaches for his laptop and the menus and price lists on his website, I see that it is. I leave the place with a decent menu and a strangely reasonable bill, in exchange for an awkward hug I didn't see coming and an invitation that he should "pop in" next Saturday night.

Saved from an hour with a caterer, I go shopping instead, honing in on a little boutique I haven't visited in an age. I treat myself, buying a dress that a sexy, grown-up Wednesday Addams would die for, and some underwear I'm pretty sure Flynn will die a *little death* when he sees me wearing them.

I'm just paying up at the counter when my phone rings again.

'*Dah-ling!*' My aunt Camilla is a little theatrical. She likes to tell people she used to be a thespian. Truth is, she still is. She just no longer gets paid for her ham-iness. But she's the one person in my family, other than Max, who really takes any interest in my life.

'I see the familial grapevine isn't on the blink.' Sliding my credit card away, I murmur my thanks to the store assistant as I grasp my bags and step out into the street.

'Strange you should say that. I *have* just got off the phone with your mother.' She says this with an air of someone having experienced a colonic. She never fails to make me smile. Or feel better about myself. 'Imagine my surprise when she inadvertently let it slip you were having a little party for your birthday.' Let slip, my left tit. She was probably complaining. 'Charlie, darling, I'll admit I was hurt.'

'Stop pouting. You know there's an invitation for you. I mailed it myself. You've probably just ignored it.'

'Oh, how fancy! No one does proper invitations these days. You young ones are all about the text.' I hear her heels echo along the parquet floor of her hall. Papers rustle then tear. 'You are a love. So we have a theme!' she exclaims. 'And will there be lots of pretty boys in attendance?'

'It's like you don't know me at all—like you didn't teach me anything!'

My aunt's ribald humour rattles down the line. 'You are a saucy one. You didn't get *that* from your mother.' Aunt Camilla is my mother's aunt. Like me, she's always been the black sheep of the family. 'You are the daughter I never had.' She tells me this at least once per call, finishing it with, 'The daughter I could never have coped with.'

If Auntie Cam couldn't have coped with me, it was more to do with her lifestyle. Because, truthfully, my parents didn't even realise I was there most of the time. In fact, most of the time, I was at school.

'Did Caroline say if she was coming to the party?' I ask, Caroline being my mother.

'She was . . . very cagey about it, dear.' I swallow a few

DONNA ALAM

times, willing the tears away. I must be due my period or something. Normally, I wouldn't give a stuff.

'I doubt Dad will come. Something to do with prior plans.'

'It'll be that floozie he's seeing. Number forty-three, isn't she?'

'Oh, you know that's not her name.' I'm not touching *that,* even if I don't like the woman. 'Nor is she girlfriend number forty-three.'

'No, I'm sure you're right,' she answers, unchastised. 'I doubt there are forty-three women on the planet stupid enough to live with him. It's a good job you got my genes, darling. So, this party. Tell me a little why you think thirty is elderly.'

I laugh loudly. Trust Cam to bring the topic back to her. We chat a little longer before we say our goodbyes. I drop my phone back into my purse, hitching it higher on my shoulder when something farther down the street catches my eye.

A family. A husband, I assume, and his wife. She has a toddler balanced high on her hip, the husband wearing one of those baby carriers, the tiny bundle dangling from his chest. On any day this might tug the strings to my heart's desire. *My longings.* But today, all I feel is panic.

'Chastity. H-how are you?'

I realise I haven't moved from my spot outside of the boutique doorway. Stupid. *Stupid!* I should've turned and walked the other way. At a decent pace.

'Miles. How are you?' I'm surprised how even my voice sounds. Surprised and grateful.

'Have you met Helena, my wife?'

'No.' I send her a quick smile as we murmur our

In Like Flynn

respective hellos, the tow-headed toddler she holds on her hip wriggling to the ground.

'And this is Isobel,' he says, smiling happily down at the gurgling bundle in his baby bag thing. 'And this wriggling fellow is Freddie. Say hello to the lady, Freddie.'

I suddenly want to be sick. Freddie. What the fuck is wrong with him? Why would he want to hurt me? And "the lady?" Is that what I am these days? I'm not the woman you used to like to fuck while you pulled her hair and called her bad names?

The tow-headed tot ignores him completely, trying to pull free from his mother's hand. That's right, Freddie, you ignore your daddy because you can tell what a twat he is already. I do the right thing—make the right noises about their family. Smile, even if it doesn't reach my eyes.

'Isobel, oh, how sweet. What a gem.' *Two children, a marriage, and a receding hairline.* 'And Freddie, such a lovely name . . . how old is he?'

'One and a half,' his mother says, smiling down at him as he prods a finger up one nostril. A habit he has in common with his father, I recall.

I do the math in my head. Eighteen months plus nine months, plus at least six months for a whirlwind romance. *Thirty-three months.* Less than three years. What have I done in three years?

I blink, my throat suddenly tight. I've made a home, started a business, and those are important things— achievements—things to be proud of. But nothing quite like bringing new life into the world. My heart suddenly aches for what could have been, for what *was,* even if for a short time. Not that the lack of physical presence ever really took the ache away.

Less than four years ago, I lost a little piece of me. A

surprise, you might say, though welcome all the same. I housed her in my body for a little while and almost as soon as she arrived, she was gone. I say *her*, but that's just a feeling I had. And this man in front of me? The man so full of his own blessings? He held my hand as I was wheeled into surgery. He promised me I'd be okay. That we'd have other children.

Well, at least one of us has.

Surgery left me with more than just physical scars.

I built a business. Made a home. Adopted new friends. And never really got over my loss. And in the face of his golden love, I want to slit his throat and dance in his guts.

Does that make me evil?

Good, because evil is better than tears.

22

I TEXT HER. No answer. I call her again and again. Nothing.

We were meant to meet at a sushi joint for an early dinner—she doesn't like the bike and insists it's madness for me to pick her up. *London Traffic*—then we'd made plans to see a movie. One we couldn't decide on. Chasity isn't a fan of action movies, and I don't fancy watching subtitles and films in black and white, which I assumed were more her wheelhouse. It turns out she's a fan of chick click and romantic comedies. But it's all good, and our disagreements are just verbal foreplay.

I would've been happy staying in, but when you're in a relationship, you've got to switch it up. A dinner, a show, an actual picnic with grass and shit, which isn't quite as good as staying in bed, feeding her figs, champagne, and my cock. But a relationship isn't solely based on bedrooms and fucking. Or bathrooms and fucking. Or kitchens and . . . well, you get the picture. You've got to get out once in a while is what I'm saying.

When she's ten minutes late, I'm not worried. Twenty and I'll admit my feelings ramp up to concerned, intermingled with a little irritation. Thirty and a couple of unanswered phone calls and my thoughts are running to frantic.

Calm down, I censure myself. *Don't go hunting her down like she owes you money.*

There must be a reason. Some kind of work emergency maybe? Family? Something to excuse a lack of preoccupation with her phone. I hope, whatever it is, runs to the former and is coupled with something as simple as a flat battery on her phone.

Like a loser, I vacate the table and grab a couple of take-out boxes and some Asahi Japanese beer, changing my mind at the last minute and swapping it out for a decent sized bottle of sake. Something tells me I might need it. A half hour later, and I'm pulling up at her door.

I knock. Ring the bell. Stand back from the door and look up at her bedroom window to where the shutters are slid shut. I pull out my phone again and just as the call connects, the front door slides open a couple of inches.

'I'm sorry.' Words almost bubble from her mouth. Her eyes are rimmed red, mascara having tracked down her face at some point before being smeared across her cheeks.

'What happened?' I ask, stepping closer to find her body blocking the entrance. She's not gonna let me in?

'I fell asleep. I'm sorry—I should've called.' She sniffs, and I nod, weighing up my options. I'm not sure what they are but accepting this bullshit sure as shit isn't one of them.

'Fuck this,' I grunt, catching her midriff with my shoulder, lifting her into the air as I stand.

'Flynn, please, I don't have the energy.'

And this is patently true, lucky for me, hey? Or else I

might now be recovering from a knee to my face. The bottle of sake in the bag wrapped around my wrist bashes against the door frame as I push my way in. I wonder distractedly if the sushi will be in any state to eat after that.

'I'm sorry. I'll make it up to you,' she whimpers upside down as I pause in the hallway. 'I promise. But just not tonight.'

'Shush, babe.' If there was ever a sign that Chastity needs me, it would be that tone right there—and words following my actions that don't resemble *go fuck yourself*.

Hallway. Kitchen. Living room. Bedroom. Where to put her down? I go for neutral, depositing her on the couch.

'I'm sorry.' Something twists in my gut as she folds herself forward, her hands in her lap, her face covering them.

'You have nothing to be sorry about.' I chuck my jacket on the opposite chair and drop to my knee in front of her to rub a few circles of reassurance across her back. The gears in my mind beginning to turn and clank, coming up blank. 'What is it, babe?' Under my hand, her body stiffens, and she rapidly shakes her head. But I'm not accepting that shit, either.

I take a seat next to her, pulling her barely resistant form onto my lap. My body cradles hers, her legs bent, feet planted on the sofa cushion to the side as I band my arms around her. I keep up with the circles, though lighter this time, the way I know she likes.

I don't speak, and I don't make demands. I just listen to her small, shuddering breaths, her face pressed into my shirt as I accept the cooling effects of her tears breaching my shirt to touch my skin.

Eventually, her breathing evens out. I think maybe she's gone to sleep—worn herself out. I don't doubt that's part of why she didn't turn up earlier. Exhaustion from tears? But what the fuck has happened and how can I help? How can I fix this? As though privy to my thoughts, she speaks.

'I saw my ex today. Miles is his name.'

Oh, shit. My heart fucking sinks to the depths of my boots. Anything that causes this much hurt hasn't been dealt with—the emotion and the pain hasn't burned itself out. But I still don't speak. I don't know what to say, but I feel the implications, the thoughts of her slipping away making me sick.

'I-I haven't seen him since we broke up. He said I was u-unstable.' Her breath catches on the final word, her chest beginning to stutter again.

'We say a lot of things we don't mean when we're hurting. And you already know men are arseholes, right?'

Her laughter is just a consonant sound that breaks free, surprising us both.

'Thing is, he was right.'

'Maybe,' I counter quietly. 'Love makes us do mad things sometimes.'

'I was crazy,' she whispers, her finger reaching out to trace the pocket on my shirt. 'I we . . . we had, *almost* had, a baby.' *A miscarriage, maybe?*

'How is this something I don't know?' I wished I could swallow the words back. What an arsehole. What a selfish prick—what the fuck has it to do with me until she says?

'No one knows. After we split up, I pretty much cut everyone from that time out of my life. I didn't have him, and I didn't have my baby, and he . . . he's just moved on. Like nothing happened. I saw him today. He's married, and he has a family. A beautiful family.' She shakes her head, her next words seeming apropos of nothing. 'His son is called Freddie. I think that hurt me more than seeing him. Why does he get to move on and I'm stuck?'

'You're not stuck, babe. You're amazing.' She doesn't seem to hear me, or maybe she isn't listening. 'Why does this son's name piss you off?'

'Because he stole my name,' she mumbles.

'I didn't know you were called Freddie.' I feel her smile weakly at my words, and as I push the fallen hair from her face, I place my lips on her head.

'I'll never be able to use it now,' she whispers.

'It's a pretty shit name, babe. I don't think I want a son with a name like that.' My lips freeze on her head as I wonder where that came from. *Way to drag out the caveman, Flynn.*

'Why would you call your son Freddie?' she asks, not latching onto the meaning behind my words—the words that caused a strange sensation in my chest. And those words? They lead to images. Things I'd never thought of until now.

Chastity, her gaze soft and belly swollen. Chastity with our child in her arms.

Fuck. The idea is crazy and exciting. I suppose I've always wanted kids. I've just never—

She twists her head, giving me her swollen eyes and sombre gaze.

'Are you still in love with him?' I almost don't want to ask, apprehensive that I might hear something I'm not ready to hear. But as she shakes her head, I find myself releasing a heavy breath. 'I'm sorry you lost a baby, and I'm sorry you've carried this on your own.' You're not alone now. You have me.

'I couldn't talk about it,' she says, her words barely a squeak. 'Not since. I've never told anyone—I was barely pregnant. I'd only just found out. One minute, we were wondering how a baby would fit into our lives, and the next, I was being rushed to surgery.'

'I'm so sorry, babe.' I wrap my arms around her and crush her to my chest as though the power of my arms holding her could bear her pain instead. 'So fuckin' sorry.'

'It was an ectopic pregnancy. Emergency surgery. I might've died.'

'Fuck.' I can't keep saying I'm sorry, even if I am. 'You must've been terrified. I'm so pleased you didn't die.' She huffs out a short laugh again. 'I mean it, Chastity. I'm out of my fucking head on you. I'd give you a dozen Freddies right now just to see you smile.' And I would. I haven't even fucked her today, but the sight of her smile, however weak, shoots my veins with the same endorphins. *I'm high on the girl.*

'You don't even like kids.'

'Just a fuckin' minute.' Hands on her shoulders, I push her away a little just to see her expression. 'Where'd you get that idea from?'

'The day at the pub. You said so.'

'Come on. I say a lot of shit.' It's true. 'Especially when I'm trying to get an invitation to your undies.'

'You said you'd make a great uncle.'

'That's true. And I do. My older brother, Byron, has a couple of the little fuckers. But I want kids. I just needed to find the woman mad enough to put up with my arse to have them with. Looks like you're it.' She doesn't look convinced.

'Then why did you say what you said? Why did you look so horrified?'

'Firstly, it's not the kind of thing a single bloke runs around saying—*let me fill you with my babies!*'

'Actually, that sounds like one of your pickup lines.' She bites her lip to stifle a smile.

'And second, I really liked you. I didn't want to frighten you off because you weren't giving off baby vibes. You have your business, and you're always so straight, when you were fully dressed, at least. And you don't go around kissing babies and pulling kooky, gooey faces.'

'No, but I'm always the first to offer to hold little ones to give mums a break.'

'Ah, sneaky. I like it.'

'I think I have a bit of a fetish,' she admits shyly. 'I like the smell of a baby's head.'

'Nah, that's not a fetish. That's biology.'

'It's like baby crack,' she adds.

'Nah, pretty sure baby crack is at the other end, and not quite so sweet smelling.' Funny how her tear swollen eyes can still manage a withering look.

'So you'd like a family.'

'If I find the right man.' A hint of her attitude returns, and though I smile, I also theatrically clutch my heart.

'Way to sling me under the bus. Are my swimmers no good for you?'

'Don't joke about it, Flynn,' she says, sounding pained.

'Who's joking? See this face? As sober as a judge and just as serious.' And as I say the words, I know them to be true. 'So, that's settled then. You want kids and so do I. Guess that makes me your ideal man a little further down the line. We just might need to get a lot of practice in first.'

'My ideal man isn't crazy. You can't just decide you want a family with someone you barely know.'

'Didn't stop my parents.'

'What?' She drags the word out over several disbelieving syllables.

'They'd been dating a month when Mum fell pregnant. Forty years later and the old fella still can't keep his hands off her.'

'That sounds like a fairy tale.'

'True. Like the ones the Brothers Grimm wrote, especially when you're a kid and you go into the laundry room to find a clean T-shirt only to find your mum sitting on the washing machine, your dad's hips working like a piston between her legs.' I shiver at the memory, feeling like I ought to cast a circle of salt or something. 'And then there are my brothers. They're like the cast of a gory fairy tale. When you meet them, you'll see what I mean.' I pull her to my chest again and sigh. 'Come on, fuckin' Miles?'

'What's wrong with Miles? Apart from him being a colossal twat?'

'It just sounds like you had a close escape from the fuckwit. He must've been an ugly kid. Who names their kid a measurement of length? Maybe the kids weren't even his. His wife might've been playing *Miles* away. A bloke with a name like Miles sounds like he couldn't organise a fuck in a brothel with a fistfull of fifties, never mind father a couple of kids.'

'And you're such an expert on fatherhood?'

'I reckon I am. I have the best kind of dad. A pretty cool family, too. Just don't tell them I said so. I'll tell you about them sometime.'

Chastity yawns, nuzzling closer. 'I have had a really shitty day. And these things you're telling me are just like . . . information overload. I just need this day to be over.'

'Sounds like a plan, babe. Lead the way.'

'What?'

'Well, you're not kicking me out,' I reply, because fuck that.

'You want to stay?' she says softly. 'I'm not ready—'

'Babe, don't. You're not getting rid of me that easily. Just let me hold you tonight.'

23

CHASTITY

I WAKE with his arms around me, and I know it shouldn't feel as good as it does, even if the admission doesn't move me from his arms. *I'll just stay here a while longer*, I tell myself. *It doesn't mean anything.* But the truth is, when I'm with Flynn, he makes me feel like there is only now; this bed, this moment. The here and the now. When I'm with him, tomorrow is a world away. And that's not safe.

My eyes are still swollen, and they feel gritty and what felt like extreme heartache yesterday, today feels like a gaping hole in my chest—like someone has punched me and ripped out my heart. I think what I'm trying to say is yesterday was painful, and today, I feel empty. I can't afford to take Flynn's words to heart, and I promised myself four years ago I wouldn't risk my sanity again for any man.

Last night, he'd carried me to bed—yes, carried me. He was insistent on that fact. So I'd let him, mostly because I hadn't the energy to argue or walk up the stairs myself. And I'd let him dress me for bed, let him pull off my clothes and slip my nightie over my head. He'd even put toothpaste on my brush, then watched me brush my teeth as he wet a flannel for my face. He didn't laugh or joke but was diligent in his care of me as he washed the mascara streaks from my face. Then he'd tucked me into bed, flicked off the light, and my heart had ached as he'd walked away.

What does that tell you? my mind whispers. The man took care of you. And you let him. When was the last time anyone took care of me but me?

Last night, he hadn't gone far, and as I'd turned on the mattress to watch him, he'd walked to the bathroom and repeated the process with my toothbrush before crawling into bed with me.

And you let him, my mind whispers again. You might suck a man's dick, but you never share oral hygiene implements.

Clearly, I've been hanging out with Flynn too much because my mind is beginning to channel him.

'Someone's up,' says a sleepy voice from behind me, sounding sexy and rumpled and all kinds of yum.

'Someone certainly has high hopes of being so.' I push back, my bottom nudging his cock and causing him to groan.

'You're a tease, duchess.'

'And you're hard.' My voice is husky, though from tears not intent, as I reach around behind me, giving his cock a solid tug.

'Not so fast,' he replies, taking my hand and pushing it up onto the pillow under my head. Big spoon to my little one, he traps me further by bringing his thigh over mine. 'How are you this morning, duchess?'

I sigh. 'How am I feeling? Like a frog.'

'Ribbit.' He chuckles, burying his nose into the space

between my shoulder and neck. 'You don't feel like one. You're more in the vein of a warm bun.'

'Funny,' I complain, trying to twist from his arms. 'My eyes are swollen, and I need a shower.'

'A shower and a cold compress. In that order. But first, I need an answer.'

I note he doesn't make any mention of the things he said last night. Those weren't promises he made. Declarations signed in blood. It was mostly just nonsense, even if it came from a good place. *Sort of.*

'Thank you for looking after me.'

He sighs an unhappy sigh. 'I don't want your thanks. I just want you to be happy.'

Happy enough to give me a child? I almost ask, but then I remember I'm not crazy.

'You were going to tell me about your family,' I whisper, desperate for a change in conversational direction.

'I did, didn't I?' His beard rasps as he rubs his cheek across the pillow I'm lying on. 'We'll be here all day if I tell you about all of them. Instead, let me tell you a little of how I was raised. Every family has rules, and with four boys running amuck, ours were pretty solid. But Dad taught us how to grow into men, good men, I'd like to think. His rules have stood us all in good stead.'

'He sounds like a good man.'

'He is. He taught us to play with passion or not at all. Said that if you're entrusted with a secret, you're honour bound to keep it. And, babe, I'm like a vault.'

'Good to know,' I murmur, wondering if he's referring to last night.

'He said never be afraid of punching above your weight where girls are concerned because that's how he ended up with Mum.' I laugh softly, swatting him away as his lips find the shell of my ear. 'I took that one to heart and ended up with a duchess.'

'Go on.'

'He said stand up for what you believe in, and be confident and humble at the same time.'

'I'm not sure you've mastered humble yet.'

'*Pssht.* It's overrated in my experience.'

'And what else?'

'He also said to find a woman you won't mind losing your heart to because you might lose your heart, but you win in the end.'

The pressure of Flynn's hand loosens on mine, so I roll onto my back to face him. The bruising on his face is tinged yellow, but it doesn't detract from how handsome he is.

'Your dad sounds like a pretty smart man. No wonder he's been married for so many years. I wonder which of his words of wisdom you've taken to heart best.' I place my hand against his cheek as he appears to contemplate. But not for long.

'I'd have to say, never waste an erection and never trust a fart.'

I set off giggling, hard, as the gorgeousness that is Flynn stretches back along the bed to grab his phone from the nightstand behind him.

'Far out—the time!' Like a shot, he's out of bed and stabbing his legs into his jeans. 'I'm sorry, babe, but I'm gonna be late for work.' His expression looks pained as he fastens his pants.

'Never waste an erection, huh?' I laugh, staring at the bulge in his jeans.

'Rain check, yeah?' With a quick peck to my forehead, Flynn grabs his T-shirt and dashes out of the door.

I flop back onto my back and consider the past twenty-four hours. I don't really want to dance in Miles's guts, but that doesn't mean I'm happy. But Flynn. What do I do about Flynn? I think he could make me happy if I let him. I like him more than is healthy. In fact, there's a slight possibility I might be in love with him.

Doesn't that just make me a glutton for punishment?

24

FLYNN

CHASTITY KEPT me at arm's length for the rest of the week, making me promise to give her space. If you ask me, space is exactly the last thing she needs, especially after what I'd seen sticking out of her purse the morning I'd left her in a hurry, late for work. Boots in my hand at the hallway, I'd dropped them to the floor to shunt my feet into them when my eyes had slid to her purse on the floor. A big slouchy purse, the contents hanging half in and half out; mail and a brightly coloured A4 brochure thing. I know better than to pry, and I sure as shit wasn't snooping, but the word *Fertility* had jumped out at me. So like an arsehole, I'd pulled the brochure out of her bag.

A fertility clinic in London.

I get why—more than ever after seeing her so devastated. I just don't get *how*. Not that it'll come to it. Not if I've got anything to do with it because this last week, Chastity has been the only thing on my mind. Turns out, absence does make the heart grow fonder. Absence makes you realise you are in love.

Call me stupid, but if she's having a kid with anyone, she'll have it with me.

But how do I go about it? Not the technicalities. I think we've got that down. How do I get her to trust me enough to let me be the one?

Hey, duchess. I wanna put a baby in you and not just for the practice.

Nah. That'll just get me a kick in the balls.

Babe, I know you don't believe me because you think half of what I say is shit and the other half ridiculous, but I want to be there for you. Give you a baby. Because I love you.

Love. How'd I get to this place, anyhow? It's like falling into an uncovered manhole. One minute, I'm happy, minding my own business, just plodding along, stoked that a girl as classy as Chastity would have anything to do with me. And the next thing? Boom! Down the fucking hole I go. I'm falling and struggling in the dark. And when I do finally hit the bottom, it all makes sense. I'm in love. Only, I'm alone and naked, and shivering, worrying how long I'll be in the hole alone.

Far out, I've turned into a maudlin fucker. It doesn't help that I haven't had more than a few minutes alone with her since I'd arrived tonight. A quick birthday kiss and a few words, and eyes that said a million things, though none of them concrete, before she's called away to greet someone else. But not before making a promise that we'd talk later.

Talk.

'Cheer up, pal. It might never happen.'

Keir passes me a tumbler of something amber. I bring it to my nose and pull a face. Music plays in the background, people milling around the open plan space, most dressed in black as the invitation suggested. It's not like the house parties I usually get invited to, but then, Chastity is a girl with taste. That must be why she likes me. And because she likes me and because I want to get into her undies, I mean good books, I've toed the line in my dress tonight. Chastity was right the day I'd ambushed her at the studio; I do like a bit of Tom Ford. Tonight, this suit is jet black and teamed with a tailored shirt and black tie.

Keir had mentioned I look like a penguin, but he's just jealous, I reckon.

'Get it down you,' he instructs. His expression is amused as he points at my glass. 'What whisky cannot cure, there is no cure for. Or in other words, it'll cheer your face up.'

I don't normally drink this stuff, but then again, I'm not normally such an introspective sap. 'I accept your magical piss water,' I say, raising the glass. 'And if it doesn't make me feel better, may the chunder be on your shoes tonight.'

Keir's gaze flicks down. 'You'd better not vomit on these. They're custom-made.'

With a tip of my head, I chuck the drink down my throat. 'Fuck! How do you drink that stuff?'

Keir laughs. 'It's not so bad. Then again, it's not Macallan, either.' He studies the amber liquid in his glass.

'What the fuck am I gonna do?'

I hadn't meant to speak because if I had, the words wouldn't have sounded nearly so plaintive or have the effect they're having on Keir right now. His expression is frozen in a look resembling horror. See, blokes don't talk about this shit. In fact, his current look reminds me of a rabbit sensing a fox. Only, the rabbit has realised the fox isn't hungry. He just wants to talk about his emotions and shit. And the rabbit? He'd rather have his flesh torn from the bone and die a nasty painful death than speak of love.

'Fuck off, would you?' I sort of grunt. 'Go hang out with your girl.'

'I would, but she's hell-bent on interfering with the catering under the guise of *help-ing*.' He makes those poncy air quotation marks with his fingers, which is difficult, given the glass he has in his hand.

'Fucking catering.'

'It's not like you to have something bad to say about free food.'

'It's not the food.' The food, in fact, is very decent. 'And fuck you very much about the freebie thing,' I add with a glare. 'You're just jealous that I can eat what I like and maintain my six pack, meanwhile you've got to watch your weight like a girl.'

'I'll watch your weight in a minute,' he bounces back at me. 'We'll see how far I can kick your arse across the lawn. What the fuck is wrong with the catering?' he asks when I don't bite.

'Him. The prick who brought the stuff.'

Keir's gaze follows the direction of my own. 'He's Chastity's neighbour. He lives across the road, apparently. And she got a good deal on the catering, Paisley said.'

'I reckon the bastard wants to give her more than mate's rates.' I glare in the direction of Chastity and the tall fucker next to her. Dark hair and slim built, he looks like he'd be more at home on a yacht rather than in a restaurant, and though I hate to admit it, the fucker looks almost as good in his suit as I do. Almost.

I've got my eye on you, mate. And if your hand touches the small of her back one more time, I might just twist the fucker off. Except I won't. At least not tonight. Not on her birthday.

Keir opens his mouth, then closes it again. 'Am I missing something here?'

'I dunno. Are you?'

'Are you and Chas serious?' I frown because I hate that nickname with a fucking passion. It's too common or garden for someone as special as her. '*Oi*. I asked you a question.'

'Are we a thing? If a thing is *in love*, then I'm half of that thing. And half of a thing just isn't a thing at all.'

'That's a load of—'

'Things,' I finish for him, agreeing.

'I was gonna say bullshit. But you know how you find out?' My head swings to his, pathetically hopeful. 'You use your mouth. Ah, fuck! Wipe that expression off your face and don't twist my advice. I don't want to know where your mouth has been.'

'Only on her lately.' I put my empty whisky glass down on the table behind me and pick up the bottle of Camden Pils I was drinking earlier.

Keir shakes his head. 'You want to know how she feels? Go ask her.'

'Oh, it's Charlie's new friend! Hello, darling.' Chastity's aunt grabs me by the shoulders, placing a heavily lipsticked kiss on each of my cheeks. She's a tall woman and, at a guess, the wrong side of seventy, but from what I can gather, she has more life in her than most twenty-year-olds. 'Flynn, isn't it?'

'It is.'

'You have a look about you like a young Cary Grant,' she says, grabbing my cheeks in one age spotted, heavily diamond adorned hand. 'But something tells me you're a little more like your namesake, Errol Flynn, than the divine Cary. He was Australian, too.' Jesus, the woman has some grip. 'I hope you're treating my Charlie well.' I open my mouth to answer, but I must look like a fish. 'Well, with a side order of naughty. In like Flynn, eh?' She lets go of my cheeks, sending me a saucy wink before immediately turning to Keir.

'Camilla Wolf.' She holds out her hand as though expecting it to be kissed, harrumphing as Keir shakes it instead. 'Well, you're no fun!' she chastises before he can introduce himself. 'I shall have to find one of those lovely film boys to get me a drink.' She strides off as quickly as she'd arrived.

'Well, that was . . . fuck if I know what that was.'

'That, Keir my friend, was Aunt Camilla.'

25

CHASTITY

I TURN AWAY from the sight of Flynn and Keir on the other side of the room, shielding the goofy grin I'm currently wearing. God knows what my Aunt Camilla had to say, but whatever it was seems to have entertained her no end. She's a handful that one, and proof age is just a number.

I can't wait until Flynn and I are alone later this evening, and hopefully I'll make it up to him about being a bit of a bitch for asking him to give me space. I missed him and I was certain I'd find difficulty not jumping on him when he first arrived, but I didn't anticipate he'd be wearing glasses. Gah! What is it about a sexy nerd?

But I appreciate everything he did for me—the care he took and the gentle way he treated me—but I've needed time this week to work out how I feel about a lot of things, including him. But this past week has given me the time and distance to make some decisions. Decisions that include him and his sexy eyewear.

'Your home is beautiful, Chastity,' Sophia, one of my actors, says. It's not a very big party; just my friends, Camilla, and some business contacts, along with a small number of people who have worked for Fast Girls. The ones I've gotten along with, at least. Sophia is one such person. She's very professional—not a diva like one or two I've come across. She's also a bit of a sweetheart.

'Thank you.' I touch her arm and compliment her on her dress. She's one of the few who chose to wear white this evening. White can be so unforgiving, but with a body like hers, the only forgiveness needed is for being unable not to stare. 'You look gorgeous, sweets.'

'And so do you.' I resist a whole-body shiver as Flynn's warm hand touches the small of my back, his lips brushing my ear. *I've been watching you*, his eyes say, *and I can't wait to get you alone.* That would make two of us. His warm gaze seems to mirror my appreciation and delight.

He looks so handsome in his impeccable suit, his soft hair pushed back from his face. And I'd say Sophia would agree, given the way she's looking at him. *Debonair* was how Camilla described him following their introduction. *Like a young Cary Grant*, she'd said. She'd also said a few other things which Flynn had very graciously chuckled about, not rising to her saucy bait. Meanwhile, her compliments had turned my complexion tomato red.

'Can I get you a drink, duchess?' His low spoken words in my ear are as unravelling as the movement of his stroking thumb. Every nerve ending seems alight.

'Chas, where did you want these cocktail sausages?' Tate asks, suddenly appearing to my right, holding a dark coloured rice bowl filled to the brim with the less than stylish offerings. That they're gourmet hasn't really satisfied Tate who holds the bowl like its contents offend him.

'These are for you,' I say, taking the bowl from Tate's hand into both of mine. I pass them to Flynn almost like they're an offering.

'You're a legend,' he says, taking one from the bowl and throwing it straight into his mouth. He winks, and if that wasn't sexy enough, I'm pretty sure both Sophia and my ovaries sigh as he swallows, then licks his full bottom lip.

'T-Tate,' have you met Sophia and Flynn?' I stutter, turning away from the Devil's better-looking twin to put the bowl on a nearby table. Unfortunately, I don't fail to see Tate's less than impressed expression. If Flynn notices, he doesn't show it as he picks the bowl up again.

'Not so fast. These were meant for me and only me.'

There's a particular note in his tone as he throws another into his perpetually smiling mouth, almost as though he's relating *me* to a bowl of sausages. Which makes no sense and is completely Flynn. I can't help but laugh even as, for an encore, he feeds me a sausage from his fingertips, his smile turning thoroughly sultry.

With a wink in my direction, Flynn holds out his hand to Tate. 'Pleased to meet you. You're a neighbour, right?'

Hands are shaken, the slight air of manly posturing permeating the space between the pair. Maybe this isn't surprising given that one of these men has carnal knowledge of me and, given the signals he's sending out, the other still want that knowledge. What does surprise me however, is the surprising amount of eyelash fluttering coming from Sophia—so much so, she's created a small breeze. *Okay, not really*. But I do find it paradoxical how her social persona is so much flirtier than her work one.

'Could I steal you for a moment?' Tate asks rather pointedly. 'The wrong champagne has turned up, but it's already on ice, and there's a slight issue with the *gougères*.'

Usually, you pay a caterer to avoid dealing with the details, but as Tate is both a neighbour and seems to be running the catering at a loss, judging by the invoice, I feel obligated to be involved.

'A drink,' I say, turning to Flynn, placing my hand on his chest. His eyes darken as I splay my hand wide under his jacket, the tip of my little finger brushing his nipple. From our position and proximity, no one notices but us. A secret between two people who are more than just good friends. 'I'd love a G and T.' And there's my promise to return.

What is it they say about the best laid plans?

When I return to the room, Flynn isn't talking to Keir or Sophia. In fact, I can't see him anywhere.

'Hey, lady,' Paisley says, planting a smacker on my cheek. She holds a champagne flute in each hand, one of which she passes to me. 'How's your birthday so far?'

'It's not actually my birthday until tomorrow, and as you know, tomorrow I'm working.'

'Bad planning, boss lady. Bad planning. You should've booked a spa day or a lazy brunch with good company.'

'I'd have settled for waking to a certain man in my bed,' I tell her.

'Ohhh. Is it a tale I need to hear over coffee?'

'We'll catch up next week sometime, and I'll fill you in on all the details.'

'I'm gonna hold you to it,' she replies, her eyes wide over her glass. 'But I can't believe that on a Sunday *and* your birthday you're off to do a shoot!'

'Oh, you're a photographer,' Tate says, coming to a stop in front of us.

Shit. 'Something like that,' I answer, probably with a slightly pained expression because the truth is bound to come out.

'That answers why your friends are all so attractive.'

Hmm. Yeah. I suppose he's partially right. Thankfully, he doesn't hang around, maybe due to the vibes Paisley was throwing out.

'Awk-ward!' Paisley sings.

'Not nearly as awkward as it will be when he finds out I'm a certain type of photographer.'

'And by that I suppose you mean an erotic cinematographer.'

I sigh. 'People are so weird. Or is it me? Am I the weird one?'

'Everyone watches porn in some form or another—look at your Aunt Camilla.'

I choose that moment to do just that. Dressed in a wide-legged pant suit, she's channelling Bianca Jagger tonight and looks every inch as stylish. Of course, if I was to say this to her, she'd reply that Bianca is the copycat because she wore it first. Either way, I'm not sure she's a good representative for "normal", whatever that is, particularly as she's currently being tended to by another of Fast Girls actors, Nathan Cox, who's probably a third of her age. But she's always been a little off the wall and is probably the only woman of her age and station who regularly quotes Anaïs Nin.

'Everyone,' Paisley repeats. 'It's just not everyone who'll admit to it.'

'But watching people's faces as I tell them what I actually do; shock, horror, intrigue. And the questions? Eww.'

'Ha, I'll bet. But at least your job is more interesting than say, running a shop. Although with a shop you have regular hours.'

'True,' I agree. 'But it is what it is.' And what it is, is actually my own fault that I'm working on my birthday.

I'd cancelled last week's shoot and barely left the

house, opting for complete hibernation. My creativity shut off, and I just couldn't contemplate spending my time around naked bodies. So while I'm glad I'd taken the time for a little reflective self-care, the flip side to that is I'm hustling now to make an upload deadline. If we don't shoot tomorrow, I won't get the filmed edited in time.

'And the airline won't reschedule the flights a second time.'

'Where are you off to again?'

'Barcelona.'

'Home of the erotic museum.'

'Darling, I think most European cities can claim that exact fame.'

'Yes, but not many have theirs on the main tourist drag.' True. *Museu Eròtic de Barcelona* is smack-bang in the middle of *La Rambla,* often complete with a Marilyn Monroe lookalike blowing kisses from the balcony to tempt people in. 'And speaking of drag . . .' Paisley raises her glass, toasting someone on the other side of the room.

'Is that. . . Stephen?'

Stephen recently starred in a solo shoot, but the buff yet shy blond from the studio and the glamorously fierce-looking redhead at the other side of the room are the same person, but with two looks a million miles apart.

'Hills.' Paisley grabs Hillary's arm as he passes, almost making him spill clear liquid from the tumblers he holds in his hands. 'Is that Stephen from the other day?'

'I told you I'd recognised him from somewhere,' he replies, his eyes widening dramatically. 'She's a drag performer over at Stella LaFella's,' Hills explains, flipping the pronoun. 'It's a new place in Shoreditch.'

'What's her stage name?' Paisley asks.

'Avery Goodsux.' Hills gives a theatrical pout. 'I'll let

In Like Flynn

you know later if she lives up to her name. If you'll excuse me, I'm just going to go get as close to sex as humanly possible while keeping on my clothes.'

'That man,' Paisley says, giggling. 'He should be in front of the camera, not behind.'

'His ego is bad enough now.'

'Hey, you should definitely go,' Paisley adds.

'What? To the naughty museum on La Rambla?' Been there, done that, bought the smutty souvenir. 'No, I've decided I'm celebrating my birthday tonight. And, you know, I think this is the first birthday party I've had since I was six years old.'

'No pass the parcel at this swanky shindig. Happy Birthday, babe.' She clinks her glass against mine. 'I think your thirtieth year is going to be a fantastic one.'

'You know what? I think you're right.'

'Oh, honey, I know I am. Starting right now.' I frown, not quite following her meaning. 'I've been tasked with a message for you. There's a man in your bedroom right now just dying to give you a birthday gift.'

26

CHASTITY

My heart beats like a drum as I dash up the stairs, excited, and eager, and apprehensive. Yes, apprehensive. The kind that comes from feeling guilty for keeping him hanging.

When I reach the top of the stairs, I quickly check my reflection, my complexion flushing at the memory of Flynn holding me captive in this exact place to torture me. *We've come so far since.* I hope he feels the same.

I turn and make my way to my bedroom but don't make it that far as a white shirted arm reaches out, pulling me into my home office.

'Flynn.' As he closed the door, my hand rises and falls over my still rapidly beating heart. 'You scared me.' The room is dark; the light from the streetlamp outside the only light in the room.

'Sorry, duchess. I couldn't wait until they've all gone to get you alone.'

I inhale a deep breath and push it out through a slight pout. 'I half expected to find you naked and spread out on my bed, a red ribbon tied around your dick. And where are your glasses?'

Flynn laughs, bringing me closer, his big hands on my hips. 'You like those, yeah?'

I nod. 'Hell, yeah.'

'Maybe I'll wear them for you next time.' His gravelly chuckle shimmers down my spine. 'But for now, I have another plan. No ribbon, but it does involve my dick.'

'Oh, I'm intrigued.'

'So I've got your attention?' In an effort to restrain my smile, I bite my lip as I nod yes. 'Good,' he says with a nod, a nod that quickly turns to a shake of his head. 'God, you look gorgeous.' His gaze is dark, but his expression earnest as he devours me without touch.

'You like my dress?' I don't mean to sound so coy, but his avid gaze is so brazen.

'It's almost a dress,' he says, his eyes roaming before landing on the ragged lacy hem. 'It looks like they forgot to put anything on under the belt.'

I laugh, and it feels so good. Time with Flynn is like stepping into a bath, only you never know what it's going to be filled with. Tonight it's warm sudsy water, a sweetly scented delight. *Preferable to a tub filled with cold baked beans.* But as he drags his hand up my bare leg, the atmosphere changes.

'I have missed you so much.' His voice is deep and his tone sincere.

'I know. I'm sorry. I've missed you, too.'

'It's mad, isn't it? A few weeks ago, I didn't have you in my life, yet these past few days, not having you near left seemed to leave this gaping hole.'

I nod because I can't speak. I know what he's saying, I

can relate to it even, because I've felt the same. But as he slips his index finger under the hem of my dress, just a fraction of an inch, my mind turns to mush. He begins running it back and forth across my thigh, electrifying my skin, making me silently will his exploration a little higher.

'I've missed you so fuckin' much.' His lashes cast dark shadows against his cheeks as I lean in and slide my mouth across his. It's just a glancing brush, but the pull of it is real as his hands on my hips pulling me in for a second touch. A touch becomes a press of lips. A press of lips turning to a slide of tongues, just a bare moment before the kiss turns to something else. Something deep and passionate, grasping and owning. My back hits the door as Flynn slides his hand up the back of my thigh, grasping it to rest it against his hip. And he pins me there, the length of his hardness pressed into my heated core, and as he hums his appreciation of the moment, I feel the deep vibration all the way to my bones.

'Are you going to give me my gift now?' My voice is needy and rasping as his lips kiss their way down my neck.

'Is that my cue to tell you I'm gonna give it to you hard?'

'Oh, Flynn.' I sigh, his tongue playing *time to make you squirm* with my ear. 'You can give it to me any way you want. I like it all.'

'What about if I want to give you it now. Nothing between us but skin.'

'I'd say it's probably not the right time of the month.'

'No, babe,' he says, pulling back to capture my gaze. 'I mean, let's make a baby.'

'What?' I can't tell if the word sounds incredulous or like a laugh. 'That's why you brought me in here?'

'Well, I always wanted to fuck in an office, too. Does that count?'

'Flynn, I have guests downstairs. People are here to celebrate my birthday. This is not a conversation for now.' Though it strikes me as kind of freaky that it appears he's been thinking the same things.

'And some people are here to try to fuck you.'

'Yes, you!'

'Not just me, babe.'

'Who—Tate? Are you talking about Tate?'

'Come on, Chastity. I might be the lowly secretary, but even I can see him for what he is.'

'And what exactly is he?' I retort, my hand suddenly finding my hip.

'A smarmy, smug, fucking chancer. The kind that would be out of your life before your undies even hit the deck.'

He might be right, but I'm not going to admit it.

'He's not a threat to you. Currently, *you're* the only threat to you,' I say, pointing one black polished nail in his chest.

'Why's that?' he counters, leaning into my nail. Leaning into it, then lifting it to catch between his teeth.

'Because it's the twenty-first century,' I whisper hiss. I want to shout, but I don't want people to hear. 'And you're behaving like an arse.'

'No, I'm behaving like a boyfriend. You're just not used to the difference.'

I shake my head. 'Boyfriend is such a pathetic title. What? Are we teenagers?'

'I want to be more than your boyfriend,' he whispers, stepping into me. 'I mean it, Chastity. I want so much more, starting with a baby.'

'You nutcase!' I place my hand on his chest and push.

'Yes,' he retorts, covering my hand with his own. 'I know you want to.'

'We're not talking about bringing home a puppy. What happens if this thing doesn't work between us? What then?'

'We'll cross that bridge if we come to it. But I don't think we will.'

'Flynn, all we do is argue and fight!'

'What's wrong with that? I love fighting with you. And I'll fight for you.'

His words and the sincerity in his tone, coupled with the look of intensity on his face blows me away. But only for a minute. Right about now maybe a cold wave of reality should sweep through the room, but I'm glad when it doesn't. What I get instead is the kind of belly licking warmth you feel when someone tells you they love you.

'You're saying,' I begin, the words slightly choked. 'You'd give me a child, even if I don't want to be with you?'

'I'm not that selfless, babe. I want a promise from you. A promise that you'll at least try to love me back. It's been the best thing ever, falling in love with you. Fathering our child wouldn't be a consolation prize.'

Who would've thought it? Flynn Phillips has the soul of a poet.

'Don't play with me.'

Like a slow burning fire, Flynn's smile is slow to grow, but he doesn't answer. And I'm not sure who reaches for the other first; all I know is we come together in that instant. I've never felt this kind of connection, this kind of need as I push him into the room, our mouths fused together and our fingers grasping. My hands shake with desperation as I fumble with his belt.

'I can't believe we're doing this. I can't believe we're doing this now.'

'You've got your hand around my cock,' Flynn rasps. 'Feels pretty fuckin' real to me. But maybe you need convincing.'

In an instant, he spins me around, and I catch myself on my hands on the desk against the adjacent wall.

I want to touch him. Feel his skin. Fill my mouth with the solid feel of him. I want to—

Breath halts in my chest as his hands drag the lace of my dress up my thighs and over my arse.

'You have a body that sonnets should be written about.' His words are a rasping kind of appreciation as he pushes down on my lower back, coaxing me to stick my bottom out. 'You are so gorgeous tonight. It just makes me wild with the need to mess you up.'

'How will you do that?' Wrong. So wrong. And yet, I can't help but provide more encouragement. His answer sends pulsing waves through my core.

'I'm gonna stick my cock in you.' His words rasp my ear as he slips my thong to the side. 'Make you come. Leave my come in you.'

'Flynn,' I whisper urgently. 'We can't be long. People will notice we're miss—'

My words halt as I note his wicked smile, feeling the string to my thong snap in his hands. I have no words, but I have plenty of noises as he drops to his feet and slips his tongue between my legs.

One lick and my legs turn to jelly. Two and I'm crying out.

'Shush, duchess,' he rasps, his tone thick with want. 'You don't want people knocking the door down thinking I'm fucking you up.'

'D-door doesn't have a lock,' I pant, my fingertips scrabbling against the desk as though to hold me up.

'All the more reason to keep your joy to yourself.'

Flynn's broad tongue swipes the length of me before he buries himself between my splayed legs. His tongue is magic and his dirty whispers divine as he tells how he can't wait to fill me. To own me. That he can feel my cum dripping across his tongue.

It's hard to remember those months I couldn't climax, not with this master between my legs, licking and tasting, whispering how my pussy makes him drunk. Feeling him spread me wider with his fingers as he grasps his cock in his hand.

He makes me frantic—makes me rock back against him shamelessly. Against his mouth and his tongue. Against the roughness of his stubble as it abrades and burns.

'Oh, God!' I dip my head to the warm surface of the desk as I lose my mind to his commands.

'That's it, duchess. Let me feel that pussy pulse.'

I'm desperate. To touch him—desperate for him to fill me. I can't think—my mind is empty for everything except the intense pressure building between my legs.

'*Flynn!* I can't . . .'

'I want . . .'

'I need . . .'

So goes my litany of pleasure as my climax, white hot and intense, explodes between my legs. And the last thing my sentient mind processes? That accent

'That's it. Ride my fuckin' face.'

Flat against the polished surface of my desk, I open my mouth to speak when the feel of him at my entrance steals my

216

breath. Steals my breath, then forces it out from my chest as he thrusts inside. I'm so wet my body offers no resistance, and in that one push, we're how he wanted us to be. *Skin to skin.*

He growls as my body pulses around him. He dips his knees, and if I'm not mistaken, grits his teeth against the pleasure. 'Ah, what this?'

The very particular tone of his voice brings my head up from the desk. I groan, a sign of desire and distress, as Flynn's studio sequence flickers to life on my computer screen.

'You beautiful, dirty girl. Have you been watching me fuck my hand this week?'

'Just once or twenty times,' I whisper, pushing back against him as onscreen Flynn undulates, his hard cock in his hand, and I shiver from pleasure as the now Flynn flexes his thighs against mine from behind.

'Oh, *God*,' I whisper, or maybe groan—quietly—as he moves back, then into me again oh-so slowly. He's so large on screen, holding himself in two hands, and so large inside me. *So impossibly hard.* How can I be quiet? How can I take this without any noise?

'You'll take it,' he grunts. 'Take it all. You like watching me wank.' The roughness of his expression and the grunt in his tone makes my inside pulse. 'Tell me,' he adds urgently—*Tell. Me*—timed with his thrusts.

'*Yes!* Yes, I like watching you.'

'Have you touched yourself?'

'Yes! In the chair. In my bed, with my laptop between my legs.'

'Did you come?'

My eyes go wide as he thrusts so hard I almost kiss the screen. 'I-I can't. Can't speak.'

'Yes, you can,' he says, as though prepping me for a race. *You can do it!*

'I-I can't concentrate when you're inside me.' My words are garbled, my hands sliding across the desk to grip the sides.

'If I can keep one eye on the screen and one on my cock between your legs, I'm pretty sure you can fuck and talk.'

I shoot him a glare over my shoulder, ignoring his near silent chuckle as he delivers another flex of his hips.

'Tell me about this.'

'Y-your expression,' I admit. 'I've never seen anything so sexy. I-I think I might have an issue because I keep re-watching the bit where you bite my knickers as though you're out of your mind.'

I recall the absolute beauty in his need. The craving I felt for him. The absolute certainty that I could come for him. My fingers as they slid on my clit as I'd reached the place that had been hiding from me.

'*Fuck, yes!*' he hisses, grinding against me. 'I am out of my mind. Out. Of my. Goddamned mind. For you.' He punctuates each of his words with his hips, then lifts my face to meet his to deliver a punishing kiss.

'Oh, God,' I gasp, as he releases my chin, his arm sliding around my body, his fingers slipping between my legs. I'm wet—so wet—I can hear it in the meeting of our bodies. Feel it as it aids his slide and coats my thighs.

'Shush.' How can *that* sound amused? And how? Is there such a thing as silent fucking?

'No . . . one . . . listening . . .would be fooled . . . into t-thinking were we're . . . doing anything else o-other than . . . f-fucking!'

'It's what we do best, my dirty little fuck doll.' I narrow my eyes even though the humour rings clear in his tone.

'Listen,' his voice rumbles, his body going still. Footsteps sound in the hallway—high heels on the wood. From under the doorway, the light cuts out as though someone is standing on the opposite side.

I bite my lip so hard I might taste blood as Flynn makes a *V* with his fingers, sliding them from my clit to between my legs, touching me and touching himself. I'm so swollen, the pressure of my orgasm making me fit to burst. My eyes roll back, my muscles trembling, taut and tense, everything centred between my legs and pulsing with my silent release.

Flynn doesn't move or speak as my body throbs around him. And as the heels draw away, I lie my cheek on the warm surface of the desk, preparing myself to take what he has to give, again and again. One solid thrust. Two. Then a third before his thrusts speed up, the sound of skin slapping and his sharp grunts and rough groans twisting my pleasure higher somehow. It's like an agenda change; from something good to something absolutely necessary as he works himself deeper and faster inside my body until, finally, he stifles a long, rough groan by pressing his mouth against my neck.

'I think I like office fucking,' he rasps, kissing my cheek.

I can't answer. I don't think I can speak, let alone think. But when he pulls out of me I groan—a groan he joins me in as he makes some comment I don't think I can repeat.

A beat later, there's a brush of material between my legs.

'What are you using?' I twist my head over my shoulder to try to look.

'Your knickers,' he replies with a sinful smile. I huff but don't truly answer. I'll just slip into my bedroom and grab a clean pair. 'It'll be like a secret between us. I know you'll have no undies on, and you'll know I'm sporting a stiffy because of you.'

I push up from my hands and turn to face him. 'You're ridiculous, you know that?'

He nods, something peculiar settling in his gaze. 'You might've mentioned it once or twice,' he answers, his lips meeting mine, brief yet sweet. 'One thing's for sure. I'm ridiculously in love with you.'

27

CHASTITY

I CHECK my appearance in the mirror at the top of the stairs as Flynn stands behind me with an expression that's a little smug.

'What are you smiling about?'

'I reckon that was good enough for twins.'

'Pardon?' I turn my head to look at him rather than his reflection, his own eyes falling over my body as greedy as his hands earlier.

'I think I fucked you so solidly, you'll be good for twins. Twins at least.'

I tilt my head to the side as I push up onto my toes to pat his cheek. 'Aw. Did little Flynnie miss the reproductive talk at school?'

'Yeah, I did. I was probably a little too busy to make that class on account of fucking some chick behind the gym.'

'Do you miss Australia?' I find myself suddenly asking.

'Sometimes. I miss my family, but I love living in London. But I won't be making plans to relocate until you've had our twins. You know, so I can steal them away back in the dead of night and move them to Sydney.'

'You've got it all worked out, haven't you?' I say as he takes my hand, and we turn to the stairs.

'Nah. What would be the fun in that?'

Paisley's brows lift as Flynn and I enter the room together. She sends me a look that speaks volumes and causes my cheeks to heat instantly. We make our way to the makeshift bar because, twins or not—and it's most likely to be not—this woman needs a drink. I've no idea how long we were gone, and I'm beginning to wonder who was outside the door, and who else, if anyone, heard. So I'll just finish my G and T before facing anyone.

'Some one ring an ambulance!' Hillary comes rushing into the room, his red hair sticking up all over and red lipstick smeared over his face. My first instinct is that this must be some kind of prank. If someone has hired me a paramedic striper-gram to give me mouth to mouth, I'm going to junk punch someone. 'Oh, thank goodness. Chas, come quick. Your Aunty Cam has taken ill.'

I follow Hills out of the room, my heart beating against my ribcage. Cam can't be ill. She still goes to the gym twice a week and does Callanetics, for goodness' sake. Out through the kitchen, Hills steps out onto the patio and I immediately know what she was doing out here. Smoking. She used to have a twenty-a-day habit but swore last year she'd kicked that habit well and truly in the butt, pun intended.

'Camilla! Camilla! Come on, lovely!' Stephen—Avery's —sequinned frock is all I can see. Then I see her legs between his, her body slumped in the chair.

'Aunt Cam!' I place my hand on her grey cheek and lightly tap. 'Come on, darling. Open your eyes.'

Please don't die. Please don't die.

I feel like a fist is squeezing my heart as horror, sickness, and fear wash through me, making my head pound and my vision blurry.

'We were just kissing—p' My head snaps up as he qualifies this. 'Not me and her. Me and Avery. She sort of staggered into the chair, complaining of pains in her arms. The next thing, she slumped in her seat.' Hills words are frantic, his hands clutching his arms as though cold.

'Stop shouting,' Camilla murmurs, though doesn't open her eyes. 'I'm not dead yet.'

'Thank Christ!' I let out a breath. 'You gave us all a fright.'

'Gave you a fright? Darling,' she says, her lashes fluttering heavily. 'I think I've wet myself.'

'It doesn't matter. The upholstery will wash.' I rub her arms, tentative relief showing in the form of the tears balancing on the rims of my eyes.

'Bugger the upholstery,' she says, suddenly clutching her chest. 'This suit is Chanel!'

'Ambulance is on its way,' Flynn says, his hand a comforting weight on my back.

'But she's awake.' Even as I say the words, I'm not exactly sure of their significance. I know she's not out of the woods yet. *The pallor of her skin and the heat on her forehead is terrifying.*

Flynn steps around me, taking Camilla's wrist between his fingertips. 'She should have some aspirin,' he asserts.

'That's very kind of you, Cary,' she says, speaking through laboured breath. 'But I'd rather have a glass of brandy.'

'I'll get the aspirin,' Paisley says, dashing off in the

DONNA ALAM

direction of the kitchen. In the commotion, I hadn't even realised she was here.

'We'll save you a glass for after the paramedics have checked you over,' Flynn asserts.

'Her breathing.' I turn my head towards Flynn, not letting go of her hand, and lower my voice to a whisper. 'It sounds awful.'

'Don't speak about me as though I can't hear, dear. If it sounds awful, you should try experiencing it.' With a pained wince, she tightens her grip on her chest.

This is so awful. 'What can we do?'

'Help will be here soon.' Flynn wraps his arm around my back, his solid presence a reassurance I'll be eternally grateful for.

'Here, aspirin.' Paisley thrusts it into the hand of Flynn, the obvious authority amongst our motley crew. *The pornographer, the makeup assistant, the drag queen.* Moments later, Keir arrives outside with a blanket in his hand as Flynn instructs that Camilla should chew, not swallow, as she sends him a withering look.

'The last time I tasted something so awful,' she mumbles, her expression one of person trying to swallow chalk, 'was when you were twelve, and you persuaded me to buy you lunch in that awful Scottish hamburger chain.'

'Stop talking now,' Flynn says kindly.

'I do like a commanding man.' Though she's full of complaints and pluck, I suddenly realise it's an act for my benefit.

I being to cry, great silent tears falling down my cheeks, my chest feeling like it hasn't the space to accommodate the thunder of my heart.

Paramedics arrive, and Camilla is assessed, blood pressure and heart rhythm, before being hooked up to preventative medication and oxygen and God only knows what, before being loaded into an ambulance.

'I'll follow you,' Flynn says, as I become part of the entourage on the way out of the door.

'No, you've been drinking,' I reply.

'Barely,' he protests.

'I don't want to worry about you having an accident tonight, please.'

'I'll follow,' says Paisley.

'Flynn and I will sort it out here,' adds Keir. 'Don't worry about anything.'

Truthfully, the house could burn down for all I care. *So long as I get to keep Camilla for a few more years,* I bargain with God.

Flynn kisses me once, fiercely, turning me in the direction of the open door. 'I'll be here when you get back. Go.'

So I follow the complaints of *'It had better be the Chelsea and Westminster hospital we're going to,'* out the door.

28

CHASTITY

'GERD?' I stare at the youth dressed in green scrubs, not fully convinced he's a qualified doctor despite what his name tag reads. *Dr. Child, of all things. It almost makes me want to look to see if he has baby teeth.*

'Yes, gastroesophageal reflux disease. The symptoms can mimic a heart attack, as seen with your grandmother.'

'Aunt,' I correct, feeling the tension draining from my body, the news, despite the word "disease" going off like a bomb of relief and confetti. Until I'm hit by another concern. 'But her blood pressure was ridiculous.' My gaze flicks to Paisley as though inviting her to back me up.

'Yes, one eighty-five over one-ten, I think,' Paisley supplies, her hand tightening on mine reassuringly. 'She was crying and so uncomfortable, the poor dear, and complaining of pains in her chest *and* her head by the time I got here.'

'Yes, how can a gastro . . . whatever kind of disease cause headaches?' What if there's been a misdiagnosis?

Dr *Kindergarten's* expression turns censorious, his finger sliding across the electronic tablet he holds in his hand. Okay, so we're painting ourselves as overwrought females in this scene.

'I see she was given trinitroglycerin,' he says, 'as a preventative. It can cause severe headaches—a common side effect of the drug. But I can assure you we're quite certain Ms. Wolf is not having a heart attack.' He goes on to discuss further investigations and possible treatments, telling me she'll be kept in overnight. Then, with a curt nod, he swings on the toe of his squeaky running shoes—*running shoes?*—and leaves.

'Oh, God.' I grip Paisley's hand tighter. 'That's . . . that's the best thing I've ever heard.

I get a few minutes with Cam before she's moved onto a ward. I hope for the sake of the nursing staff that it's a private room on a side ward and nowhere near geriatrics.

With a quick goodbye and a promise to return in the morning, Paisley and I find ourselves in an almost silent hall, the smell of disinfectant and old building stretching the length of the long corridor.

'I'll take you home.' She reaches into her bag pulling out both her car keys and phone, flipping the latter open to check for messages.

'No. It's late and you've done enough. I'll get a cab.'

'No way.' She looks up from the screen, her expression firm. 'I mean it. There's no way you're getting a cab after tonight.' Her kindness forces the tears I've been holding back to stream down my cheeks. 'Oh, honey,' she says, wrapping her arms around me. 'Don't cry. It's your birthday.'

She's right; midnight has come and gone long ago. I am officially thirty years old and I feel at least ninety years older than that.

'I can't lose her.' My voice is watery and sort of warbling. 'What will I do without her when she's gone?'

'That's a worry for another day. Camilla has acid reflux, she's not dying anytime soon.' I sort of snort through my tears. 'She'll be so mortified tomorrow and probably insist on a second opinion from Harley Street. Or need to convalesce in Barbados.'

'That's not a bad idea. Do you think she needs a companion?' Paisley jokes. 'I might be available.'

Pulling my shoulders back, I use the tips of my fingers to wipe the tears from my face. 'God, what must I look like?' I catch a glimpse of my reflection in the darkened window, my soft curls have begun to frizz and I'm currently sporting panda eyes again.

'We look fabulous.' She makes the sort of clicking motion with her fingers that would stand her in good stead on a drag show stage.

'Speak for yourself. I look like a five-dollar whore.'

'I'd pay you at least double that,' a familiar voice says.

My heart then beats with a mixture of pleasure and surprise as Flynn takes me into his arms.

'What are you doing here?'

'I've come to take you home. No need to look so worried. I haven't brought my bike.'

'Donor cycle,' Paisley mutters. 'If you're not careful, you'll end up in here one day.'

'I reckon,' he replies, 'but hopefully it'll be on the maternity ward.'

'What's that supposed to mean?' she asks, letting the question hang in the air as her gaze flicks between us.

In a flash of panic, I open my mouth, overly effusive words just tumbling out. 'You say some of the most ridiculous things, Flynn. Random, ridiculous things!'

A look of something resembling hurt flits across his expression, but before I've had time to process or examine this, Keir arrives.

'Is this some kind of a meeting?' he asks. So we all make our way to the elevators.

Keir and Paisley head to the carpark while Flynn and I call a cab. By some unspoken agreement that I'm grateful for, it's seems Flynn is coming home with me.

It's almost three in the morning when the cab pulls into my street, the tire sounds as they rumble along the road a strange sort of comfort. Flynn pays the cabbie as I shuffle along the garden path and before I can reach the door, he's taken the keys out of my hand.

Once inside, he silently wraps me in his arms. My cheek pressed into the hardness of his chest.

'Come on.' His words are both a rumble through his chest and a burst of warm air on my neck. 'Let's get you upstairs.

I let him lead me, grateful that he seems to understand that I don't have the brain capacity for speaking. He makes a beeline for my bathroom, flicking on the shower before coming to the doorway, curling his fingers in a sort of *come hither* motion.

'It's almost three thirty and I have to be up in the morning.' My protest is as half-hearted as I feel. Perched on the edge of my mattress, I peel off the torture devices some women would call shoes. Flynn seems unmoved, smiling indulgently at me, his shoulder leaning against the doorframe. 'I really am too tired,' I repeat.

'Come on, babe. Let me wash your day off,' he says, still holding out his hand. 'I promise I'll behave.'

'I'm not sure you know the meaning of the word,' I mumble even as I shuffle across the room.

'She's gonna be okay,' he promises, his mouth pressing a small kiss to my hairline. Until I tilt my chin, offering him my mouth instead. It's a tender kiss, yet one that still leaves us breathless. Wordless. Both of which I'm thankful for.

I shiver as he pulls on the zip of my dress, the heat of his body so compelling behind. But I don't turn. As he pushes the lace from my shoulders, I'm conscious of the tiny catch in his breath as he loosens my bra.

'Nice undies,' he says softly. *Noi-ce.*

'I can't believe I went to the hospital bare arsed.'

'Sorry,' he mumbles. 'Kinda, anyway.'

I chuckle at his candour as I press my hand against the wall to step from the pool of my clothes. It's refreshing to know I'll get nothing but honesty from Flynn.

'I wore really pretty lingerie tonight.'

'And I went and spoiled it all by being a caveman.' His knuckles ghost the swell of my bottom. Despite the warmth of the room, I shiver.

'I quite like that side of you,' I admit, wanting to match his honesty. 'And I can always wear them another time.'

'I reckon it's true what they say. If a woman wears matching undies, you're getting lucky because she planned it so.'

'So my underwear forced your hand? Sent you telepathic messages?'

'This issue is, I just can't keep my hands off you.'

My heart does a little leap—the way he looks at me and the things he says? Flynn's brand of adoration is certainly heady.

The steam swirls around us as I turn to face him and watch as he strips from his own clothing without fanfare or words, providing me with the opportunity to just appreciate the sight of him. The pop of muscles at his biceps, and the coarse hair on his chest. The strong lines of this thighs, and the ridiculous *V* that leads to places I won't be visiting tonight.

Flynn steps into the shower pulling me in behind him, allowing the heat of the water to bite at my skin in the most delicious of ways. My muscles unlock and relax in the heat and steam, the last vestiges of tension disappearing as Flynn smooths a scented soapy sponge over my skin.

'Head back,' he murmurs, his finger under my chin. *I was right to allow him to coax me into the shower*, I think, as his long fingers massage shampoo into my hair. Eyes closed, I just allow myself to revel in his care.

Then later, I dissolve in a different kind of pleasure as I slip naked and clean between my sheets.

Flynn is solid presence behind me and though it's dark and it's mostly quiet, the early birds have already begun to chirp.

'Don't forget to set your alarm.'

'I can't find my phone.' His deep voice rumbles in the quiet of the room, his fingers trailing light circles across my arm.

'I'm sure it'll turn up.'

He makes a noise of inconsequence, pressing his lips to my head. 'Whatever you need tomorrow, I'm there. At your disposal.'

'You've done enough today.' I sigh heavily remembering the chaos that awaits me in the morning, or rather later today.

'I'm a pretty decent PA,' he says. 'Just ask Keir. I've taken the day off. Best case scenario, you might have need of a handsome tea boy.'

'But where would I find one at this hour?' His chest rumbles against mine. 'I was so scared,' I whisper in the dark.

'I know, babe. But she's gonna be all right.'

'But she won't be here forever and that scares me so much. The number of people I love isn't large, but the people who love me is smaller still.'

'Shush.' He can't fail to have heard the watery quality of my words as he pulls me closer, his arms holding me tight, his hand splayed on my belly as though to remind me of his promises. 'You are loved,' he whispers fiercely.

Tears dampen my pillow as I place my hand over his arm.

'Flynn Phillips, I love you, too.'

29

I AM HAVING the best fucking day.

She loves me. Last night, in the darkened room she'd whispered the words, then turned in my arms to press her sincerity against my lips.

The woman I love? She loves me, too.

I woke stupidly early feeling about as happy as a dog with two dicks. Just *that* happy. Flat on my back, Chastity lay splayed across my chest, her thigh over mine and her foot pushed between my legs. I wasn't exactly comfortable, physically at least, though it improved once I'd pushed her mad hair out of my face. I think part of the problem is my morning stubble attracts those golden curls like Velcro.

'I must look a sight,' she'd mumbled, stifling a yawn.

'You look like a ninety-year old penis, babe.'

It might not have been the most sensible response, as far as responses go, but at least it had gotten her attention. She'd pushed up onto her palm, almost crushing my diaphragm in the process.

'What's that supposed to mean?'

I set off laughing and it took me more than a few minutes to compose myself.

'You're not much of a morning person, are you?' I ran my hand down her bare back trying to keep my eyes on hers. A hard task, I can tell you, with those cherry ripe nipples in my face.

'If you don't stop dicking around and answer my question,' she'd said, her warm chocolate eyes shooting me daggers. 'You won't be a morning person either.' As quick as a flash, her hand shot out to grab my dick. 'I'll make it so *this* won't work and wear your balls as earrings.'

'Though she be but little, she is . . . *feisty!*' I'd bucked up into her hand, the shock of the movement giving me the momentum to roll her onto her back. I'd pinned her hands either side of her head.

'It's *fierce*,' she corrected with a sexy little growl. I planked over her body, dipping down to brush my lips against hers. *And my dick.*

'Same thing, duchess. Yeah, that's it. Wriggle your hot self a little more while I explain, birthday girl.'

'Oh, so you do remember,' she said, squirming harder. 'And yet you're still being a horrible arse!'

'Just saying it as it is. You're all wrinkly. In a good way.'

Her eyes narrowed. 'From the birthday party from hell to the birthday where my boyfriend tells me I'm looking old. Well, you know what? Your dick is wrinkly.' She'd stuck out her tongue and I'd laughed again.

'Babe, it's not very wrinkly at the minute.' It was rock fucking hard. 'Let me start again,' I said smiling down at her. 'Happy Birthday, oh gorgeous one. You don't look a day over twenty-five. You've just got pillow creases on your face that I'm finding oddly erotic.' Or maybe it was the fact that waking up to her this morning was different. Real.

Maybe it was more that I've been imagining waking up with her every day for the rest of my life, looking forward to that point in the not too distant future where we'd be lying under the covers, squabbling over who was going to get out of bed first to tend to our wailing child.

Her gaze narrowed then she burst out laughing herself, her next breath little more than a sigh as I'd shut her up with a kiss. She'd arched her nakedness against mine and I'd spent the next hour in a blissful kind of exploration, devouring her like the delicacy she is. Finding all those places that made her sighs curl through the air and breath stutter in bursts from her mouth. Then we'd fucked, skin to skin, and it was glorious.

After a soapy and very slippery shower, with a tone much sillier than last night, I'd made coffee, insisting she open my birthday gift. The rest of her gifts could wait but I wasn't going to miss the opportunity to see her reactions. I'm not sure she appreciated the coupons for sex. Or the candy G-string. But she seemed to like the mug I bought her to use at her studio. *She laughed, anyway.* It had originally read "I love cock" but I'd added the word "Flynn's" with a little arrow after *love*. You know, just in case anyone around her needed confirmation of that.

There was also the dirty weekend away I'd booked for us in Brighton next week, though I feel a bit of a tit for passing that off as a birthday present 'cause it's as much a gift for me as it is for Chastity.

There are good times ahead.

'Who does the car belong to?' Chastity glances at the car in question then back at me.

The morning is grey, the sky full of the kind of clouds you know promise a drenching. I click the fob and open the passenger door for her, ignoring the wanker, I mean, *caterer*, Tate, watching from the other side of the road. *Hands off, mate.*

'The car? It's mine.' *A Jaguar XJ.* 'I had the F-Type before this one. When Rafferty, my brother, visited London last year, he refused to get in it. That was a pretty good incentive to keep it, but I got tired of only having two seats.' I kiss her, just one brush of my lips against hers. Maybe it's an arsehole move, like a dog pissing on his favourite tree, but I reckon that's okay as I really want to kiss her, too.

She slides in to the car, knees together like the lady she is, still looking a little confused as I close the door behind her. Not confused about the kiss—*that* made her smile. It's probably the fact that I own both a high-end car and bike. *European manufactured and expensive.* But there's time enough to explain these things. It's not like I'm a total rev head or a wastrel. I just like nice things, including quality vehicles. But at the end of the day, they're just a means of getting from A to B, and with London traffic, you usually stay between those two points for far too long. So the way I look at it, I may as well be hanging around in style and comfort.

'Go on, belt up.'

'I thought you had a motorbike.'

'I do. You've seen it.' As I start the engine, I turn to look at her. *My girlfriend.* The mother of my future offspring. My future wife, if I've got anything to do with it. I can't believe I get to see this woman naked whenever I want. Within reason, of course. 'You know I don't catch the bus carrying that helmet, don't you?'

When she smiles, I smile. When she giggles, it feels like a contact high or something. I pull out into the road feeling like a fucking king.

We go to Camilla's London bolt-hole, aka her apartment and escape from the bucolic boredom of her country house. Charity ducks in and picks up clean clothes before we head over to the hospital.

'Cam, it's overcast out there. It's going to rain.' Chastity sighs with an air of long suffering. 'There really is no need for sunglasses.'

In answer, Camilla swirls her Burberry poncho thing over her shoulder, catching me in the face with the fringe.

'Don't worry, darling, it's cashmere,' she says by way of apology. 'Now, lead on, Charlie, get me out of this godforsaken place.'

Chastity smiles apologetically at the ward sister, taking the notes for the GP and further appointment cards that Camilla appears to have no intention of taking. She begins jogging along behind her aunt.

'Must be the trauma,' I say as I pick up her abandoned bag.

'Hmm. I expect so,' replies the ward sister with barely a smile herself.

Once restored to her rightful place, Chastity fusses over her aunt. I'm beginning to wonder why Camilla is her favourite, to be honest. She seems a bit of pain in the arse.

'I'm sure you must have other things to attend,' Cam insists. 'I've called Doctor Randolph and he'll be here this afternoon to discuss this hellish experience.'

'It could've been much worse,' Chastity replies sternly.

'Yes, the ambulance could've taken me to that awful place. You know; what's the name of that hospital again?'

'You know fine well that isn't what I mean. You gave

me an awful fright, Cam. You have to take better care of yourself. For you *and* for me!'

For the first time today, Camilla looks chastened as she takes her niece in her arms. 'There now. There's no need to be upset. You aren't getting rid of me quite yet. I have the last of your uncle's wine cellar to deplete before I pop off this mortal coil.'

'Cam!'

'It was a joke. You know I'm living until at least one hundred and fifteen. I've too many things to do. Off you go now,' she says, turning Chastity in the direction of the door. 'I'm sure you have lots of naughty things to get caught up on at work. And thank you, Flynn, for taking care of my favourite niece.'

'Your only niece,' Chastity grumbles.

'Semantics,' she replies with a vague wave of her hand. 'Can we expect to see you around more?'

'Absolutely,' I say with a grin. 'I'm almost part of the furniture now.'

'I didn't think you were coming in today.' Keir barely looks up from his laptop as I throw myself onto the leather sofa in his office. 'I tried to ring you earlier.'

'I've lost my phone.'

'Shit.'

'I need to cancel the sim and get a new one.' But first things first.

'How's Chas doing today?' Keir asks, concern showing in the pinch of his brows.

'My *loving girlfriend* is very . . . loving. And also doing fantastic.' Well, she's as okay as can be expected for someone who's still fretting about losing her favourite relative.

'It's like that, is it?' he says, looking up. 'You finally pinned her down to absolutes?' Too fucking right, not that he needs to know the exact details of my morning. 'I thought you were losing your touch.'

'My touch is just fine,' I answer, rubbing my hand through my hair. Past complaints have been aimed at my lack of heart, not touch. But not this time. This time I'm all in—heart, head, fingers, dick—everything.

'So you blinded her to your many faults and moved into the serious zone. Well done, young padawan.'

I chuckle, which turns into a belly laugh. 'Padawan? So that makes you the Jedi Master, does it?'

'Speaking as someone who's been married twice, aye. And I'm trying to give you a bit of advice. You'd better treat Chas right because Paisley can use a gun.'

'Of course she can. But it's one of those ones that spray-paints makeup on her client's faces though, right?'

'You don't want to find out, 'cause I'm warning you—'

'No need to, mate. It happened. I'm in love for keeps. Chastity is the woman for me.'

'Well, fuck me sideways.' Elbows on the arm of his chair, Keir holds his Mont Blanc between the fingertips of both hands. He must've gone snooping around my desk to have found it. 'And she hasn't impaled you with an umbrella yet?'

'Not yet but I have high hopes.' He doesn't answer but shakes his head. 'Obviously,' I begin, 'your sex life isn't as adventurous. My commiserations to Mrs Keir.'

'Leave Paisley out of it.'

I nod, accepting the warning, empathising for probably the first time. Wives and sweethearts are off limits, even from the mildest jab. 'Anyway, speaking of adventure. I think it's time I moved on.'

Keir's eyebrows almost retract to his hair line. 'You're serious?'

'As a heart attack.' Fuck, bad timing. 'Chastity has stolen my heart and only this morning threatened to make earrings out of my balls. What was I to do but give in?'

'Because she has your balls?' he repeats, confused.

'And my heart. I wouldn't be giving up my position in perpetual servitude if she didn't.'

'Piss off,' he counters mildly. 'You wanted to learn the ropes, do the thing without bearing the responsibility, and that's what you've done.'

'But now I want it all.' A wife, family, a home life. It's time to grow up.

I've worked for Keir for a couple of years now. I've learned from the best but it's time to stand on my own. I'd never had the incentive before. I was happy with my life, switching off from work at six o'clock, no responsibilities beyond that hour. Weekends spent playing rugby, going out, and getting lucky.

It's been good to know Chastity doesn't care how I made my living. She's a cool kind of chick, I know. She realises I'm more than just a pretty face but has appreciated me for who I am, and not for what I appear to be.

What she doesn't know is that I'm actually decently well off. Rich, some might say. Not the yacht dwelling kind, though I'd previously spent enough years bumming around and squandering my inheritance. When I met Keir, the deal he offered me was pretty sweet. I'd assist him, be his back up, and meanwhile learn to become a killer property developer.

'You'd better find yourself another slave,' I tell him with a grin. 'Because I'm off to the bank to transfer some cash. I want in on the Walton job.'

Keir nods, holding out his hand. 'Welcome to the land of grown-ups, man.'

30

CHASTITY

'HOW'S YOUR GRANDMOTHER?'

I open my front door to find Tate on the doorstep, another bouquet of flowers in his hands. His shirt is crease free and his hair looks recently brushed. Meanwhile, I look like something the cat dragged in. And possibly vomited up. I've spent the afternoon in my home office apologising for missed bookings and paying compensation for loss of time, so my hair is currently corkscrewing all over the place, and my t-shirt might be slightly stained from where I've spilt a little coffee from my *I love Flynn's cock* mug. It's safe to say I don't really have the time for niceties and don't bother correcting him on the point that Camilla is actually my aunt. *Great aunt.* Besides, what would be the point? Because while I don't believe Flynn was completely right about Tate's intentions, I don't think he was too far off the mark, either.

So best not to encourage him.

'She's okay, thank you for asking.' I take the proffered bouquet. 'It wasn't a heart attack thankfully. And thank you for the flowers,' I add, glancing at the pink blooms. 'I'm sure she'll love them.'

I'm not entirely certain the flowers were for Cam, but it's best to assume they are or else why would he be bringing flowers to a girl who's already said she has a boyfriend—a boyfriend he's been introduced to, no less. It's not the kind of bouquet you buy a neighbour for their birthday and I'm beginning to feel a little awkward keeping him at the door, especially as he's showing no signs of buggering off.

'Actually, I have to get on,' I begin, stepping back. 'I've got so much work to do today.'

'Sophia seems like a nice girl.' My hand pauses on the partially closed door because there's a particular note in his tone that tells me that's not quite what he means.

'Yes, she is,' I agree, shifting my body. It's strange, but something tells me I should just shut the door in his face. *And be done with this exchange.* But then he seems to shift himself, or at least his demeanour does.

'Look, Chas, I didn't just come over here to give you flowers. Flowers for your granny, I mean. I just . . . ' He reaches into his back pocket, pulling out a black iPhone.

'Oh, you found Flynn's mobile! He'll be so pleased. He's been looking all over for it. I did suggest it might've been packed away by one of your staff. Did he call the restaurant?'

'Actually, I accidentally picked it up last night,' he says. 'I thought it was mine.' He shrugs modestly, casting his gaze down to the thing in his hand. 'The thing is, Chas.' His eyes rise then, their sharpness contradicting his tone, daring mine to look away. 'This is so awkward. I didn't want to bring this over to you, but I also thought you deserved to know the truth.' He passes the phone into my hand. 'You see, when I said Sophia seems like a nice girl, that's exactly what I meant. *Seems.* Appearances can be deceptive.'

As the phone touches my palm, my eyes are drawn to the screen by movement.

A video.

Is that . . .

Oh, God. I think I'm going to be sick.

'Why are you sitting in the dark?'

Afternoon has turned to dusk, dusk to full dark since I'd mumbled something to Tate before slamming the door in his face. I've been sitting in the same spot on the couch torturing myself, watching the video again and again, trying to make sense of what I see.

Trying to prove to myself that it isn't what my brain tells me this is.

Flynn switches on the light, concern flickering across his face. 'What is it,' he asks, coming to his knees in front of me. His warm hands hold my colder ones. Colder, whiter, bloodless, almost. Because these are hands that have held something abhorrent all afternoon. 'Is it Camilla? Why didn't you ring? I sent you a text from my new phone.'

I don't answer, unless you classify an undignified sniff as such a thing, as I fight tears and the tell-tale tingle in my nose. I pinch the flesh from the inside of my cheek between my teeth in an effort to remain composed. *Is it working?*

'Chastity, babe, you're worrying me.' I force myself to look at him as I pass him the phone I have hidden under my thigh. 'You found it.' His expression doesn't remain cheerful for long, his eyes staring at a frozen frame. I lean over, hitting the screen to play the video again. *The video dated last night.*

I don't watch it play out because I don't need to. And despite the fact there's very little audio, I seem to know what he's looking at almost frame by frame. Her mouth sliding down his wet penis. She gags a little as the head hits the back of her throat. The heavy sounds of his breathing as he uses her mouth like a receptacle.

'What the fuck!' His gaze flicks to mine. Is it angry? Confused? It's hard to tell. 'That's not me,' he adds quickly. 'Is that the girl from last night? The one in the white dress —what was her name again?'

I don't know whether to be upset or relieved that he doesn't seem to remember. But maybe this is an act, too.

'It's your phone,' I answer flatly instead.

'Yeah, but that's not me,' he says more forcefully. 'Someone must've picked it up at the party—recorded the fucking thing!'

'Really, Flynn?' For someone who feels she might be on the edge of losing her mind, I sound eerily calm. 'That's all you have to explain . . . this?' I want to shout, be angry, but I'm afraid. Afraid I might be right.

'What the fuck do you want me to say? It's not me!' he yells passionately. 'It's some woman who works for you, sucking off some random bloke in the dark. You can't tell who it is, for fuck's sake. Have you asked her?'

I shake my head. Of course I've called—repeatedly. But she's not answering her phone. Guilt riddled, maybe? Or maybe she only gives blowjobs, never really giving a fuck about anything, other than perhaps professionally.

'So you're okay to accuse me? The man you professed

love for last night? But you haven't asked the one person in this we *can* identify?'

Identify her by her dark hair concealing his hand. Identify her by the familiar roll of her eyes, the practiced look of ecstasy. And by the way she stares up at him pleadingly.

More. Deeper. Harder. Give it to me.

'She won't take my call,' I say between gritted teeth.

'So let's go visit her,' he demands, pushing to his feet.

'I don't know where she lives! She moved last month, and I haven't updated her file.'

'Right, so. What are we going to do then? Because this needs sorting the fuck out. That isn't me, Chastity.' His hand shakes a little as he pushes it through his hair. 'The fuck it isn't.'

I stand myself, feeling like I could run a hundred miles just to get away for myself. From him. From this situation. My mind swirls with hurt, anger, and confusion—am I being used again? Why me? Why now? What did I do to deserve to be duped again?

'I don't know what you're going to do.' My voice is devoid of emotion because that shit? It's brimming in side. Brimming. Boiling. Ready to burst like a volcano.

'Where are you going?' He catches my arm as I turn away.

'I'm going to bed,' I say calmly.

'So that's it then?' Flynn's expression hardens into something I've never seen before, his anger barely restrained as I pull free. I turn at the bottom of the pale wooden stairs just as he begins to pace, anger the source and the fuel of his sudden motion. 'You've made up your mind,' he half yells, dragging his hands through his hair again, making it stand on end. 'I'm guilty and that is fucking that?'

'I can't argue with facts. With proof.' I can't think about what Sophia might say—can't live on that hope when there's a risk it'll be for nothing.

Was he always this good at acting? Was she?

'Fuck proof,' he spits. 'I'm standing in front of you— the man who loves you. And you don't believe me.'

'Tell me why—why is that video on your phone!' In an instant, my anger flares. I told myself I wouldn't do this. I wouldn't get myself into this state. 'Tell me how it got there,' I sob—I shout. 'Tell me how I'm to believe it isn't *you!*'

'What's the point,' he answers flatly. 'You think you know the truth. And you're not willing to take a chance. On me. On us.' The room falls silent before he speaks again. 'A man goes to his psychiatrist,' he says, apropos of nothing.

'Flynn, no,' I plead, tears tracking my cheeks. 'Why can't you be serious—just for a minute. Just now.'

He ignores me.

'The man says, Doctor, you've got to help me. I keep thinking that I'm a well-known psychoanalyst. And the shrink replies, *how long has this been going on? Well,* says the man, *it all started when I was Jung.'*

'Am I supposed to be laughing?'

'It's the best medicine, babe. But that's you. It doesn't take a shrink to see that you keep expecting the worst from people. Expecting them to leave. I reckon you've been like this since you were a kid. But at some point you've got to grow up. To take a chance on someone. You've got to believe that *you're* enough to take a risk on.'

'I fail to see how a video of someone deep throating you could be my fault.'

'That's just it, babe. You're not listening. That's not me. And do you know why? Because I love you and I would cut off my right arm rather than hurt you.'

I look away as I begin to climb the stairs, my demeanour dignified.

At least until I get to the top of the stairs.

At least until I hear the *click* of the front door, when I allow myself to finally fall apart.

31

CHASTITY

THE NEXT DAY it rains heavily, the skies as grey as the rain-slicked pavements, and a perfect backdrop to my mood.

'Just a hand?' Paisley says, her tone careful. She'd turned up about an hour ago, taking one look at me before opening her arms. But I couldn't cry. I don't want to be consoled. 'Nothing else to prove either way?' she continues in the same tone.

'Just a white shirt, no watch on his wrist.' I shake my head, the images alive in my mind for the millionth time. Her eyes. Her mouth. His cock.

'Does Flynn even wear a watch?'

'What does it matter? What I'm trying to say is, I couldn't tell either way. But it was on *his* phone.' I rub my hand over my face, so sick of thinking about this. 'What the fuck am I supposed to think? Tell me—am I wrong? Did I react in the wrong way?' Because the more I think about it, the more I wonder.

'I don't know what to tell you, Chas. If I were in your shoes? I just don't know. But I don't think I could say *that's it—I give up.* I'd need to know for certain.'

Discomfort hits me in the centre of my chest, a million things still swirling through my head. Isn't it better to cut my losses now? Chalk up my mistakes to a rush of baby-seeking hormones? Blame the chemical attraction for allowing my heart and head to overrule my brain, constructing a world all of my own where I believed our love was real? Because anything that felt as good as being with Flynn had to be genuine. Enduring. So what if we annoyed the shit out of each other? It might've been impractical and a pain in the arse, but love overcomes all things, doesn't it? Until you're looking down at a phone, your arm banding your waist because you feel like you're coming apart.

'I shouldn't have gotten involved,' I mutter vehemently. 'Then I wouldn't be feeling like this—looking like this.' I jump up from the couch, clutching my grimy T-shirt as though to prove my point.

Twenty-four hours and I'm still stuck in yesterday. I want to call him. And I don't. But either way, my mind has gone there plenty. I've had silent conversations where I've ripped him a new arsehole, then moments when I've begged him to just hold me in his arms. I've planned whole new lives for myself and our phantom child, picturing his regret as I tell him *I don't need no man*.

I wonder if he'll get in contact over the next few weeks to see if I'm actually pregnant. I'm not. I did the numbers and to cap it all, this morning I got my period. *Yay for hormones.* But still I wonder. Would he have proven to care? Been compassionate or combative?

'You do look like shit.'

'Thanks, Paisley.' I blow out a long breath, my rage over once more for the moment. 'That really helps.' Like a hole in the head, actually.

'Friends are supposed to tell you the truth.'

'Am I wrong?' I repeat; is that what she's saying? 'Tell me, because if you've got any advice on helping me *not* feel like this, spit it out.'

'Actually, I have,' she says, sliding her phone out of her purse. 'Go and shower, tie up your hair, and put on a little mascara, for God's sake. We're going out.'

'This wasn't the kind of solution I was expecting.'

'Oh, honey, this isn't a solution,' Paisley chuckles. 'This is more like a Band Aid.'

'One that'll hurt like a mofo tomorrow morning as you peel your head from the pillow, wishing you could rip it off.' Hills and Paisley clink their glasses, rowdy shouts of, *You tell it, sister!* coming from the table behind. I'm not sure if theses words are for Hillary or for the heavyset drag queen belting out *Respect,* Aretha Franklin style. The *sisters* on this particular table are fierce in heavy makeup, big-hair, with one or two sporting full beards.

The place is loud, the décor gaudy, and the tunes being belted on the stage for open mic night a little too much for my mood. But otherwise, I'm glad Paisley forced me out of the house. Even if I initially put up a fight.

We're at *Stella LaFella's,* Hillary's new favourite hangout given that Avery, the new person in his life, works behind the bar several nights a week.

'I'm so fucking stupid.' My head *thunks* on the table. It's safe to say, buzzed was two drinks ago.

'I used to be fucking stupid,' says Paisley, her tone a touch trivial. 'But then we broke up, thankfully.'

'Oh, God,' I groan, sitting straight again. 'I need less

comedy act and more reassurance that I've done the right thing.'

'Your ex is that famous singer—the ginger one, right?' ask Hills, clearly ignoring my cry for reassurance. I think they might be a little tired of this question tonight.

'One and the same.' Paisley raises her glass as though toasting the waste of space. 'Good bye to bad men!'

'Was Flynn bad?' At my plaintive tone, the pair fall quiet before Paisley turns her slightly hazy gaze to mine.

'Only you can be the judge of that.'

'He was awesome in bed,' I say with a sigh. 'I'll miss that.'

'Relationships have to be more than good times in bed. And more good times than bad, come to that.'

'What she said,' adds Hills. 'I like my men to be good in the kitchen, too.'

'He was good in the kitchen. That one time. Really fucking good.' Elbow on the table now, I prop my chin on my fist as I sigh.

'He cooks?' Paisley tilts her head enquiringly.

'Not that I know of. Kitchen fucking on the other hand . . . '

'Right,' she replies. 'When he turned up dressed like Mellors.'

'All sweaty and dirty. And let me tell you, he really does know how to handle a hoe.'

Paisley sniggers as Hills screeches, 'He role plays in the bedroom? And you let him get away?'

'Don't try to make my sex life seem special,' I say, pointing my finger his way. 'Not when you're dating a man who's comfortable wearing red sequins. And Flynn looks like Henry Cavill!'

'Honey, I think it's time to stop your drink.'

'I had the best orgasm in months, right there in my kitchen. I don't think I'll ever be able to eat there again.'

'Me either,' replies Hills with a queasy look.

'I'm going to smash Sophia's face when I see her next!' I might not ever orgasm again. *God, what a depressing thought.*

'Why? She didn't have sex in your kitchen, too, did she?' Hills asks.

'Have you not paid attention to anything I've had to say?' I know it's after hours—that he's no longer on the clock but come the fuck on! Pay attention to your boss in her hour of need, please.

'Of course I've listened,' he says, counting items on his fingers with an air of supreme disinterest. 'You shagged in the kitchen. You're drunk. And you found a video on your new boyfriend's phone of someone who may or may not be him—'

'What?'

'That's the way it looks to me,' he answers with a shrug. 'But I still don't know what Sophia has to do with it.'

'Because she's the one on the recording,' Paisley answers for me. I can't answer for the blood pounding painfully between my ears.

'Oh. Really?' He takes a mouthful of his mangotini looking thoroughly unconvinced. 'Have you spoken to her about it?'

'She's not answering her phone,' I growl through gritted teeth.

'Shall I call her now?' He picks up his phone from the table. 'I spoke to her yesterday. I must say, it doesn't seem likely,' he says, swapping his glass for his phone at the same moment I try to snatch it from his hand. But Paisley

DONNA ALAM

is quicker and even Hills complains. 'Watch it! That's a new phone!'

The phone disappears under the table before she takes both my hands in hers.

'Not now,' she cautions. 'Not when you're overwrought and a little drunk.' Smashed. I'm totally smashed. 'Tomorrow,' she adds, her firm gaze sliding to Hills. 'Tomorrow, we do this together.'

Not satisfied with punishing me by sending me the hangover from hell, the universe fills the sky with brilliant sunshine the following day. Birds sing, bees buzz, and blossom blows in the breeze. Meanwhile, I sit in my office in the studio, wrapped in a large cardigan and feeling as attractive as a hungover Ebenezer Scrooge. With the flu.

Strangely enough, I get three visitors, too.

The first is Paisley. There's nothing for her to do here, and she isn't scheduled to work today. Yet she insists she's inventorying, which isn't even her job. *I mean, what's she counting? Anal beads?* The truth behind the excuse is that she's my support network of one. She wants to be here when Hillary turns up with his phone and Sophia's number.

Maybe I should've just called Sophia last night, drunk or not.

'So, this is where it all goes down?'

I'm in the kitchen fighting with the coffee machine when Keir's voice tugs at my attention, and the thing splatters coffee-coloured milk all over my pale cardigan. *Shit.*

'I think it's fair to say there's a reasonable amount of *going down* that goes on in here.' He smiles, almost

254

studying me—whether for cracks in my exterior, or the stains on my clothes, who knows. 'What are you doing, Keir?' He doesn't normally come into the studio. In fact, I don't think I've ever seen him here before, and he's certainly never sought me out like this at any other time.

'Paisley's car is in the shop for a service,' he answers mildly, tugging on his ear.

'I know. There's a courtesy car parked out front.'

You can hardly miss it; it's the same colour as baby poo. He refuses my offer of a coffee, not that I blame him, so I turn and make my way in to the studio, though note how he's a little slow to follow.

'She's in the store cupboard.' His gaze lifts briefly and he nods though makes no effort to ask where that is. 'And you don't have to keep your eyes glued to your shoes. There's no one here today.' Apart from Paisley and me.

'Oh,' he answers mildly, his shoulders relaxing. Guess he was worried about seeing things. Naked things? Like that's all we do here. I know from Paisley Keir isn't at all a prude. Maybe he was trying to be respectful.

'Well, I never was a very good liar,' he says firmly. 'I'm sure you've already guessed I haven't come to collect Paisley, so I'll get to the point. I'm here about Flynn.'

'What about him?' My first instinct is to ask if he's okay. But I won't. Instead, I put my cup down on the windowsill and lean back against it, crossing my legs at the ankle.

'Well, he's currently walking around like he's been punched in the guts.'

That doesn't make me feel any satisfaction at all.

Since discovering last night I *can* contact Sophia, I've been like a bear with a sore head—a bear with a sore head, dancing on hot bricks. And I don't care if I'm mixing my metaphors or similes or whatever because I feel like the truth is in reach. I'm antsy and angry and worried how this will play out. If it was Flynn in the video, and I find this out definitively, I'll feel the absolute devastation again. And if it wasn't, then how that will change things I'm not entirely sure. How would I feel in his shoes? *Betrayed. Angry. Hurt. In no place to forgive.* But there's also a third possibility; Sophia might lie. And a fourth, I suddenly realise; maybe she'll tell the truth and I won't believe her anyway.

This is the current mess that is my brain.

'I like Flynn,' Keir says, coming to stand in front of me, his expression concerned. 'He's a solid guy. But I can't see him doing the dirty on anyone, let alone someone he loves. Someone he's willing to change his life for.' As I open my mouth to speak, Keir holds up a forestalling hand.

'But I get where you're coming from, too. I've been on the other side of infidelity and that shit hurts.' *Of course; Keir was married before, but I didn't know him then.*

'You and me, we don't know each other all that well. What I do know is, last year you took Paisley in when that fuckwit of a fiancé hurt her. You barely knew her, but you set her on her feet and in a way, you sent her to me. Look, I doubt Flynn would appreciate knowing I've been here, but I just felt compelled to say I think you're selling him— and yourself—way short. Whatever happens, you can't pretend you two didn't mean anything to each other.'

My third visitor comes as a bit of a shock. I'm expecting Hillary. And I'm trying to be very understanding while waiting. *Waiting. Stressing. Aching.* But Avery, or Stephen this morning I suppose, worked late last night. He and Hills are probably still sleeping. That I understand. What I don't understand is when Sophia knocks on my office door.

Actually, she doesn't knock so much as say, 'Knock-knock.'

'Sophia!' Paisley notices her first and at her exclamation, my heart sinks to the pit of my stomach . . . before rising again, my blood pressure along with it. 'Thanks for popping in.'

There are so many puns I could go for here. Understandably, I'm not in the mood .

'I wasn't expecting you.' I'm surprised how even my voice sounds.

'Hillary. He explained what had happened, and I had to come and see you to explain. To apologise. I didn't know he was your boyfriend, Chas, I promise!' I thought I was hurting before. I was wrong. 'He didn't tell me until after . . .'

'After he came down your throat?' My jaw begins to ache from the pressure of staying composed.

My boyfriend. My love. My torturer. My fucking hate!

'I can't believe I did such a thing,' she continues, the lilt of her Spanish accent peeking through. 'It's not an excuse, but I'd taken strong pain medication. I strained my back last week and I was uncomfortable wearing such ridiculously high shoes. So I took a couple of pills, not intending to drink more than one glass or two. But I was having such a nice time, and he was *so* attentive.' I wonder if it's acceptable to punch her, even though it appears she did no harm willingly. 'He kept filling my glass, and I kept drinking it. Which was stupid, but do you know how hard it is to meet nice men in this line of business?'

'I think I might have some idea.'

She has the good grace to look chastened at my reply. I take a seat behind my desk because I think a heavy lump of wood between us might be a good idea right now.

For at least one of us.

'You didn't seem to be interested in him,' she says in a quiet tone, her eyes now on her shoes.

'What?' From the heat of my anger, my blood suddenly turns cold. The absolute gall of this woman! I grip the arms of my chair, willing myself not to respond. Physically, at least.

'I thought he was single.' She shuffles backwards as though afraid of my sudden change in tone. 'N-not your boyfriend,' she adds quickly. Her dark eyes are almost beseeching as they find mine again. 'I know I have sex for a living, but that doesn't make me immoral.'

'No one's accusing you of anything,' Paisley interjects, her voice calm. 'Just tell us what happened. Chas needs to hear your side of things.' From beseeching to calculating, Paisley's gaze has other things to say. *Wait. Listen. Don't throat punch her yet.*

'We were laughing,' she begins. 'And drinking. And then he went outside to smoke a blunt. I might have taken a couple of tokes.'

Fucking great. Sex, drugs, and alcohol; the idiot trifecta.

'Did he smell of weed?' Paisley asks, her gaze sliding to mine. But I shake my head. *I don't think so.*

'We started kissing, and things got a little heated. And then you know . . . '

'And you let him film you.' At this she blushes—*this!* That's like, I don't know. Charity work?

'Afterwards, he got nasty,' Sophia says, hurrying on quickly. 'He told me he was dating you, that if you found out, you'd be angry. But not nearly angry as he would be.'

'He threatened you?' That doesn't seem like the Flynn I know. But then again, the Flynn I know wouldn't have done this. *Do you ever really know someone,* whispers my consciousness. *Especially after such a short time?*

'I suppose. Maybe?' Sophia says. 'But I didn't know what to do. So I took a cab home.'

'Was this before or after the ambulance?'

'There was an ambulance? What for?'

'Never mind,' I interject, thinking back to how I'd introduced Sophia to Flynn.

'Sophia, just to be sure, he has dark hair and was wearing a black suit and a thin neck tie?' She nods as it occurs to me I could be a little more specific. 'The guy with the sausages?'

'Yes, that's him. You introduced me to him—to Tate.'

32

CHASTITY

I DON'T KNOW how long it takes me to get to Tate's restaurant, or if I get there by running a dozen traffic lights, by broomstick, or by ruby fucking slippers. But the one thing that consoles me as I pull up on double yellows is that this isn't the first time I've driven on autopilot and lived to tell the tale. We've all been there at one point, I'm sure. One minute you're turning the key in the ignition, and the next you're pulling up outside your destination without any recollection of the journey. Difference is, I think, as I slam the door to my car, this time my mind was filled with discernible thoughts. Angry thoughts—no, rage filled thoughts. How the fuck—no, how about *why* the fuck would he do this?

I push open the door to the restaurant, assailed by the smell of garlic and rosemary, my eyes flicking around the light filled space. The lunch crowd have mostly departed though there are one or two tables with paying customers still seated. I feel sorry that I'm about to spoil their afternoon coffee, tapas, or whatever the hell they're partaking in.

'Table for one?' A young waitress appears in front of me. Dark haired and pretty, she wears the bistro staple of white shirt, black skirt and wrap around apron. A menu is pressed between her folded arms and her chest, her eyebrows raised in expectancy. *The girl next door type.* I mentally kick myself for slotting her into a trope or a category—professional hazard, I suppose.

'Actually, I'm here to see Tate,' I reply. Maybe I should be in the movies. That devil-may-care answer was almost Oscar worthy. Meanwhile, something resembling lava swirls and builds deep inside my chest.

'Oh.' Her brow furrows but straightens almost immediately. 'He's just popped out to the bank. Would you like to take a seat while you wait?'

No, I would not. Righteous indignation won't have the same effect if I'm sitting. I'm more likely to stand *on* a table and *Lucha Libre* his ass, though without the mask because I want him to be sure that it's me that's taking him down. You know, just in case he has a troop of irate women after him. Not that irate really covers how I feel. How did he do it? And more to the point, why? What kind of low-life scum does that sort of thing? *The mentally ill kind?*

'Chastity! What a lovely surprise.' I'm brought out of my musing with a snap at the sound of Tate's cultured voice and his pleasant though measured smile. 'Were you meeting someone or waiting for me?'

There's just something about his tone; a certain smugness, an almost imperceptible *something* that provokes me immediately. As the waitress makes herself scarce, words begin tumbling from my mouth. Though not the kind of I would've anticipated. *Less swear-y for one thing.* My mother would be so proud.

Camilla not so much.

'Why, Tate? Why would you do such a thing?'

'I'm sure I don't know what you mean.'

'Yes—yes you do.' This I know for sure. What I don't know is, 'What could you have possibly thought you'd would gain from it?'

His laughter is bitter. 'Well, *Chastity*.' There's such venom in his delivery. 'Your parents didn't think your name through very well, did they? Perhaps they were duped by that pink mouth and peachy skin? I'm sure you must've been a beautiful baby. And your parent's fooled into thinking their cherubic child would grow to be a woman of virtue and taste.'

Ah, so that's where this is going. I have no taste because I didn't choose him. And because I produce erotica, I have no virtue. *What a colossal tit.*

'Do you think you're the first person to ever remark on my name and my looks as some kind of antonym to my profession?' I fold my arms across my chest defensively, my words reasonable, my expression probably anything but.

We're standing almost at the front door, out of the way of the main restaurant, but I wonder how long we can keep up our exchange in spoken terms.

'Profession,' he spits. *So not long, apparently.* 'I suppose even whores can lay claim to the nomenclature.' His eyes roam over my body, full of distain. 'At least, the ones that get paid, anyway.'

Big words and a superior attitude. Well, fuck this for a game of soldiers. This pathetic kind of boy's club pisses me off no end.

'Get over yourself, you complete fuck nut! I have no idea why you would do such a thing—why you would want to

262

hurt me this way. And what gives you the right to use Sophia in such a despicable manner.' Each word fuses the heat in my veins. Each reminder of the transgressions of this . . . *person*, because I refuse to call him a man, makes me feel sick.

'The woman has sex for a living. Don't expect me to feel anything for her.'

'You're fucked up.' This is my official diagnosis. There is no remorse or feeling or guilt. There isn't a flicker of anything decent in his expression. How could I have been so fooled?

'She deserved it. What's more, she probably liked it. Girls like her are so worthless, they're familiar with being used. As for you?' His gaze flicks over me again, the lazy distain turning to hate. 'You brought this on yourself. You led me on—let me believe you were interested, then you fucked another man while I wandered around your kitchen serving food!'

I realise three things at this moment, as angry fricative-spittle hits my face.

1. He's moved closer
2. He's completely delusional
3. He's possibly dangerous.
4. That was him outside my bedroom door, listening like a perv.

Okay, four things. I'm a little stressed. I can't be held responsible for counting.

'No one asked you to serve food,' I answer calmly, reasonably. 'I paid for waiter service, just as I paid for the food.'

'And do you honestly think the paltry sum you paid covered even the raw costs of the produce?'

'That's on you, Tate. I didn't flutter my eyelashes at you

to get a better rate.' It's not my fault you're a crappy business man.

'I thought you'd be opening your fucking legs.' Although quietly spoken, his words are rage filled as he reaches for my arm, his fingers pinching instantly.

Time to leave. There's getting your point across to sane persons and there's putting yourself at risk. These two things are *not* the same.

'You insulted my manhood and my intelligence. You're a cock-tease. Nothing but a filthy cock-tease'

'Let go of my arm, Tate.' I begin to feel a little sick. Not the ill kind, the anxious kind. Yes, there are people around, but they're behind me. The floorspace is L shaped and the customers seated some distance away, probably out of Tate's line of view. Can they see this happening? And if they can, will they just watch if he gets physical? I'd like to think people stand up for others, but I know this isn't always true. 'I want to leave.'

'Oh, she wants to leave now,' he snarls, towering over me. 'Now that she's heard a few truths. What'll you do now, Chastity? Will you go back to your cunt of a boyfriend and suck his little dick?'

I might laugh if I wasn't so stunned. Or suggest we call Flynn over and get a tape measure out. Instead, I struggle, trying to pull my arm free but his just tightens. Fear swells in my throat, but I don't want to give him the satisfaction of hearing me call for help. It's broad daylight—nothing can happen here, right? Even as I'm reassuring myself, I can see how my reaction fuels the fire in his gaze.

There are names for men like him. Men that get off on power over women. *Rapists*, my mind whispers. But no, not here.

I put my whole body weight into one shove, and yank

on the door as he stumbles back. I can't get my keys out of my purse quick enough before his shoes sound on the pavement behind. Cars whizz by; it's the mad rush hour centred around school pick up time.

He won't hurt me—not in broad daylight. Not with all the traffic rushing by. Pedestrians bustle past, their shopping bags almost brushing my back.

'You're a cunt,' he growls, coming up behind me. 'It's women like you who give your gender a bad name.'

Ignore him. Get in the car, drive away.

Finally, my fingers grasp my key. I click the fob, put my fingers on the door handle and cry out as he grabs my hair.

Fear zips down my spine as he slides his other hand around my waist. We might look like lovers—my head pulled back and resting on his shoulder as he whispers in my ear, my whole being caught in his embrace.

'*Fucking slut.*' He elongates the insult as though it wasn't already frightening enough. I'm no shrinking violet. I stand up for what I believe in. Stand up for those I love. I never once imagined that, should a man put his hands on me, I would react like this.

Tears prickle from the force of his hand, but my fear is debilitating and like a punch to my chest. I have no breath for breathing. I want to run but don't have the freedom or the wherewithal to do so.

And then, I'm suddenly free. Slumped against the car, my heart beating as though I've just taken part in a marathon. *And I don't run. Not by choice, at any rate.*

'Chas!' Paisley's voice is like a balm as she throws her arms around me, pulling me back from the car. 'What was that about? Did he hurt you?'

As I turn, her eyes flick over me as though to discern

my state of wellbeing. But you can't always tell what's broken just by viewing the surface. All the same, I shake my head. He didn't hurt me. At least, not physically. *And at least, not this time.*

It's about then I notice the motorbike and the man. Two men, really. Keir stands off to the side, almost refereeing the fierce looks being exchanged between Flynn and Tate. Looks that speak of violence and hate.

I open my mouth, to what purpose, I'm not sure, but I'm pleased I don't take that moment to look away, not as Tate pushes Flynn. Not as Flynn retaliates by bringing his fist to Tate's stomach, hard and fast, making his body bow. I wished I could hear what Flynn says as he places his hand on Tate's shoulder, lowering to whisper something in his ear.

And then it's over.

And he's walking over to me.

And he looks so pissed.

And I want to cry but I can't let myself do it.

His hands on my upper arms, his jaw flexes under the stubble covering his skin, and his eyes are just so . . . unyielding and grim.

'You look like shit,' my mouth seems to say, though I'm almost certain my brain meant to ask him what he's doing here.

His tongue darts out to wet his lips, and even in this state I can see that this is a delaying tactic . . . for a smile. A smile that is a precursor to laughter.

'I wished I could say the same.'

'You wished I looked like shit?' I answer, bemused, though I'm sure I must look like someone who's just had the piss frightened out of them. *Try not to look down. If you had peed yourself, I'm sure you'd know by now. You'd be feeling a little cold down there, surely.*

He inhales, and when he exhales, the merriment seems to drain out of him. 'Yeah, I wished you looked like shit. It'd be easier to walk away.'

'I'm sorry.' I sound like a cartoon mouse—a blubbering, eye-watering, snot bubbling mouse. 'I know it's not enough, but I really am so, so very sorry.'

'I know.' He nods, his hands tightening. 'Me, too.'

And then he turns away.

33

FLYNN

Part of me wishes I could walk away. It would make life easier, for sure, but I'd be poorer for the experience. I know this—feel this—on so many levels. I know it intellectually; Chastity is a good person whose experiences led her to believe she couldn't trust her own judgement. I know it viscerally; just being around her is enough for me to learn how her mind works. She believes *in* people. And she's a good person with a generous heart. The place she falls short is trusting her own judgement. And that I know in *my* heart. We may not have known each other for very long but a litany of small incidences tells me all I need to know. The text check ins with friends, the way she holds an infant. The love and concern she has for her family, both blood and chosen, the way she cares for her own staff. In an industry dominated by men and rife with exploitation, she stands strong. She's an advocate of the industry in her own right, standing up for the rights of people—to watch porn and be watched, ethically. Then there are the smaller things that endear her to me. Her love of romantic comedies and her abhorrence for anything glorifying horror or death. The way she smiles at me with a dozen variations, my favourite of which is when she's not buying my bullshit and not calling me out on it, either. A smile that's cute and exasperated and elevates my joy to ridiculous rates. The way she hums to herself as she works in her home office and the way her body seeks mine in her sleep.

The way she looked at me when I told her I loved her, and the delight in her voice as she'd said it back to me.

The woman has a hard shell and a tender centre, and I can't help but want it all.

Besides, how could I miss out on a woman whose name includes my favourite part of her anatomy? Chastity. Well, almost.

Keir stands at the restaurant doorway, presumably where the food fucker slunk off to. He's lucky to still have his own teeth after I saw the look on Chastity's face. I've seen her smile a dozen ways, and loved them all, and I've watched her face wear a thousand expressions, yet until a few moments ago, I'd never seen her fearful.

'Do you want me to sort Chas's car?' Keir asks, tipping his chin. 'She'll get clamped, or worse, left there.'

I nod, though Chastity's car is the least of my concerns and I act on instinct rather than intellect as I swing on the toes of my oxfords and storm my way back to her. She looks worried, which is near enough to frightened, but I can't think about that. Not as I take her head in my hands, my gaze fiercely demanding of hers.

I just stare at her because I know if I open my mouth, the words won't make sense. So instead, I tilt my head and slant my mouth over hers.

She squeaks as I kiss her, kiss her hard, kiss her as though I could press my frustration into her. *Or maybe some sense.* This woman is going to be both the bane and the joy of my entire life, I can tell. The agony and the ecstasy. The person who drives me crazy, as well as driving me to be a better man. But so long as she wants and needs me like she does right now—her hands hooked under my suit jacket, one fisting my shirt at my back—I reckon I'm okay with that.

As I pull back, her eyes are a little hazy, her fingers finding her lips as though to contain the power of our kiss.

'Do you trust me?'

'I do, and I'm sorry,' she begins, hazy turning to threatening tears. 'I was wrong, but try to see it from my position—'

I shake my head because that's not what I meant at all. I have thought. I have tried to see it from her side—the evidence and the weight of her experience balanced against a man she thinks she barely knows. But I've been honest with her. *Mostly.* What you see is what you get. *Mostly there, too.*

I take her hand in both of mine, looping the ring holding her keys around my fingers only to deposit them in Paisley's hand, all without letting go of her hand. It looks so small and slender in mine, her fingers widening as I draw one of my own the length of her palm.

'What are you doing. Why are you giving her my keys?'

When she called from the office, Paisley was in a bit of a state—all broken sentences and emotion as she'd dashed out to her own car to follow. Because Chastity, on learning the truth behind the video, had shot out of the carpark in her little car like a bat escaping hell.

'Because you're coming home with me. It's time to let someone else look after you.'

Her gaze softens and she exhales a soft breath, the tension dropping out of her. For at least a beat, before her eyes widen then flit to the bike parked in front of her car, the wrong way in the road.

'On the donor cycle?' she sort of yelps. 'No. No way. People die on those things!'

'Do you trust me,' I repeat, not just talking about our mode of transport. And though I can tell she has a million things to say, provisos and addendums and fuck knows what else, she bites her bottom lip to stem the flow and nods her head.

'I do trust you. I trust you not to break me. But I'm not sure,' she says, her gaze sliding fearfully to the bike again, 'I trust whizzing through the streets on a hunk of metal with wheels not breaking me.'

'Just think of all that power between your legs.'

Her next look my way borders on contemptuous. 'Really? At a time like this, you want to talk about sex?'

'I don't want to *talk* about it,' I reply with a sly half smile. 'So why don't you just get your arse on the bike and we can go do something about it.'

As I help her pull the helmet from her head, I don't know if it's the ride, her brush with Tate, or the subterranean parking garage that has her eyes the size of dinner plates.

'Where are we?' she asks as I feed my fingers through hers to pull her to the lift.

'Home.' I bite back my grin. 'Tell the truth, you

thought I lived in some grotty flat share in Islington, didn't you?'

'I'm well aware of my privileges,' she answers snippily. 'There aren't many under thirties living in London who don't have housemates.'

'Keep your undies on.' I slide my gaze over my shoulder and shoot her a saucy wink. 'At least until we get upstairs.'

The elevator comes to a stop. It's not the penthouse, but a thirteenth-floor apartment overlooking the river Thames. Mutli-million dollar real-estate, the kind most personal assistants only get to dream about. As I slip off my jacket and drop my keys on the table in the hall, I can tell that's where her mind has gone.

'Do you rent?' As the words hit the air, her expression turns a sort of wide-eyed horrified. 'Ignore that.'

'I think it's time I clued you in on a few things,' I say, placing my hands on her shoulders from behind. I push the old Parker she'd had in the boot of her car from her shoulders, dropping it next to mine. I'm pleased she had something to wear as bike rides are wicked cold in spring. 'I work for Keir,' I begin, lowering my mouth close to her ear. 'Mainly because it saves me from being one of those rich arseholes who don't work. I also work for Keir because I've been learning how the property development market works.' *Slotting away the insights to his killer instincts.* 'But none of that alters the fact that I am one of those rich arseholes.'

Her eyes stay resolutely on the bank of windows and the terrace beyond, filled with greenery. The apartment is pretty stark; white floors and upholstery, the only real colour from a massive parlour palm and my huge TV on one wall. The space is light and bright, and I suppose in some ways, I've subconsciously brought a little bit of home here with me. Sadly, I can't say the same for the sunshine.

'And you didn't think to mention any of that to me?' Her tone is even, her voice clear.

'Not until this week.' Not until I offered Keir a cash injection and a partnership.

'I don't think I understand.' And why would she? I'm the only one of my brothers that hasn't really done much for themselves. Granted, we all went through that mad playboy stage coming into our inheritance after uni, but the Phillips clan are over-achievers, professionally. Apart from me.

'You're asking why not work for myself from the start?'

'Maybe. Yes?' she says, turning her confused gaze to me.

'That's easy.' I step around her and take her hand in mine, leading her to the sectional sofa. 'Because some of us don't have the drive that you do. Or are half as brave.'

'That's . . .' Baffling to her still, I can tell. 'But why not mention it?'

'Dunno. I suppose I don't tell anyone. It's not impressive or earned. It's a family thing.' My grandfather owned a small hardware store, passed down from his father. Don't ask me how, but he designed and patented a multifunction tool table that took off like a rocket. Aussie blokes like their sheds and their tools almost as much as they like their beer. 'Speaking of family, when I called them this week and told them about my plans, I also told them about you. You know, before you gave me the flick.'

'Before I gave you what?'

'My marching orders—the boot.' She looks horrified, whether because of my phrasing or the thoughts that I have a family, I'm not sure. But they're not bad, really. 'Mum seems to think you're some sort of miracle worker. Her and dad are going apeshit to meet you.'

'Meet me?' she repeats.

'Anyone who's had . . . how'd mum put it? *Such a positive effect on me must be a very special person.*'

'But I didn't do anything,' she says, totally bemused.

'You're helping me live up to my potential. Or some such shit. Making me grow the fuck up, according to one of my arsehole brothers.'

'But I like you the way you are.' I feel like she has my heart in her hands for the purpose of giving it a good hug. 'I don't want you to change.'

'You might feel a bit differently when we have kids.'

'Flynn.' She places her hand flat on my chest, her soft brown gaze turning solemn. 'I'm not pregnant.'

'Maybe not yet. We've got plenty of time to change that though, hey?'

'You really want to do this? With me?'

'Well, I'm not here to fuck spiders, love.'

When she laughs, it's the very best of things. 'Am I even supposed to know what that means?'

'You know, the sooner you stop talking, the sooner I can show you my big bed.'

'Your family—I won't hide what I do.'

'Who's expecting you to? In fact, if you get any new subscribers with Aussie ISPs, feel free to block them. It'll be my brothers. They've already decided you're a dead-set legend. Just be grateful we live half a world away.'

'You told them?'

'Yeah. I'm in love with you; of course I did.'

'You are the most perplexing—' She shakes her head, her hand falling away. 'I really don't understand.'

'I reckon we'll work that into our wedding vows. Neither of us understands, but yet we know.' She inhales sharply her mouth falling open, her expression filling my head with images that have no business there. *Yet.* 'That wasn't a proposal by the way. When I propose, you'll know.'

'Do you think we're moving too fast?'

'Maybe. But it works for me. Don't overthink it,' I say, taking her into my arms. I feel like a duck; calm on the surface, but under the water line, I'm manic. Or at least my heart is. 'I can see right now the conversation you're having with yourself,' I say tapping her forehead. 'Analysing. Criticising. Second guessing, babe. I dare you to act on instinct, Chastity. I dare you to take a chance.'

Her tongue darts out to wet her pink lips. 'You want me to take a chance on you?'

'Not me, duchess. Us. What do you say?'

Her mouth is just a whisper away as she slides her hands around to the nape of my neck. 'These brothers of yours . . . are they as handsome as you?'

'Nah, they look like a hat full of arseholes.' She laughs softly, the swell of her chest brushing mine.

'I might pass, then,' she says, screwing up her cute nose.

'We're going to make such beautiful babies, you know.'

'Then I think we'd better make a start on that.'

She squeals a little as I lunge for her like a man possessed, pressing her back against the sofa as I begin covering her in kisses.

EPILOGUE

CHASTITY

'W ELL, looky who I've found here ...'

I jump at the sound of Flynn's voice. I hadn't realised he was still in the house.

'You're not supposed to see the bride before the wedding.'

'I'm pretty sure you're also *not* supposed to sleep in the same bed as the prospective groom the night before. Or have sex with him. Unless you're the stripper, of course.'

I shoot him a glare. 'Strippers aren't sex workers.'

'And that was a joke that fell flat on its arse.'

'That's okay, I'm used to your poor sense of humour,' I reply, turning back to face the mirror to tame my hair. 'And no one has their bachelor party the night before the big day, anyway.'

We're getting married in a couple of hours and though I've said those words out loud at least a dozen times this morning, it still doesn't seem real.

'Christ.' Behind me, Flynn shivers, no doubt recalling his own buck's night. It took him two days to recover from what he described *as feeling a bit dusty*, when wrecked was clearly a more suitable word.

'I've a confession to make.'

I don't turn, rather lift my eyes to his reflection again. Dark pants and a crisp white shirt, the jacket to match hangs on a wooden hanger on the back of the door. Which is unusual in itself—the man is a bit of a slob. But that's only obvious when contrasted against my type A personality, apparently.

Yes, we're still keeping up the verbal foreplay.

It's safe to say that things haven't really changed between us in a lot of ways. In the year we've lived together, I've lost count of the number of times Flynn has driven me to the edge of despair just to drag me back again by kissing the grouch out of me. *The grouch he's often responsible for in the first place.* We still bicker and argue but that just means we get to make up more. You could say we're experts at that bit. Just like we're experts at loving each other, too.

'Do you want to hear it?' he asks.

'Your confession? Go on then, but make sure it's worth hearing.' I put down my comb, grateful for the distraction. 'You're eating into my beautification time.'

His mouth hitches in one corner and he shakes his head. 'You can't improve on perfection, babe.'

Something bright and warm and perfect blooms in my chest but I don't have long to ponder it as, in several large strides, he's in front of me, grabbing my chair by the arms. Like it weighs nothing—like *I* weight nothing—he lifts it, turning me to face him.

I might squeal and giggle a little, my heart pounding as he drops to his knees.

'Forgive me, Chastity,' he begins, his tone a fake kind of sombre. 'For I have sinned.'

I place my hand on his head in a gentle benediction. He's recently had a haircut, the short dark hairs on the back of his head a soft bristle against my palm.

'You weren't a choir boy, or else you'd know confession isn't done with your head in your confessors' lap.' At least, not last time I went to church.

'Depends on the church of your choosing, duchess.' His tone takes on that husky bedroom quality of his as he trails his hands up the backs of my legs, from ankle to knee. 'Because you are the altar at which I worship.'

With a deft flick, he moves the sides of my robe open, our collective breaths hitting the air in a rush as he pushes his hands between my thighs, spreading me wider.

'You're fucking perfect,' he whispers. His eyes roam my skin, setting my every nerve ending alight.

'Flynn . . . ' I'd meant it as a warning, not a encouragement as he lowers his head, slipping his thumb between my slick lips to expose my clit.

'So pink and perfect.'

I'm aware of everything and nothing all at once. The knot in my belly under his splayed hand. The tremble in my thighs as he lifts my leg over the arm of the chair, spreading me impossibly wide. The devil in his expression as he raises his gaze to mine, his tongue flicking out to deliciously caress my heated flesh. His first touch is electric, my back bowing as I thrust against him.

'*Oh, Jesus,*' I cry out, tightening my hand in his hair as though to contain the pressure—the sensation.

One flick, one lick of my full length, Flynn begins spreading open mouthed kisses along my wet flesh as he begins making out with my pussy.

'Last time I get to eat you out as your boyfriend,' he rasps, the words echoing through my insides. 'Better make it good.'

'So good,' I whimper. 'So fucking good.'

'There she is. There's my dirty girl.'

I feel so swollen and desperate and kind of dissolute. We're supposed to be getting married in a couple of hours and I suddenly don't feel very bride like—not at all. And he's right. I am a dirty girl—*his* dirty girl, as I tighten my grip in his hair and begin rocking into his mouth, taking my pleasure from him.

I ache, my pussy pulsing emptily, every inch of me hungry for his touch. And as though he could discern my wishes just from my moans, his lips cover my clit as he thrusts two fingers deep inside me. *Sucking and thrusting. Licking and finger fucking.* His actions undo me, picking apart my soul, stitch by stitch, only to put me together again in a rush.

'Come on, Chastity,' he'd whispers. 'Come for me. Come on my tongue.'

Everything inside me draws tight, my spine an impossible arch as I throw my head back against the chair. I want to watch, want to see the slide of his fingers and his tongue. See the pleasure on his face as he groans against my flesh.

But it's all too much—my arms grasp the back of my chair as though to prevent my fall. But I do fall. I give into him. Give into the needs of my body.

'God. *Oh, God*. I'm—I'm—'

Unable to process the waves of pleasure pulsing through me, the rush and sensation of a heat so thick and overwhelming, I feel I'm sure to burst. And when I come to, dizzy and panting, Flynn stands above me, loosening his pants.

This man owns me, body and soul. Just as I own him.

His fingers slide from my throat down, the backs of his knuckles ghosting the hardness of my nipples.

'How did I get to be so lucky?' His next breath is sharp as I lean forward, wrapping my hand around the base of his cock.

'Looks like you're about to get *very* lucky,' I reply, sliding my tongue the length of him. I kiss his tip, swirl my tongue around his silken head.

His eyes squeeze shut as though he's struggling to control himself. When he opens them again, it's with a masculine groan as he slides his hand to the back of my head.

Pleasure shimmers through me; joy, power, ownership. Flynn isn't what I'd call a man of few words. Quite the opposite. That I can make him lose the power of speech is some achievement.

He shifts his hand through my hair, snagging his fingers on a knotted curl. My complaint is non-verbal though it makes his body bow, his hips jutting forward as an encore, feeding me as much of his length as I can take.

'*Chastity* . . . Fuck, look at us. Look at you.' His hand still in my hair, he twists my gaze to meet his in my dressing table mirror. 'You look so beautiful with my cock in your mouth.'

My breasts bounce a little and my cheeks are hollowed as I continue to work him with my tongue and my lips.

'I'm going to fuck you,' he rasps. 'I want you to feel me everywhere. And when you're standing in front of me in your pristine dress, I'm gonna know what's going on under it. I'll know how aching and wet you'll be, just waiting for the next time we fuck. But this time as husband and wife.'

His words and dark expression deepen my arousal. My breathing erratic as I groan around his cock. His languid gaze slides from the mirror, dark lashes almost kissing his cheeks.

'Put your fingers inside your pussy,' he demands. 'Spread your legs.'

I do as I'm bid. I don't think I've ever seen an expression so avid, his eyes flicking from the mirror where he fills me to between my legs, where I fill myself.

'Fuck, that's it. Faster,' he commands.

I try, but it takes some co-ordination. It's like rubbing your tummy while simultaneously patting your head. But I'm wet, so wet, the sounds on my slick fingers seeming to do something to him.

'Circle your clit.' He moves the hair from the side of my face to better see himself sliding in and out of me. 'Make yourself come for me.'

Oh, God. Just the sound of his dark command is almost enough. *Almost, but not quite.* But it doesn't take long, a second orgasm building on the first.

In the year I've loved Flynn, I've had more orgasms than I've eaten roast beef dinners. *Fact.* I no longer have problems in that department at all. Not with him and not without, though my *ménage à moi* is enhanced by his sometime audience.

As I begin to pant around him, he pulls me up from the chair, his hands hooking around my thighs as he carries me to the bed, following my body down to the mattress.

He enters me slowly, his dark blue gaze intent on my own, our joint appreciation hitting the air as hungered, helpless sounds. My arse in his hands, he lifts me, setting the pace and depth as I pulse around him, squirm under him. He fucks me deeply, thrusting from tip to base, then feeding me short jabs of his hips.

And I love it. Love it all.

'I can feel you pulsing around me,' he grunts, driving his cock into me like my body is something he owns. 'Tell me how it feels.'

'I-it feels like I'm yours.'

'That's right,' he rasps, pinning me into place. 'I own this pussy. I own every inch of you. From your wild curling hair to your abundant heart.'

I grind against him as he whispers his sweet filthy promises, whimpering and calling out his name again and again, the edges of my last orgasm tied to this one.

And when I'm an aching and sated, a sensitive twitching mess, Flynn brings my hands to my head, pinning them there against the bed. His arms shake as he delivers long urgent strokes, his face contorted in ecstasy as he finally comes.

EPILOGUE

FLYNN

'I RECKON her IQ must've dipped since she's been hanging around with you.'

I turn my head to my brother, Rafferty, and scratch the centre of my nose . . . with my middle finger, my eyebrows raised like a taunt.

'She's a stunning woman,' he continues, ignoring the insult, 'but I don't know what she's doing with a drop-kick like you. Just look at you.' *Look-at-cha.* 'You've got a face like a dropped fucking pie. A woman like her should be with someone who's got their life together. Someone who takes care of himself.' As though to make a point, he turns to the window, straightening his tie in his reflection.

'Mate, if there was ever any chance of you stealing Chastity away, today was not that day.'

'You reckon?' he asks with a quirk of his brow. 'She might not have cold feet yet, but you never know when she might need pair of warm strong arms to fall into.'

'She seemed pretty hot for me this morning. And pretty happy when I married her an hour ago.'

His gaze snaps to mine and I realise what I've said.

'Fuck, my bad.' Still, I can't help but chuckle at his expression. I thought Camilla was the only attending maiden aunt.

'Fucking hell . . .' He blows out the curse on a long breath. 'You're not supposed to root on the morning of your wedding.'

Now, there's an Aussie term for you. Root, verb or noun.

To root: to fuck

Rooted: you're fucked.

A good root: a desirable sort. *So, not Rafferty, then.*

When in Aus, never say you root for your favourite sports team. And if you're *rooting around in the cupboard* I hope you're both having a damn good time.

'Let me get this straight,' I begin. 'On the morning of my wedding—on the morning of the day I tie myself to one woman for life, I'm not allowed to show that woman a little affection?'

'I don't make the fuckin' rules,' he grumbles. 'And is that what you're calling your cock these days—affection? I remember the days when you used to call it Peter the Dancing Penis.'

'I was three years old. And piss off, those stories are for mum to tell.'

'You fucking root rat,' Rafferty complains good naturedly. I think that insult speaks for itself. 'You've got no decorum. You're supposed to wait 'till your wedding night—and then be too drunk to get it up.'

'I suppose that's where you'll come in?'

'I am the best man,' he reasons. 'Some would go as far as to say the *better* man.'

'You're a tosser,' I return as he shakes his head, slapping his manicured hand on my shoulder. 'How long before we can expect the news of the pitter-patter of tiny feet?'

'Kids? I've only been married five minutes.' And living with her for twelve months. Living with her, sleeping with her, fucking her like it's going out of fashion. And every month like clockwork, she gets her period. I don't know who's more disappointed; me or her. But we know these things take time. So in the meantime, we're just keeping up our practice hours.

'You did good, kid.' Raff squeezes my shoulder and I let him have his big brother moment, despite there being only a couple of years between us. 'Chastity is a keeper. You hit the porn peddling jackpot.' He's still laughing as he walks away. *The wanker.*

I'm a married man. *Who'd believe it?* I think, my eyes sliding to the vintage red London bus ambling along the road. Today has been perfect. Low key and low fuss, just as my bride intended.

We'd married at eleven this morning at Chelsea Registry Office on the Kings Road, much to the consternation of Chastity's family. They wanted pomp and circumstance—a fucking cathedral wedding. But Chastity wanted none of that. Just a quiet day with a few friends. *And family, if we must,* she'd said. As there was no chance of hiding a wedding from my lot, or forgiveness after the fact, both sets of parents are here, along with my brothers, and Max and Camilla. But still, Chastity's mother isn't pleased. That the building we married in is beautiful—Victorian Greek revival—and that it was deemed good enough for James Joyce to marry in, didn't seem to matter at all.

Honestly? I don't give a fuck. I would've have married

her stark bollock naked in the middle of Leicester Square, if that's what she'd wanted.

The London bus pulls up outside of our favourite pub. Yep, we had our wedding breakfast in a pub. Roast beef and veggies, and enough champagne to sink a ship, and to add to the theme of low key, we didn't hire wedding cars, we hired wedding busses.

I spot my bride as she steps down from the vintage vehicle, a tiny silver clutch and flower corsage in the place of a bouquet. She looks like a summer sprite as she jumps from the last step with a dainty swing of her dress. Knee length and almost silver, it covers all my favourite bits of her in lace, with the exception of her back, her creamy skin exposed by a deep *V*.

Paisley steps down from the bus next, passing a glass of champagne into Chastity's hand as the pair laugh at something Mac's little boy has said.

My wife. Mine. Every inch of that treasure belongs to me, and not because of the ring on her finger, but because we were meant to be.

She wanted a simple day with no fuss and a plain wedding band. And I gave her it all but took her choice of ring into my own hands. I was certain I did the right thing, though almost confessed to her in the bedroom this morning. For more reason than one, I'm happy we ended up fucking instead. Yes, fucking. Not making love, because even when we're fucking, we are love. We're not making it, we just *are* love.

Not content to watch and compelled by the sight of her, I make my way out into the sunshine.

'Mr Phillips.' Her eyes are soft and warm as I bend to press my lips to hers.

'Mrs Phillips,' I return, shooting her a sly smirk and

enjoying the colour rise in her cheeks. 'Have I told you how beautiful you look today?'

'Oh, not for at least ten minutes,' she replies, smiling up at me.

'Well, that's what happens when you take the bus to escape.'

'We weren't escaping, Flynn,' Sorcha interrupts, as she jumps from the steep step. 'We were just taking the bus for a joy ride.'

'And stopping for ice cream, it seems.' At least, if the chocolaty stain on her pretty dress is any indication. I pretend to point at the stain on the smocked front of her dress, flicking her nose when she looks down.

'*Fl-ynn*!' she complains indignantly. 'I'm too old for you to play silly tricks on me.'

'When you get to double digits, then we'll talk.'

'What's a summers day without a little indulgence?' Paisley interjects, taking her step-daughter by the hand. She shoots us a sly wink over her shoulder as she walks away. Louis trails behind, using a tiny plastic scoop to scrape the remnants of watery ice-cream from the small tub in his hand. It mostly ends up on his little suit.

Man, kids are fucking ace.

'Do you think she was suggesting we grab a little after-noon delight in the bus?' As I turn back, I catch Chastity staring down at the diamond band. 'I did okay?' I ask hesi-tantly. 'If you don't like it—'

'I love it,' she says, placing her slender hand on my arm. 'And I love the inscription.' *Today. Tomorrow. Always.* 'But I'm still not shagging you in the bus.'

'Eh. It was worth a try. You might want to bear it in mind for work, though. A new take on taxi cam shots?'

'Eww. Just no. That premise is so awful. You can't

afford the cab fare, so you screw the taxi driver instead? There's nothing very erotic about that. It's just sad and a little desperate.'

I slide my hand into my pockets, pulling out a handful of change. 'So I'd better not ask what this would get me?'

Chastity sets off laughing, the flowers woven into her hair moving in the slight breeze.

'Today has been everything,' she whispers quite suddenly. 'I wanted to give you something, too.'

'So we are getting on the bus?' I wiggle my brows expectantly as she passes the glass of warming bubbles into my hand.

'I wanted to do this better but I haven't had a chance really to prepare. Bear with me. And don't laugh.'

'I wouldn't dream of it, love.'

'Here goes,' she says, pressing a shell into my hand. 'I picked this up from the beach the night of Paisley's wedding.'

'Okay,' I answer, rubbing my thumb over the smooth surface as I try to keep my bemusement to myself.

'That's something old.' Something I think might be delight pokes me in the centre of my chest. 'This is new,' she begins, pulling from her purse a silver Mont Blanc pen. It's engraved with my name. 'It's for you. It means you don't have to keep stealing Keir's. My amusement this time breaks free from my chest in a burst of laughter. 'You don't work for him anymore. Stop stealing the office stationery. You're paying for it, too.' She pats my cheek indulgently.

'But it's fun!' I protest, kissing her head and inhaling a deep breath of her floral scent.

'This—'

'Borrowed, I've got it,' I reply, holding out my hand. But as she pushes up onto her toes again, she kisses me on the mouth. A chaste kiss, but with a little nip of teeth against my bottom lip as she pulls away. *A promise of things to come.* 'Now remember, that's borrowed. I want it back.' She giggles cheekily.

'Don't worry. I'll give it to you all right.' If I have my way, I'll be giving it to her all night long.

'Final item,' she adds in a much more sombre tone.

'Something blue,' I assert as she dips her fingers into her purse.

'Close your eyes.'

'Kinky,' I mumble, smiling like a loon. *Another pen*? I think, wrapping my fingers around something that feels plastic.

'It's blue,' Chastity says softly, a certain hesitancy in her tone.

As I open my eyes and look down . . . there's a pregnancy test in my hand.

Blue.

Positive.

'You mean you're . . . we're . . . ' She nods. 'We're going to have a baby!' I exclaim.

Well, fuck me blind!

A RIDGY-DIDGE AUSSIE GLOSSARY

(JUST FOR FUN)

- Arvo - Afternoon.
- Arse - Ass. Derriere. Bottom
- Biscuits - Cookies. Also biccies
- Bluey - a redheaded person
- Carpet Grubs - Children
- Chooks - Chickens
- Crack a fat - get an erection
- Dag/daggy - uncool
- Daks - Trousers.
- Daks (trakkie daks) - sweatpants
- Dakked - to pull someone's pants/shorts down swiftly and without warning
- Didgeridoo - Australian Aboriginal instrument made form a hollow branch
- Dingo - wild Australian dog
- Drongo - a stupid fellow
- Dusty - hungover
- Fair Dinkum - a proclamation of truth
- Far out! - and expression of surprise or disdain

- Feral - wild
- Flat-chat - very busy
- G-string - Thong underwear. Also bum-floss. Also G-banger
- Go (what's the) - what's going on?
- Going off - mad and/or fun
- Good onay - well done
- Gourd (off your) - an extreme (mad?) state. Or high (stoned out of your gourd)
- Hanky - handkerchief
- Hard Yakka - hard work
- Jeez - a mild expression of surprise or annoyance
- Little tacker - Child.
- Malle bull (as fit as) - in excellent health
- Nightie - Nightdress
- Ridgy-didge - the genuine article
- Root - Have sexual intercourse (lucky!)
- Root Rat - A person notable for their sexual endeavours . . .
- Rough as guts - coarse, uncouth, unpleasant
- Sangers - Sandwiches.
- Sangers (a few sangers short of a picnic) and idiot
- Spunk - a hottie! Good looking
- Also on the topic od sangers: A few sangers/sandwiches short of a full picnic - crazy
- Septic tank - An American. Rhyming slang for Yank (Irreverent, yes. A slight, no)
- Servo - Gas station. Short for service station
- She'll be apples - All will be well/okay
- She'll be right - All will be well/okay

- Sparrow's fart - Early morning
- 'Straya - Australia
- 'Strine - Australian language
- Sunnies - Sunglasses
- Swag - camping bedroll
- Tickets on (yourself) - Conceited/vain
- Thongs - flip-flops
- Wank -masturbation
- Wanker - an insult
- You beauty (sounds like bewdy) - exclamation of approval

ACKNOWLEDGMENTS

I'm so grateful to so many people for helping and generally being my little cheer squad.

To Aimee Bowyer, or Aimee Boo-yaah! Thanks once again for stepping in at the last minute, for your quirky yet spookily on-point observations and general take on the world. Also, your eagle eyes.

To Natasha Harvey, the Queen of OCD, thanks for listening, OCD-ing. I know you've had it rough recently and I appreciate you doing what you can.

To Lisa her help and support and helping me perve, and to Waleska for being a good sport, and Michelle, though be she new, she be mighty. Or something.

To Jenny for editing and always making space for me.

To the Mo-Fo's. The secret society. Or society with secrets. It's hard to tell!

Not least, thanks to my family. I know, I'm getting worse but it's the werdz, not dementia—I promise! Thanks to M for the pep talks and my little mammy Jeanie-Jean for just being fab.

And thanks to the Lambs for putting up with my general lack of timing and surprise releases. And thanks to the people who pick up my books. I have no words. So I'll save them for the next book!

ABOUT THE AUTHOR

Donna writes dirty stories, according to her family. She hopes you find them funny, too. When not bashing away at a keyboard she can usually be found hiding from her family and responsibilities with a good book in her hand and a dog that looks like a mop by her feet. She likes her humour and wine dry, her mojitos sweet, and her language salty.
You can join in all things Donna by signing up for her newsletter or by becoming part of Donna's Lambs, her reader group over on Facebook where the best romance readers on the interwebz hang.
(She might be biased)

Keep in contact

Donna's Lambs
Donna's VIP Newsletter
mail@donnaalam.com
www.DonnaAlam.com

Made in the USA
Middletown, DE
14 August 2022

71333441R00179